"YOU MAY KISS THE BRIDE."

Georgiana shuddered as the reverend recited the words. A hush fell over the drawing room while every person in it stared at the newly wedded couple.

The air between Georgiana and the viscount crackled with tension. Her instincts told her to flee, but common sense reminded her that there was nowhere else to go.

"Do not be frightened." Lord Seybourne's whisper was inaudible, except to Georgiana.

He lowered his head and pressed his lips to hers.

It was an undemanding kiss, yet it knocked her world off its axis. Conflicting feelings of desire and apprehension coursed through her veins. It simply wasn't possible to reconcile her terror with her urge to kiss her husband back!

Kiss him back? Had she completely lost her senses?

BOOK YOUR PLACE ON OUR WEBSITE AND MAKE THE READING CONNECTION!

We've created a customized website just for our very special readers, where you can get the inside scoop on everything that's going on with Zebra, Pinnacle and Kensington books.

When you come online, you'll have the exciting opportunity to:

- View covers of upcoming books
- Read sample chapters
- Learn about our future publishing schedule (listed by publication month *and author*)
- Find out when your favorite authors will be visiting a city near you
- Search for and order backlist books from our online catalog
- Check out author bios and background information
- Send e-mail to your favorite authors
- Meet the Kensington staff online
- Join us in weekly chats with authors, readers and other guests
- Get writing guidelines
- AND MUCH MORE!

**Visit our website at
http://www.zebrabooks.com**

THE MINX OF
MAYFAIR

Bess Willingham

Zebra Books
Kensington Publishing Corp.

http://www.zebrabooks.com

ZEBRA BOOKS are published by

Kensington Publishing Corp.
850 Third Avenue
New York, NY 10022

First Printing: June, 1998
10   9   8   7   6   5   4   3   2   1

Printed in the United States of America

This one is for my mother, Betty Harris.

Prologue

London, 1820

Inside Sir Hester Abercorn's Farringdon Street study, the air was stale, slightly sour, the result of nine men having spent half the night there, drinking and sweating, arguing and taking snuff. Dust motes powdered the late-morning sunlight that slanted through venetian blinds. Olive-green velvet drapes, shabby golden-fringed upholstery, and faded Axminster carpets washed the room in colors reminiscent of an antique map. The room itself seemed world-weary and cynical, smothered in an oppressive air of neglect.

The flick of a black cat's tail. The tap-tapping of Sir Hester's steepled fingertips. These were all the sounds that broke the morbid silence.

Twelve hours earlier, the room had been the setting for the weekly meeting of the Kit-Kat Club, a Whig debating society named after an eighteenth-century drinking club and dedicated to the disparagement of King George IV's Tory ministry. When, well after dawn, the Club's meeting adjourned, its members were, without exception, foxed. Sir Hester's study was in shambles, carpets stained with claret and littered with snuff, tables laden with empty bottles and glasses, debris strewn like flotsam throughout the room.

Servants had set about immediately to mend—or at least patch up—the carnage wreaked in the study. Sir Hester, meanwhile, was so deep in his cups that his valet was unable to persuade him to disrobe and repair to his bed.

Instead, the political satirist, whose poison pen and acid tongue had estranged him from the society of all but the most enthusiastic of Whig sympathizers, experienced a rare moment of playfulness.

Vertigo, brought on no doubt by the vast quantities of brandy he'd consumed, anchored his bulky body to the study floor. There, under the watchful eye of his valet, he remained for the better part of an hour while wary servants skirted him with brooms and brushes. Laughing, rolling on the carpet, crawling about on all fours, he played like a child with the pet cat he'd rescued two years earlier from a Wapping wharf.

It was then that Georgiana the cat batted the crumpled piece of paper into his hands. Curiosity compelled the baronet to unfold the paper. Instantly sobered, he suffered the shock of his life. Someone had written an anonymous note referencing a plot to *destroy* the king and overthrow his Tory ministry. That someone, its author evidently a previous visitor in the baronet's study, had lost the note in Sir Hester's study.

Perhaps, in a fit of drunken pique, the author had wadded up his seditious writing and tossed it to the floor. At any rate, Sir Hester found it—or rather, his cat Georgiana did—and there was no way on God's green earth he could ignore it. His Whig sympathies did not extend to regicide.

The note had rattled in Sir Hester's trembling fingers. Hours later, seated behind his cluttered desk, the baronet still trembled. Possessing no friendly acquaintances other than the members of the Kit-Kat Club, he'd been hard-pressed to choose a man in whom to confide his enormous discovery. Inasmuch as the author of the note was probably a member of the Club—after all, how many visitors had he entertained in his study the past few days?—the list of men the baronet could trust was short indeed.

Sir Hester settled at last on fellow Club member Lawrence deWulff, Viscount Seybourne, a convicted smuggler and murderer. Long before the fashionable denizens of Mayfair arose from their beds, he took up his pen and fired off a missive requesting the viscount's immediate presence. After dispatching a footman to Seybourne's town house, he fretfully awaited the man's arrival.

It seemed an eternity passed while he waited. With beefy fingers laced across a waistcoat straining at the seams, Sir Hester contemplated the wisdom of having summoned Lord Seybourne. Seven years ago, Lawrence and his twin brother, Francis, had been found in possession of French contraband. The brothers had resisted arrest; a scuffle ensued and a Bow Street Runner was shot and killed.

Francis deWulff was cleared of all criminal wrongdoing, but Lawrence was convicted of smuggling and murder. Sentenced to transportation, he'd spent five years in Australia before the prince regent, now king, had granted him a royal pardon and recalled him to London.

The reasons for the king's actions were never made public, but it was bruited about gaming-hells and gossipy ballrooms that Lawrence, whose Whig sympathies were well-known, had threatened to disclose some embarrassing tidbit about the king's personal life. Considering the notoriety the king's love affairs had already attained, Sir Hester doubted Lord Seybourne blackmailed his way back to London. But he reckoned the true cause of the pardon didn't signify. It was enough that the king's leniency obviated any motive Lord Seybourne might have had to overthrow the government.

The crash of the brass knocker on his front door shattered Sir Hester's uneasy reverie. His eyes flew open as he rocked his heavy body forward. Accompanied by a symphony of creaking joints and cracking stays, he stood.

As he did, his gaze locked with the green-eyed stare of Georgiana who, perched regally on the edge of his desk, appraised him with her usual cool detachment. She was a fine black cat of indeterminate age and pedigree, who treated him with the identical top-lofty indifference that he directed toward the rest of humanity. In one respect, he reflected gloomily, the cat and he were the same; they treated the world with disdain in order to cover up their pathetically vulnerable and needy hearts.

"Fly now, Georgie, and stop that gazing at me as if I were the most fascinating creature on earth! I'm expecting an important visitor, and I daresay he won't appreciate being stared at by a sphinx while he learns what a bumble broth he's been drawn into. Besides, I have it on good authority that Lord Seybourne is a dog-man."

A muted exchange of masculine voices drifted from the foyer, then two pairs of unhurried footsteps trod the stairs to the second-level landing. Anticipating his guest's appearance, Sir Hester paused to run a cupped hand over Georgiana's sleek head. The cat squeezed her eyes shut and lifted her chin, offering her long, graceful neck for a tickle. When Sir Hester obliged, a familiar rumble evidenced Georgiana's satisfaction. *Ah, if all women were so easy to please,* the baronet thought wistfully.

Suddenly, the atmosphere in the house shifted from lazy stillness to menacing tension. From outside the closed study door, a loud thump sounded. The muffled groan that followed provoked an alarming acceleration of Sir Hester's heart rate. Georgiana leapt from the desktop and fled across the room toward her customary sanctuary, the shadowy underneath of a pedestal table draped by a faded Egyptian shawl. Peering from behind a fringed and tasseled corner, the cat observed every inch of the baronet's study.

The deadly silence succeeding the thump-groan was ominous. Huffing, Sir Hester skirted the desk. Had someone tumbled down the steps, or been stricken with a heart attack? A volley of pain burst inside his chest as he hurried across the room. When the study door exploded inward, his bladder spasmed. Frozen, he stood horrified in the center of the carpet, watching the tall, black-clad figure who strode toward him.

A black silk mask, with thin slits cut out for the eyes, disguised the man's features. A many-caped coat swirled elegantly around his tall, thin body. A beaver hat, pulled low over his ears, concealed his face in shadows.

"Lord Seybourne?" Sir Hester faltered. "Is that you?"

A slash of bloodless lips twisted, as if Sir Hester's erroneous identification were amusing. Advancing into the room, the tall man extended his gloved hand. Sir Hester, too scared to be rude, thrust out his own and, to his shocked dismay, received the familiar secret Kit-Kat Club handshake. The gesture was a mockery of the Club's traditions, but now the baronet knew that the plot to destroy the king had sprung from within the small Whig debating society.

Sir Hester's right hand fell to his side, where it shook as if he had the palsy. There was something vaguely familiar about the black-clad man, but the hat and mask effectively disguised his face, while the elegant Weston cloak could have belonged to any one of a thousand men in London.

"Forgive my impromptu call, Hester," the interloper said. "But I fear that something belonging to me was misplaced in this very study, and I have come to retrieve it."

Sir Hester cupped one hand behind his ear, struggling to recognize his visitor's voice. But he could do no more than note its oily cruelty and its familiarity; it could have been any one of the nine voices that contributed to the drunken babel of last night's meeting. In his nervousness, he unthinkingly asked, "Did Lord Seybourne send you?"

"Then you have told Lord Seybourne about the note already?" The black-clad man clucked his tongue.

"And what should I have told him, sir?"

"Don't play games with me! You have found the note, and I daresay you have read it. You are far too curious not to, and far too loose tongued to keep quiet about it!"

"Who are you?" Sir Hester demanded weakly.

When the menacing figure didn't answer, the baronet instinctively backed away. Retreating to the other side of his desk, he slowly lowered his ungainly body into his chair. "Sit down, then, sir."

The man remained standing. "Where is the note?" he repeated, his soft voice connoting the most violent threat.

But the cagey old baronet wasn't going to make it easy for

his interrogator. "I don't know what you're talking about," he replied through lips suddenly gone dry.

"Do not lie to me, Sir Hester. I shall shoot you dead if you do not produce the note—now!"

Sir Hester's peculiar brand of sarcasm surfaced in spite of his rising panic. "Would you be meaning that odd scrap of paper I found on the floor last night, after the adjournment of the Kit-Kat Club meeting? Dear me, I am afraid I crumpled it into a ball and tossed it onto the floor for my cat to play with. Old Georgie played with it for about an hour, as I recall, and then one of the servants tossed it into the fire."

"Don't be an idiot, you cannot fool me. You have requested Lord Seybourne's counsel, have you not? That is why you asked if he had sent me here. Obviously, you read the note and you were terrified by its contents, as any coward would be!"

Rapidly concluding that there was nothing to be gained by dissembling, the baronet replied, "So, you think it is I who am the idiot? Well, perhaps I have been for not recognizing the radical undercurrent of the Kit-Kat Club. But I thought it was all friendly disputation and debate that we were interested in. So, tell me, how many of the members are part of your plot to destroy the king?"

"That is none of your concern, Sir Hester. But since you are about to die, I shall tell you. Only one other. The rest are like you, as innocent and harmless as lambs. And equally ineffective."

"You think assassinating the king will actually further the Whig cause?" Sir Hester scoffed.

"True reform comes only through revolution; the French have taught us that. And besides, destruction in this case does not necessarily equal murder. I am surprised, sir, that a political satirist and writer of your caliber would be so literal minded as to interpret my correspondence as a threat to kill the king."

The baronet gripped the edge of his desk and glared into his adversary's eyes, eyes that gleamed through the narrow slits of a black mask. There was something cruelly familiar about those eyes . . . yes, he thought he knew who the man was now! His heart thundered. "Look, here," he finally sputtered. "I tossed that note into the fire, I swear it! Do you think I wanted to be in possession of such a vile, seditious writing?''

''But you summoned Lord Seybourne, sir. You should not have.''

''He knows nothing of the contents of the note! My missive merely asked that he come round. There is nothing unusual about that.''

''For his sake, I hope that is true.'' The unsmiling man slipped his hand inside his coat and withdrew a small black pistol.

A deafening report of gunfire cracked the room's dusty, stale air. The bullet that pierced Sir Hester's chest thrust him back in his chair. Clutching at his shirtfront, he stared down at his bloody fingers, amazed and saddened. Then he looked up through bleary eyes, his vision clouding as death quickly encroached.

''When you get to Hell,'' the black-clad man said, ''say hello for me to the old mad king.'' Then, he slipped his pistol inside his breast coat-pocket.

''Tell him yourself,'' the baronet croaked, his body tilting precariously over the arm of his chair.

The executioner moved swiftly around the corner of the desk, reaching toward Sir Hester, threatening under his breath to find the note regardless of where the old man had secreted it. The baronet slid to the floor where, in the last remaining seconds of his life, he witnessed a bizarre tableau.

From beneath the pedestal table, a streak of black fur emerged. Georgiana the cat sprang through the air, her limbs outstretched, her ears laid flat against her head. With a bone-chilling shriek, she flung herself at the black-clad man, her claws fastening onto the front of his cloak. As the man arched backward, she hung on tenaciously, every hair on her body bristling, her usually sleek tail as bushy as a chimney sweep's brush.

''Aargh! Damn cat, be gone with you!'' The man whirled like a dervish, attempting to shake the cat off his body, clutching and grabbing at her neck, cursing a blue streak.

Growling, Georgiana hung on, digging her claws ever deeper into the man's chest and arms.

At last, Sir Hester's killer throttled the cat and, yanking forcefully, managed to disengage her from his person. He drew his arm back, then slammed her to the floor with as much force as he could muster.

With a sickening thud, Georgiana landed against the thick mahogany leg of the baronet's desk. Her skull struck the hard surface with blinding force, shattering her vision, robbing her of breath. The pain was like nothing she had ever known—it wasn't remotely comparable with the wounds she'd suffered in catfights when she clawed out a living along the docks at Wapping.

Her heart slowed to a dangerously erratic rhythm. Summoning her last ounce of strength, Georgiana dragged herself the scant inches it took to reach Sir Hester's body.

As she struggled to fill her lungs, she heard the baronet's murderer mumble a sanguine oath about the lateness of the hour. Then, he lurched from the room and stumbled noisily down the steps. The house fell eerily silent.

Except for the baronet's horrible death rattle. His fingers fumbled inside his breast coat-pocket and he extracted a piece of paper, creased and bloody, blackened by gunpowder. Crumpling the paper, he tossed it on the carpet between himself and Georgiana, a rapidly fading flicker of amusement in his eyes.

"There you go, Georgie. Something for you to play with. Now, don't let it go into the fire, old friend; you must see to it that Lord Seybourne finds the note. Dear God, what am I doing . . . entrusting the king's life to a cat? Well, I suppose it can't be helped. I need you now, Georgie, more than ever. And though you won't admit it, you have needed me a little, too."

The cat made a pitiful mewling sound.

"Don't look so sad, Georgie! You can make it on your own again, now can't you, old girl? Surely you can, you've survived worse . . . haven't you . . . old girl?" And with that, the baronet exhaled his last strangled breath and died.

At the same instant, darkness descended on Georgiana and

she fell into a deep, restless slumber. She dreamed of her past lives, and of the day Sir Hester found her on the wharf, when she was injured and dying. Dear cantankerous Sir Hester . . . he had clutched her to his breast, wrapped his cloak around her and carried her home. And, having patched up her wounds, he never asked a thing from her.

Georgiana reckoned she had, in fact, given him very little in return. Why had she shown such indifference toward him? Why had she made a game of it—winding her way around his ankles, then flitting off like a coy debutante when he reached down to stroke her ears? Why had she refused to admit she needed him, if only just a little?

In the depths of her subconscious, Georgiana wished—no, she prayed—that she could relive her short tenure in Sir Hester's protective care. If she could, she would show the unhappy man the true measure of her gratitude; she would never be so cagey and coquettish in response to his unstinting care and affection. She would, if given another chance, prove to him her devotion.

Ah, they had been a fine pair, those two. Georgiana with her battle scars; Sir Hester with his world-weary cynicism and mind-numbing drink. But then, the old man had seen things in Paris during the early days of the Revolution, things that no living creature should witness. And in his drunken slumbers, he talked of those things, and they'd been so horrible that the hairs along Georgiana's back had bristled instinctively at the pain in the baronet's voice.

The cat and the old man *had,* indeed, been very much alike. They were survivors, pretenders who weren't as tough inside as they appeared on the outside. And their similarities had forged a strong, albeit unspoken, bond between them.

But now the baronet was gone, and there was nothing Georgiana could do to bring him back.

So, as she slowly struggled upward from the blackness of her subconscious, emerging into the land of the living for the ninth time, Georgiana vowed she would do things differently from now on. She would remember the lessons she learned. She had learned them well and she would not forget them.

Or would she? She was a cat, after all. Perhaps it wasn't in her nature to love selflessly, to show her vulnerability, to admit that she needed someone else. And the pain of being abandoned again might prove too great to allow her to risk an attachment to another mere mortal man.

All *that* remained to be seen.

All that, and more.

Chapter One

Outside the baronet's town house, traffic was brisk and pedestrians unusually reckless. Horses leading a gleaming black curricle round the corner of Theobold Street narrowly avoided clipping the heels of a man who darted into their path. Without so much as a backward glance, the black-clad man continued east down Farringdon and disappeared into a churning throng of carters, vendors, and strolling window-browsers.

"Whoa, there!" a coachman yelled as he reared back in his perch to rein in a pair of magnificent matched grays. Stiffening their forelegs, the horses slid to a grinding halt while the equipage bounced to a bone-jarring stop. "Damme, man, ain't ye got no eyes in yer head?"

Inside the carriage, Lawrence deWulff, Viscount Seybourne, massaged the back of his neck and uttered a colorful oath. Tossing aside a creased copy of *The Examiner,* he hooked a finger beneath his crisp white cravat, and, thrusting forth his jaw, tilted his head from side to side. After a moment, assured that the sudden braking of his carriage hadn't resulted in any serious damage to his neck or spine, he slid across the leather squabs. Flinging open the door, he leaned out and peered up at his driver.

"What happened?" he demanded. "Are you trying to stand me on my head? Or are you attempting to chop my cattle into skittish nags?"

"Damn fool man almost got hisself run over, m'lord," the agitated driver replied, his yellow-and-black-striped waistcoat in splendid sartorial contrast to his raw Cockney cant. "I swear, the streets of London are gettin' so crowded, a chap can't even drive his rig in'm widdout fear o'barreling over some jackanapes who ain't lookin' where he's go—"

"But we've arrived, man," the viscount interrupted, ducking to avoid scraping his beaver hat as he emerged from the carriage. Slanting an amused look at his driver, he said, "No sense in getting in such a pother. You didn't hit the man, did you?"

"By the grace o'God, no, m'lord," mumbled the man.

A shrug of Seybourne's broad shoulders strained the seams of his dark-blue coat. Then he flexed his fingers, smoothing the perfectly snug fit of his kid-leather gloves. Hardly the sort to fret over a disaster that hadn't materialized, he shot his cuffs and dismissed his coachman with a nod. Sir Hester Abercorn awaited. Striding toward the baronet's front door, Seybourne banished all thoughts of his driver's missish complaints concerning the carelessness of London pedestrians.

Sir Hester's front door stood slightly ajar. Deducing that a negligent servant had failed to close it behind an earlier caller, Seybourne entered.

Seybourne was familiar with the layout of the house. Crossing the threshold, he removed his hat, allowing his eyes to adjust to the semidarkness while he stripped off his gloves. He stood in a small vestibule from which a rather grand staircase ascended to the main living areas. Without closing the door behind him, Seybourne called out, "Hello, there! Is anybody home? Hester, where are you?"

Answered by silence, an incipient dread crept up Seybourne's spine. He stole up the stairs quietly, his hand sliding beneath his coat to extract the small pistol he sometimes carried on his person. At the top landing, he froze, every muscle in his body tensing. The butler, a man well known to Seybourne, lay in a crumpled heap beside the balustrade. Blood pooled beneath his battered head, filling the air with a strong metallic smell.

Swallowing hard, the viscount stepped over the butler's body. Clearly, the man was beyond help, but Sir Hester might yet be alive.

Seybourne pressed his back to the wall, gliding along the dimly lit corridor with his gun held at ready, barrel aimed at the ceiling. At the end of the corridor was Sir Hester's study, the door hanging half open to reveal a wedge of Oriental carpet and swatches of heavy mahogany furnishings. Having spent the better part of the previous evening in that room, Seybourne knew it well. The site of Sir Hester's political salon, it was also where the man sat daily behind his desk, poring over newspapers, both liberal and radical, writing his articles, conducting his correspondence—in general, plotting government reform through prolific sarcasm.

Every hair on the viscount's body tingled with apprehension. He paused at the door to the study, senses alert. Not a sound or squeak broke the silence. The stillness that hung in the baronet's house was ominous.

With the toe of his high-topped Wellington boot, Seybourne gave the door a violent kick. He sprang across the threshold. Feet planted wide apart, arms extended, he stood in the center of the room. Pivoting, haunches tensed, he scanned the room, noting instantly the undisturbed positions of the refectory tables, armchairs, and sofas. Not so much as a single leather-bound book appeared out of place in the study.

Turning full circle, Seybourne's gaze fell to the baronet's desk, its cluttered top, the heavy armchair behind it, empty and pushed back against the paneled wall. His stare traveled downward to the floor where a spill of lustrous black hair—a mane of it, long and silky and distinctly feminine—blotted a segment of the intricately patterned carpet.

Black hair? A woman's hair? Beneath the baronet's desk?

Seybourne's masculine instincts were aflame. Tucking his gun away, he flew toward the desk and rounded its edges. At the sight of a woman lying on the floor, he froze and stared disbelievingly.

Completely nude, she was on her side, facing away from Seybourne and nearly nose to nose with the entirely clothed body of a similarly posed and equally unanimated Sir Hester. Her perfectly rounded bottom, accented by the gentle curves of a slender waist, was startlingly white against the rich oranges and browns of the carpet.

Crouching beside the woman's still body, Seybourne let out a breath he hadn't known he was holding. For a moment, presuming both Sir Hester and the mysterious nude woman were dead, he simply studied the strange placement of their figures. Sir Hester's eyes bulged in a grotesque death mask while a trickle of blood snaked down his chin. The lifeless baronet's nose was mere inches from the woman's. Her arms were thrown about his neck; the fingers of one pale, slender hand curled at the lapel of his coat and clutched a crumpled piece of paper.

"Christ on a raft!" Seybourne muttered his favorite imprecation as he gently grasped the woman's bare shoulder. Then, he rolled her on her back. A reddish swelling at her temple evidenced a severe blow to her head. Pressing his fingers to the hollow of her throat, however, he detected a strong pulse. When she gave a convulsive shudder, the viscount's own heart skipped a beat.

The paper fell from her fingers onto the carpet, where Seybourne quickly snatched it up, unfolded it, and read it. With each word he read, his teeth clenched tighter, so that by the time he was finished, his jaw was as taut as a steel panther-trap.

The day of reckoning is growing ever closer. Your courage must not falter; indeed, your participation in this enterprise grows more important daily. Rest assured that when the king is destroyed and his Tory ministry toppled, no man will dare sneer at you again. The Kit-Kat Club shall achieve instant notoriety—more than Abercorn's pen ever could have wrought. Keep your eyes open and your ears pricked ... we cannot afford exposure! As always, burn this note when you have read it. Need I tell you that our greatest enemy, beside the Tory coxcombs, is indiscretion?

Seybourne studied the inked words, softly swearing as he mentally compared them with Sir Hester's familiar, untidy scrawl. The baronet hadn't written this note, that much was certain. Nor had Lord Pigott, whose wide, loopy letters were also well known to the viscount. Whoever had authored the incriminating message found in the naked woman's hand was not someone who corresponded regularly with Seybourne, not in writing anyway.

The diabolical implications of Seybourne's discovery produced a ferocious pounding in his head. Entanglement in a scheme to overthrow the government was not what he'd bargained for when he'd joined the Kit-Kat Club at the king's *irresistible* request.

The king could not have predicted just how profound Seybourne's spy mission would turn out to be. Quite apart from collecting a repertoire of limericks chronicling the queen's Italian escapades, the viscount had stumbled smack into the middle of a murder investigation, political assassination plot and—with the addition of a beautiful naked woman—a social scandal the likes of which the *ton* hadn't seen since Lord Devonshire took up residence with his wife *and* mistress. For a man struggling to repair his reputation, this imbroglio did not bode well.

A faint whimper escaped the woman's lips.

"Thank God, you are alive." The viscount slipped the blood-stained paper in his pocket, then gathered the woman in his arms. He stood, pausing for a moment to stare down at her pale complexion, upturned nose, and rather smallish, bow-shaped mouth. Mounds of luxurious black hair spilled over the viscount's arm as he surveyed the creature nestled against his chest.

Without warning, her flesh warmed beneath his fingers. A quite unexpected and unbidden surge of protectiveness engulfed him. For a moment, he stood stock-still and drank in the sight

of her, from the tips of her shapely toes to the top of her head.
And everything in between.

Her weight in his arms, her head on his shoulder, her long
legs draped over the bend of his elbow, all produced sensations
that Seybourne found intensely uncomfortable. He didn't want
to feel protective toward this or any other woman. He didn't
want to open his heart to another female, only to give her the
power to destroy him.

He had found a certain solace in his status as a dispassionate
loner; as long as he kept his female acquaintances at emotional
arm's length, no one could get near enough to wound him. He
hadn't allowed his lover of two years to break through the
barrier he'd erected around his scarred heart. He certainly
wouldn't allow his strange tender feelings for this mysterious
minx to penetrate his invisible coat of armor.

It was just a passing momentary reaction to her intense
beauty, Seybourne told himself. Just a natural, physical, masculine reaction to the sight of a naked woman. He was, after
all, notoriously virile and possessed of an almost animal-like
appetite for sex.

Still, breathing in the mysterious woman's unusual perfume,
slightly musky with the sweet undertone of a baby's breath,
he couldn't help but think how satisfying it was to hold her in
his arms and know that she wasn't afraid of him, or that she
didn't want a significant allowance from him. He couldn't help
but wonder if she would be as vulnerable and enticing when
she awoke. Or would she be like his mistress Lady Mercy Mary
Spraddlin, a feisty, ill-tempered and demanding termagant, who
harped constantly on what a tremendous favor she did him by
appearing publicly on his arm?

A stifled cry jolted Lord Seybourne back to the present.
Lifting his head, he locked startled gazes with a young maid
who stood in the doorway.

"Come in, gel, and tell me everything you witnessed in this
house today."

"I ain't seen anythin'!" The young girl, her face as white
as her apron, appeared on the verge of fainting. " 'Cept a dead
butler and a naked woman!"

Omitting to offer her a peek at her employer's corpse, Sey-bourne sighed. He wasn't surprised when the terrified maid turned and fled. But as her boots pounded down the steps and out the back door, he realized the import of having been seen—even by a servant—with a naked woman in his arms.

Seybourne's reputation, so recently restored, would again be torn to shreds. And Lord Pigott's political campaign, which Seybourne presently managed, would be destroyed.

That wasn't the worst of it, though. Seybourne instinctively knew that Sir Hester's murderer was the author of the treasonous note. Further, the killer must have left the naked woman for dead. When he learned she was alive, he would come looking for her.

The thought made the viscount's blood run cold. Moreover, it negated any notion of calling in the Bow Street Runners until the mysterious woman was safely removed from Sir Hester's study. Seybourne might be subverting the administration of law enforcement by failing to apprise the Runners of all the details surrounding Hester's death, but his obligation was to a higher authority. The king himself had asked Seybourne to infiltrate the Kit-Kat Club and determine whether there were any radical elements at work plotting to destroy him. Sir Hester's death and the note found in the girl's hand were glaring confirmations of the monarch's worst fears.

It was now crucial that Seybourne maintain his membership in the Kit-Kat Club, as well as safeguard his continued friend-ship with Lord Pigott. For the king's sake, he had to find the author of the threatening note, and Sir Hester's killer. And to do that, he had to somehow avert the scandal that would erupt when the news broke that he'd been found with a naked woman in a dead man's study.

Holding the girl snugly to his chest, Seybourne allowed himself another long, hungry perusal of her figure. He'd been holding her for several minutes and his muscles were stiffening. Yet he found he could have held her much longer. Tenderly, guiltily, he rubbed his thumb along the smooth skin of her upper thigh. Shifting her in his arms, he just managed to press his lips to the top of her head. A silly thing to do, he admonished himself. Then he laid his cheek atop her head and closed his eyes.

The makings of a grand scheme slowly took root in his imagination. Seybourne opened his eyes. He knew nothing about the woman he held in his arms, except that she was the key to finding Sir Hester's murderer. In order to expose the author of the traitorous note, Seybourne had to keep the mysterious girl under his own guard.

At the same time, he had to dangle her in front of the killer's nose, tempting him to make a misstep, to unwittingly betray himself. A wild idea occurred to him, but it would require a great deal of finesse, as well as the cooperation of his aunt.

At last, Seybourne strode toward an inviting *chaise longue* in the corner. When he was halfway across the room, a feminine gasp outside the study door drew him to an abrupt halt. Glancing over his shoulder, Seybourne rankled. The curtain had just gone up on his outlandish plan to marry the mysterious naked woman.

Into the room burst a small, dumpling-shaped woman wearing an unfashionably dowdy hat and an incongruously excessive amount of lip rouge. Evidently shocked by the sight that greeted her, Lady Inez Twitchett, Seybourne's dowager aunt on his mother's side, froze in her tracks, palms pressed to her puffy cheeks.

"Thank God you are here," Seybourne said as he lowered his delicate cargo onto the shiny, worn velveteen cushions of the sofa-chair. He stripped off his coat and covered the woman as best he could.

"It appears that I have arrived in the nick of time," his aunt replied with a sniff. "When I beseeched you yesterday to consider upping your contributions to the Society for the Rehabilitation of Wanton Women, this was not precisely what I had in mind."

"Anything for a good cause," Seybourne said dryly, grinning. As he turned and approached his aunt, however, his smile vanished.

Standing in the doorway was Lady Mercy Mary Spraddlin, the viscount's female companion for the previous two years. With obvious displeasure, she stared alternately at Seybourne and the naked woman on the *chaise longue*. After a moment of stunned silence, she advanced toward the center of the room, where she stood beside Lady Twitchett.

With a spine as rigid as a lightning rod, Lady Spraddlin skewered the viscount with one of those peculiarly female expressions, a long-suffering gaze full of hurt, anger, unrequited love, and the potential for violence.

"Mercy, this is not what it appears—" Seybourne began.

"Who is the dead man in the corridor, Lawrie?" Aunt Inez interjected.

"That would be the butler," he replied without taking his eyes off Lady Spraddlin. Alarm ricocheted off his nerve endings. He knew his mistress well enough to recognize her puffy lower lip and snapping eyes as the prelude to a nasty scene.

Thinking to deflect Mercy Mary's ire, he turned his body sideways and gestured toward the desk and the area behind it, where the baronet's body lay in a pool of blood. Both women craned their necks to peep at the corpse.

"Oh, my!" Aunt Inez cried, holding a lace-edged handkerchief to her nose.

"Is he dead?" Mercy Mary paled considerably, despite already having stepped over the butler's dead body.

"He is quite dead," Lord Seybourne said. "Someone shot him in the heart, I'm afraid. Poor bugger never had a chance."

"How very tragic!" Mercy Mary wrapped a protective arm around Inez's ample shoulders. "Have you seen anyone suspect-looking on the premises? Was anyone here when you arrived?"

"No. By the way, what on earth compelled the two of you to call on Sir Hester this morning?"

With a bob of her head, Aunt Inez, apparently unable to speak, prompted Mercy Mary to answer this question.

"I visited the baronet yesterday," the younger woman explained. "The purpose of my visit was to request another donation to the Society for the Rehabilitation of Wanton Women. I have taken quite an active role in the administration of the organization, you know, Lawrie. At any rate, Sir Hester was noncommittal, but promised he would discuss the matter with his clerks. I was supposed to pay another visit this morning to receive the baronet's answer and hopefully, a sizeable contribution. So I asked your aunt to accompany me on the theory that it would be harder for Sir Hester to turn down two forceful women with their gloved hands out.''

Seybourne couldn't resist a wry chuckle. ''I daresay, the two of you present a formidable team. So the baronet was expecting you, then?''

''Yes,'' Mercy Mary replied. ''And when we saw the front door ajar, Inez—the bolder of us, actually—ventured in. I had thought to return to the carriage, assuming as I did that Sir Hester was not at home. But after a few minutes, I became concerned for your aunt's safety, and so I followed. I am still suffering from the shock of seeing that poor wretched butler dead. And now, the baronet, too! It is just too tragic by half! Who do you think killed them, Lawrie? Do you suspect the motive was robbery?''

''Robbery?'' Seybourne was suddenly aware of the blackened, bloody note in his breast coat-pocket. Resisting the urge to slip his fingers inside the jacket, he said, ''What would Sir Hester have possessed that someone might have killed him for?''

''I really don't know,'' Mercy Mary said.

''Perhaps he had gathered up the cash he was to donate to the Society,'' Lady Inez managed, her voice a trembling falsetto. ''Perhaps one of his servants saw the money and decided to kill the baronet, abscond with the blunt, then escape to the countryside where no one would ever find him. Or her.''

Mercy Mary warmed to this theory of the crime. With unsuppressed excitement, she added, ''Yes! And the butler, having witnessed the crime, attempted to apprehend the villain in the corridor. That's when the desperate criminal killed the butler and ran out the front door. How do you think he killed the butler, Lawrie? With a candlestick to the back of his head? Or a club, perhaps?''

''Or the butt-end of a gun,'' Seybourne remarked. ''At any rate, Sir Hester and his butler are quite beyond help. But the young lady on the *chaise longue* is not. Mercy, why don't you go and fetch the doctor?''

Mercy Mary's eyes flashed. Stiffening, she tightened her grip on Lady Inez's arm. "Are you out of your mind, Lawrie? You'll not send me off to do your dirty work!"

"Dirty work?" Lady Inez slanted a suddenly sober, dry-eyed look at Mercy Mary. "Pray, dear, do not forget we have dedicated our lives to rehabilitating women less fortunate than ourselves. It is our duty to assist this unlucky chit if we are able."

Coloring, Mercy Mary responded in a sweet yet crisp voice. "Be that as it may. Do you have any idea who she is, Lawrie?"

"None at all. I found her on the floor beside poor Sir Hester. She was unconscious and naked as a jaybird, I'm afraid."

"So, she hasn't said a word to you?" Mercy Mary asked. "Not a one."

Inez said, "Don't be missish, child. Go out to my carriage and instruct my driver to take you to Dr. Peeps's house on Gower Street. Tell him he must come here at once—"

"I do not wish to." Mercy Mary's tone was childishly vehement.

Seybourne thought his mistress's jealousy a trite tedious. But thinking on it, he deduced he could use her feminine obstinance to his advantage. At length, he said, "Perhaps Mercy Mary is correct. I believe it would be preferable to transport this young woman to my home. She requires protection as well as medical treatment. After all, a murder has been committed here. She most certainly witnessed it and may still be in danger. When the perpetrator of this dastardly deed discovers she is alive, she will be in grave danger indeed."

"Don't be silly, Lawrie." Mercy Mary's pretty features screwed up in a decidedly unattractive scowl. "You cannot take that creature home with you."

She cast a defiant look at Lady Twitchett. It was common knowledge that the two women, despite their shared passion for rehabilitating wanton women, were not the coziest of friends. Lady Spraddlin was clearly intent on marrying the wealthy and socially rehabilitated Viscount Seybourne. And Lady Twitchett was equally dead set against that match.

Precisely why his aunt objected to his marrying Lady Spraddlin, Seybourne did not know. But he appreciated his aunt's protection; if she had not served as a buffer between him and Mercy Mary these past two years, he feared he would be leg shackled to the volatile redhead by now. One of the great advantages to marrying the mysterious minx on the *chaise longue* was that it would eradicate any chance of his ever wedding Lady Spraddlin.

Or would it?

For reasons the ladies couldn't have guessed, a wrinkle formed on Seybourne's forehead. He meant to marry the mysterious woman solely for the purpose of luring Sir Hester's killer into the open. He had no intention of entering into lifelong matrimony with her! Which meant he would have to invent a method of extricating himself from this fraudulent marriage once Sir Hester's killer was apprehended. Since divorce was practically impossible, a more creative means of slipping through the shackles of marriage would have to be found. Already, Seybourne's mind was ticking off the few options available to spouses unhappily bound to one another.

"Well, we certainly cannot leave the poor miss here," he finally muttered. "She has not yet regained consciousness, Mercy. If we were to leave her to the devices of the Bow Street Runners, the bumblers would have her in Newgate before sundown. I simply will not hear of it."

Lady Mercy Mary, arms crossed over her chest, said, "She's probably a cyprian or some fancy lady, who was hidden beneath the desk when Sir Hester was shot."

Lord Seybourne smirked. "Perhaps it was a jealous husband or patron who killed Sir Hester."

"Oh, fiddlesticks," Aunt Inez said. "What an imagination you young people have. There's probably a very logical explanation for this unseemly picture—though God knows I haven't a clue what it might be. And it doesn't signify anyway. The girl might be a duke's daughter, for all we know. But, her reputation will be in tatters when the gossips hear she's been found naked in a dead man's study."

"Well, I certainly won't tell anyone!" Lady Spraddlin cried.

"Sir Hester's servants are bound to talk, dear. No doubt

there is a cleaning wench right now in next door's kitchen, sobbing her eyes out about the horrid shock of finding Lord Seybourne with a naked woman in his arms. Never mind the dead butler and poor Sir Hester! And I'm afraid there is another matter to consider. Odd that you haven't thought of it, Lawrie. But you've got *your* reputation to consider. And that of Lord Pigott.''

Seybourne resisted a broad smile. His plan was taking shape, and Aunt Inez, quite unwittingly and for reasons radically dissimilar to his own, was proving to be of remarkable assistance. "Yes, Aunt, I see what you mean. Two years it has taken me to salvage my reputation, despite the king's pardon of my crimes—''

"Oh, Lawrie,'' Mercy Mary broke in. "You mustn't take her home. I won't hear of it! She belongs at Newgate, locked in a cell without a key!''

Seybourne appraised his mistress coldly. She was a beautiful woman, whose former husband the Earl of Spraddlin, had donated a fortune to Lady Inez's Society for the Rehabilitation of Wanton Women. When Seybourne had returned to London, Mercy Mary, a widow, had been the first woman to receive him socially. For that, he'd been grateful; but he'd never been quite as grateful as she thought he should be. Her present fit of pique only deepened his indifference toward her.

"I will not send this poor woman to Newgate,'' he told Mercy Mary firmly. "She is going home with me and Aunt Inez.''

"Pooh! Why are you doing this to me, Lawrie!'' With a stamp of her feet, the pretty redhead drew Aunt Inez's most steely, admonishing stare.

"Inez was perfectly right in what she said,'' Seybourne pointed out. "I've a political campaign to run, after all. Lord Pigott's bid for a seat in the House of Commons would be ruined were I to become embroiled in a scandal that soured the public's image of me. Sorry, old girl, but in politics, one's image is everything!''

"But everyone shall know you took a naked woman home!'' Mercy Mary protested. "Won't that cause a scandal in itself?''

Aunt Inez gave her nephew a conspiratorial wink. She was a great deal sharper than she appeared. "If he were to marry her," she said, smiling slyly, "that would make a world of difference."

"Yes, Aunt. I quite agree."

"The two of you cannot be serious!" In a rustle of pale-green lawn and linen, Mercy Mary sauntered up to the viscount. "I will not allow you to bring scandal down on my head, Lawrie. I've risked enough of my reputation by associating myself with you as it is. If you take this naked woman home with you, you will be ruined in Town, and I shall not be able to do a thing to repair your reputation. Not this time."

Seybourne suppressed a grin. "I think you quite missed the point, dear. But you are right on one thing. Taking home an *unmarried* naked woman would be a horribly boorish thing to do. Scandalous."

"Ruinous to your reputation," Mercy Mary said. "Not to mention our friendship."

"Then there truly is only one thing to do." Seybourne turned toward his aunt. "And that is to marry the chit."

Lady Twitchett nodded. "I've always been able to count on you to do the right thing in the end, Lawrie."

"Do you think we can arrange an impromptu wedding, Aunt Inez?" he asked.

"Boy, with your connections, you can get married this evening if you like. Send round a note to Lord Pigott, and you'll have your special license before the day is up! Meanwhile, I'll handle the arrangements for the wedding. I do so love weddings! The footmen can deliver invitations to your friends tonight while cook whips up a grand feast. It will be a challenge, no doubt, but we can do it."

Lady Spraddlin gasped, one white-gloved hand clamped over her mouth.

"Come, dear." Aunt Inez grasped Mercy Mary's arm. "You of all people should applaud Lord Seybourne's decision. After all, he is sacrificing his bachelorhood for the sake of saving an unfortunate woman."

"But you know nothing about her!" Lady Spraddlin jerked

her arm away from Lady Twitchett. Standing nose to nose with the viscount, she said, "You are making a terrible mistake!"

"If she awakens and tells me she has a husband, I shan't insist on going through with the marriage," Seybourne conceded. But in his heart, he doubted the pretty minx was married. It was far more likely Mercy Mary's speculation was true: It appeared to him that the young woman was a cyprian and had been servicing Sir Hester when the killer arrived.

At any rate, when word got out there was a witness to Sir Hester's murder—and it was bound to, for Aunt Inez was absolutely correct about the propensity of servants to gossip— the killer would come looking for her.

And then, Lord Seybourne would apprehend not only a murderer, but a traitor, as well. Even if the killer were not the author of the note found in the baronet's pocket, he undoubtedly would lead Seybourne to him. Or her.

Using the mysterious naked woman as bait to draw out the murderer and traitor seemed a stroke of genius. Aunt Inez's complicity in urging the marriage was a stroke of superb luck.

The specter of marriage, however, created an entirely new nest of complications. In the short moments he'd held the woman in his arms, the viscount sensed a certain vulnerability about her that made him loathe to betray her.

Yet he couldn't tell her he was using her as bait! No, he'd simply tell the pretty minx that he was marrying her to save both their reputations. She'd be relieved to hear that when Lord Pigott's political campaign ended, she could seek an annulment, move to the country, or simply disappear.

Ushering the small party from the room, Seybourne said, "Now, if you will all please vacate the premises. All except Aunt Inez, of course. I shall need your help, dear, in dressing this poor lady so that she is suitable for travel. Mercy, may I borrow your pelisse?"

With an angry frown, Lady Mercy Mary ripped off her elegant pale green outer garment and tossed it at Seybourne. "I shouldn't say this to you, Lawrie, but despite everything, I still care for you. I only hope you know what you are about. I fear that you are headed for trouble."

"Care to translate?" he shot back at her, vaguely annoyed by the oblique threat in her voice.

She thrust out her lower lip and shook her head. Red curls bobbed as she flounced from the room. Pausing at the threshold, she cast him a backward glance and said, "Just watch your back, Lawrie. You know nothing about that woman or the trouble she will bring down on your head! And I, for one, predict you will rue the day you thought to offer her your protection!"

Chapter Two

Georgiana was brought to her senses by the heady tingle of hartshorn waved beneath her sensitive nose. Her eyes flew open, and alarm shot through her body like a hot poker. *Where was she? What was she doing in someone else's bed? And, most importantly, where was Sir Hester?*

A portly gray-haired woman and a handsome shaggy-haired man peered down at her. Georgiana wondered what they were whispering and why they wore such grim expressions.

And then she remembered. Her mind flashed on that black-clad masked man with the cruel voice and the gleaming pistol. Poor old Sir Hester's face had paled with shock. Then came the report of the gun, loud and final, clanging in Georgiana's sensitive ears like a cannon blast. Instinct had flung her across the room, talons unsheathed, fur bristling. She had leapt at the man in the many-caped coat, latching onto his clothing with her claws. He tossed her to the floor like a scrap of offal, and her head banged the leg of Sir Hester's desk so hard that she saw stars.

Vaguely, she remembered being scooped up by the tall, broad-shouldered man. It was *that* man who stood at her bedside now. His scent—dense and masculine—still tickled her nos-

trils. The strength of his embrace continued to comfort. And
that was passing strange, because Georgiana abhorred being
held. She had always struggled out of Sir Hester's arms the
moment the old man captured her.

Yet the sensation of this handsome stranger's hands on her
flesh still burned inside her. What in the world had happened
to Georgiana? It was unthinkable that she'd actually enjoyed
being held, that she'd actually taken comfort in a man's
embrace. What had happened to her in the confusing moments
following Sir Hester's murder? She wasn't the same little black
cat that Sir Hester had taken in off the wharves, that was certain.

She stretched her aching limbs and studied her surroundings.
She was in a bed, a big soft bed with crisp white linen counter-
panes and floral chintz coverlets. Mounds of soft feather pillows
cradled her head.

Her movements drew the attention of the couple standing
beside the bed.

"I think she is coming out of it," the woman said.

Digging her nails into the bedclothes, Georgiana pushed
herself to a sitting position. She was surprised to find herself
staring at a painting situated on the opposite wall above a lady's
dressing table. It was a portrait of a pale woman with long,
flowing black hair. She challenged the woman with a penetrating stare, until at last, she realized she was gazing at her own
reflection in a mirror.

Seized with fear, she let loose a bloodcurdling howl.

"Oh, my! Lawrence, do something!" The portly woman
with the powdered hair stumbled backward, her palm pressed
to a pudgy cheek.

"What would you have me do, Aunt Inez?" the man replied,
with perfect equanimity. "It appears our houseguest is a bit
confused. Not surprising given that awful lump on her head
and the shock she has suffered. Quite natural under the circumstances, I should think."

Georgiana couldn't tear her gaze from the mirror. Good Lord,
she really *was not* the same sleek black cat she'd been when
Sir Hester rescued her. Now, she was a full-grown, two-legged
lady clothed in a white linen night rail scooped low at the

neck to reveal a generous amount of creamy *decolletage*. And evidently she'd found her way into a very elegant home. That handsome man must have brought her here—it must be *his* home, she concluded.

Hissing at her own reflection, she panicked at the prospect of living as a lady the rest of her life. She never had buckled under to anyone else's fiats; she knew how to survive, but she knew nothing of domesticity, much less subservience.

Slipping from beneath the covers, she scampered to the dresser and put her nose to the mirror.

Grasping her companion's arm, the older woman spoke in a hoarse whisper any barn cat worth its salt could have detected at fifty paces. "Do you think the little wretch is a bit soft in the head?"

A warm, throaty chuckle escaped the man's lips. As Georgiana studied her reflection, turning her head side to side, she met his frankly admiring gaze in the mirror. With one hand raised to her cheek, she froze, every muscle in her body tensed, every hair seemingly on end. She stared her best unblinking stare, and the man stared back. It was a contest of wills to see who would look away first.

And it was a contest that awakened in Georgiana a deeply buried awareness, an uneasy need she fought to suppress. A long-dormant bud of feminine awareness unfolded in the pit of her stomach. The man's icy, pale-blue gaze was both disturbing and welcome, challenging, yet strangely comforting. Somehow, he managed to caress her entire body with just a look.

But, when the predatorial hunger in his stare sharply focused, Georgiana experienced a frisson of fear. There was no mistaking the animal appetite smoldering behind that man's eyes. She knew that look; in her day she had met a few toms who wore that identical rakish expression. And, she knew what that man was thinking as he scanned her backside from top to bottom.

She might be new to this Regency lady act, but she had been a female all her life.

Luckily, the older woman's high-pitched voice shattered the

disturbing magnetic bond that linked them. "Really, Lawrence, I think the poor dear is mad."

"Wouldn't you like to rest a bit longer?" The man gestured toward the bed. "I think you should. You're a trifle peaked around the eyes, if you don't mind my saying so."

Georgiana moved toward the bed in long, slow strides. Once beneath the counterpane, she held out her hands, spreading her fingers and studying with unabashed amazement her smooth, oval-shaped fingernails. They were so different from the sharp talons she remembered; so different and so much more pleasing to her. How very odd, she thought, catching the quizzical glances exchanged by the handsome man and pudgy woman.

Not one to worry over what others thought, Georgiana sank further into the soft mattress, pulling the covers tighter to her chin. She stretched her limbs again and enjoyed an open-mouthed yawn. Sleep had always been her sanctuary; now seemed as good a time as any for a long, cozy nap.

As her eyelids grew heavy, she noticed that the gaze of the shaggy-haired man remained intently fixed on her. Falling asleep beneath his stare was like curling up in a bright patch of sunlight. The corners of her mouth tugged upward in an involuntary smile.

"Why, that is the strangest creature—" the old woman began.

But, the man cut her off with a lift of his hand. " 'Tis all right, Aunt Inez. Let her sleep some more. I will talk with her later."

He reached down and pressed the back of his hand to her forehead, as if to measure the warmth of her flesh. His touch was as pleasurable to Georgiana as a stroke on the head, as luxuriously delicious as a dollop of fresh cream in her milk bowl. Sleep enveloped her. Perhaps being a lady would have its rewards, after all.

Three hours later, Aunt Inez reentered the room to find her nephew Lord Seybourne seated in a chair beside the bed. Chin resting in his hand, he stared at the sleeping woman as if he were mesmerized. He barely acknowledged his aunt's presence before returning his gaze to her peaceful expression.

"Land's sakes!" Inez said, trundling to her nephew's side. "Is she still asleep? Do you reckon the little termagant will sleep all day?"

The viscount shifted uncomfortably. If she did, he was quite content to keep his vigil.

"Shall I shake her awake?" he asked, his tone indolent.

"Why don't you, then?" Inez propped her meaty fists on her ample hips and stared at him. "I should like to ask her a question or two. Such as, who is she and where did she come from?"

Abruptly, the viscount stood and returned his chair to its original place. "This woman has suffered a great shock, Aunt, and she needs her rest. Wake her now, and you risk ruining her health, as well as frightening her to death. She needs sleep and she shall have it—as much as her body craves.

"Moreover," the viscount continued, "I want her to tell me what she saw at Sir Hester's house. And if we frighten her to death, or attempt to intimidate her, she might never disclose what she knows of Sir Hester's murder. My instincts tell me that she's a skittish one—we'll have to *earn* her trust, I'm afraid."

His aunt opened her mouth, then promptly clamped it shut.

"And those are my orders," the viscount added.

His aunt's bottom lip trembled a bit, but she nodded. "If that is the way you will have it. I shan't wake the girl, then. Let her sleep until Sunday, see if I care!"

Breathing a sigh of relief, Lord Seybourne wrapped his arms about his portly aunt. She laid her head on his chest and whiffled. When he was unable to tolerate it any longer, he gently set her at arm's length. How could he tell his aunt that he was protecting this woman like a mother lioness, not because he was concerned about her welfare or his reputation, but because he needed her as bait to trap a killer? How could he tell his aunt he intended to marry a complete unknown for the sole purpose of waggling her beneath the nose of a murderer?

The ton of stones resting on Seybourne's chest settled heavily, crushing his scarred heart. When he looked at Georgiana's sleeping face, the pressure in his chest intensified. As hours passed, and he remained at her bedside, a fissure formed in the brittle barrier surrounding his heart. *A hairline crack to be sure, but an opening nonetheless.*

The clock on the ormolu nightstand ticked off six hours. Georgiana's eyes blinked open and she stared first at the heavy-set woman, then at the tall shaggy-haired man who stood at her bedside like watchdogs. *Good heavens, they were still there! Were they ever going to leave her alone?*

Her gaze locked with the man's, and a prickly awareness ruffled the fine hairs on the back of her neck. Scrabbling at the bedclothes, she clutched them beneath her chin and tensed for battle.

But there was to be none. Disputes would no longer be solved by clawing eyes, or biting ears. Releasing a pent-up breath, Georgiana smiled. Or at least she tried to. What emerged from her lips was a sort of guttural meow. She cleared her throat and tried again.

"What was that, my dear?" The older woman leaned closer and squinted at Georgiana.

In her previous life, she would have hissed and arched her spine, but instinct instructed Georgiana to be circumspect, deferential—even submissive, if necessary. As soon as she felt at ease in her surroundings, she would say plenty. But it wasn't in her nature to lower her guard quickly. She preferred to sit back and watch for a while.

"Can you understand me?" the man said, in laboriously slow, stentorian tones.

Georgia nodded, amused. Good heavens, they thought she was dumb. Well, she'd show them she wasn't dumb. *But not yet.*

"Can you speak English?" the woman asked.

Georgiana nodded. In a former life, she'd lived on a ship that sailed from England to France to Spain to Portugal. She had traveled to the Orient, too. Truth be known, she could understand at least four languages other than English. But she supposed that was more than this pie-faced woman needed to know.

"Are you hurt or injured anywhere?" the man asked.

Georgiana stared at him. He was inordinately handsome with his rather prominent nose, piercing pale-blue eyes, and shaggy gray-brown hair. He had a wolfish look.

Not that Georgiana had ever encountered a wolf and, frankly, she hoped she never did. But, she couldn't deny this man his due; he possessed an incredible animal magnetism.

Georgiana dismissed her errant thoughts with a shake of her head. She had more important things to worry about now. Like figuring out the identities of this man and woman who seemed to be staring at her every time she wakened from a nap. And deciding what sort of Banbury tale she would tell them about her identity and her past. Even a clanker would be more plausible than the truth.

"Might I have a bowl of cream?" she asked, pleasantly surprised by the feminine sound of her own voice.

"A bowl of cream?" the man repeated, tilting his head quizzically.

Georgiana detected a glimmer of wit behind his wolfish gaze. He gave her a warm smile that sent the same ripples of pleasure through her body that Sir Hester's affectionate hand-strokes had induced. Snuggling deeper in the bedclothes, she narrowed her eyes. It was never wise to let a man know you were staring appreciatively at him. Might give him the impression you admired him, or worse, might lead him to believe you were indiscriminate with your affections.

The woman, whose complexion reminded Georgiana of clotted cream, assumed a much more jaded look. "A bowl of cream, my dear? Don't you mean a cup of milk? Or perhaps a spot of tea?"

Georgiana realized her mistake. "Oh, yes! A cup of milk, that is precisely what I meant."

The woman pulled a bell cord, and minutes later, a servant appeared, nodding deferentially as the order for milk was placed, then rushing off to fetch it. A short time later, the servant returned with a silver tray, which was set with white

linen and laden with a small beaker of milk. Georgiana sat up
and the tray was placed across her lap. The film of heavy cream
on the fresh, lukewarm milk tantalized her. Clasping the ceramic
cup with both hands, Georgiana dipped her nose into the beaker.
Then, her tongue darted out and lapped at the surface of the
thick, creamy, delicious milk.

The older woman gasped. "Whatever is the matter with that
creature?"

Georgiana's head popped up. She took in the woman's horrified gaze and the man's expression of puzzled amusement.
Belatedly, she realized her second *faux pas*. Carefully, she
raised the beaker of milk to her lips and sipped. Ridiculous,
she thought, as milk trickled down her chin. It would be so
much easier to lower her head and lap it up.

Seybourne, meanwhile, stared in amazement. He thought
he'd never seen a more delectable woman—slightly confused
as a result of that nasty blow on her head, perhaps even a bit
dotty—but delectable nonetheless. Her complexion was as pale
and flawless as a blanket of snow. Even beneath the counter-
panes, the outline of her long, sinewy limbs was an alluring
picture. If Aunt Inez had not been hovering at his elbow, he'd
be sorely tempted to run his fingers through the lady's thick
mane of silky black hair.

Instead, he removed the silver tray from her lap, took the
empty beaker from her fingers, and placed them on the ormolu
nightstand. "Clearly you have suffered quite a shock, my dear.
And I am afraid I have got a bit more distressing news to share
with you. Do you think you could stand a little conversation
just now? Are you strong enough to talk?"

The young woman rubbed her green eyes with the back
of her hand, an affectation that Seybourne found strangely
endearing. She shrugged lightly, seemingly indifferent to the
viscount's request, as well as his presence. Her nonchalance was
both irritating and irresistible. Seybourne had inspired many
reactions from many women. But he had never met a woman
who was *indifferent* toward him.

He was surprised when she looked at him and spoke. Other
than her request for milk, she hadn't uttered a word since he'd

found her. Now he experienced a heady rush of sensual pleasure at the sound of her soft, throaty voice.

"What could be more distressing than the situation I find myself in?" she asked. "I do not know where I am, nor do I know how I got here. I haven't the faintest notion who you are. Either of you. So what can you tell me that would be more distressing than that?"

Aunt Inez huffed and wrung her lace handkerchief in exasperation. "What kind of little upstart is so impertinent as to insult the very man who saved her life?"

"Saved my life?" The woman's marvelous green eyes darted from Aunt Inez to the viscount.

"Yes," Seybourne replied. "I found you this morning in Sir Hester's study. He was dead and you were lying beside him . . . quite naked, I'm afraid. Rather than leave you to the devices of the Bow Street Runners, I saw fit to bring you home with me. Of course, that, in itself, raises some very troubling issues. How best to keep you under my protection, for example, without creating a scandal that will ruin us both."

"And how do you propose to do that?" the mysterious woman asked, tossing her head so that her lustrous black mane swished across the pillow.

Seybourne swallowed a painful lump in his throat. "I intend to marry you."

"You intend to do what!" A flash of yellow ignited in her green eyes. But, just as quickly as her temper flared, she seemed to gain control of it. She let out a soft, sibilant hiss and sat as still as a statue, waiting for Seybourne to explain himself.

Her intense, unblinking stare unnerved him. But, he stared back, refusing to be intimidated by her. "You are not already married, are you?"

Georgiana hesitated a moment, uncertain how to proceed. If she said yes, the viscount would toss her into the street, an unpromising place for a defenseless female. "I cannot remember being married," she answered, at length.

Seybourne's eyes flickered to her hands. "You are not wearing a ring, so I believe it is safe to proceed on the assumption that you are alone in the world."

Seybourne turned to his aunt and leaned toward her, quietly whispering in her ear. The woman nodded, gave Georgiana a watery, skeptical smile, then left the room. The atmosphere altered dramatically once Georgiana found herself alone with the man who'd scooped her off Sir Hester's floor. Instinctively, she pushed against the bolsters and pillows at her back.

"I suppose formal introductions are in order. I am Lawrence deWulff, Viscount Seybourne." This was followed by an elegant low bow. "And you are?" he asked, straightening.

"Georgiana."

"How lovely. Last name . . . title?"

Good lord, she had not anticipated such difficulty in answering the man's questions. And these were just the easy ones!

Well, best to stick as close to the truth as possible. After all, the man was quite aware she'd recently suffered a horrible shock. It wasn't entirely impossible that her memory was temporarily dislodged, perhaps even permanently lost. It would be far easier to plead that she'd forgotten her past than attempt to invent one from whole cloth. And she certainly couldn't tell the viscount the truth.

Georgiana batted her sooty long lashes and lowered her gaze. All of her feline instincts melded with her feminine ones, resulting in an uncanny ability to read the viscount's moods. She also had an exhilarating desire to toy with his emotions the way a kitten trifled with a skein of yarn. Shifting languorously beneath the bedcovers, she allowed the counterpane to slip off her shoulder and expose the ruffled low-scooped neck of her night rail.

Seybourne's expression instantly tightened. Beneath his immaculate white cravat, his Adam's apple bobbed convulsively. His gaze fell to Georgiana's creamy *decolletage,* then darted upward, guiltily and hungrily.

A purr, deep and throaty, rumbled from Georgiana's diaphragm.

Seybourne's eyes widened. "What was that you said?"

Startled, Georgiana cleared her throat. *What was she thinking? Did she really want to tweak this giant's nose?* "I am afraid I am catching a rather nasty cold, my lord. Forgive me."

Visibly relaxed, he shifted his weight and clasped his hands behind his back. " 'Twas the milk, I suppose. I shall see to it that you are sent some hot tea. That will prove more efficacious for your sore throat, I assure you."

Tea. Georgiana nodded glumly. Unless it were brewed from catnip, she truly didn't believe she would be able to stomach it.

After a few moments of uncomfortable silence, Seybourne reiterated his intention of marrying Georgiana.

"There is really nothing else for it," he concluded. "You see, just as I scooped you up from the floor where you lay curled around Sir Hester's neck—naked—my aunt Inez burst into the room. I regret to inform you that she is the current president and chief benefactor of the Society for the Rehabilitation of Wanton Women. I believe she felt she could kill two birds with one stone by marrying me off to you."

"I am not sure I understand," Georgiana said.

The viscount sat on the edge of the bed. Clasping her hand, he leaned toward Georgiana. Pale-blue eyes intent, his nose was so close to hers she could feel his breath on her skin, and could study the slightly weather-beaten texture of his dark features. His nearness kindled an odd warmth in the pit of her stomach.

But, Seybourne—seemingly disconcerted by the warmth generated between them—quickly released her hand and slid away. "Our marriage and your subsequent *redemption* will validate my aunt's lifework, I'm afraid. Why, we'll be mascots of her pet charity ere long."

"You do not look the sort of man who would allow his aunt to browbeat him into a marriage he did not want. You do not appear the sort of man to do anything he did not want to."

Seybourne chuckled. "Just so. However, the scandal of refusing to marry a woman with whom I was caught in a compromising circumstance would be treacherous, indeed. I can ill afford that sort of negative publicity. Both *ton* and commoners alike will forgive a man his indiscretions if he behaves honorably toward the woman whose reputation he has sullied. But no one, least of all Aunt Inez, would forgive me for tossing you into the streets.''

The room fell quiet again until Seybourne said, ''I cannot help but ask you: were you present when the baronet was murdered? Do you know the identity of his killer?''

''I have no idea who killed Sir Hester.'' And that was true enough; she hadn't recognized the man behind the mask.

''Can you remember anything about the minutes preceding the baronet's death?''

''I cannot even remember who I am. Don't you think if I knew my name and address, I would demand to be returned to my home immediately? I hope you do not think I am actually enjoying this charade!''

''I am certain the idea of marrying me is repulsive to you,'' Lord Seybourne said stiffly. ''But you must be totally honest with me, particularly if we are to be married and I am to protect you. I don't mean to offend, but I must know the nature of your relationship with Sir Hester.''

Georgiana gasped. ''Are you suggesting that I carried on some sort of illicit relationship with Sir Hester? Do you insinuate that I am a *professional* woman?''

''You were found with your arms around his neck and you were naked, Georgiana. What other assumption should a reasonable man make?''

''If you believe that, why on earth would you want to marry me?''

''Because I was caught red-handed holding a naked woman in my arms, and therefore I must either marry you or risk bringing a very public and shameful opprobrium down on both our heads. I cannot risk that just now. I am in the middle of conducting a very hotly contested political campaign on behalf of a friend.''

''I do not care about your reputation. Or mine!''

''Then I am offering you respectability, a roof over your head, food to eat and enough pin money to satisfy even the most flagrant spendthrift's demand for fashionable fribbles.''

On the one hand, Georgiana wanted nothing more than to leap from the bed, race across the room, and hide beneath a piece of furniture. She thought of escaping the viscount's house and leaving this nightmare behind. If she could find her way to the kitchens, she might steal a wedge of cheese and escape through the back alleys toward the docklands, the area of London where she'd scrounged her way through eight previous lives. She could survive there; she'd done it before.

But the thought of being stranded in such a cruel, wicked environment where only the fittest survived held no appeal. She no longer possessed her claws and her sharp teeth. Her unerring senses of direction, smell and hearing were quickly diminishing. And she was fearful that she might have lost her ability to land on her feet when tossed into the air by drunken sailors or pitched from open three-story windows by exasperated prostitutes. On reflection, surviving on the wharves might not be as easy as it once was.

Her gaze locked with Seybourne's and she reacted to him as woman to man, not cat to human, or chattel to owner. With a jolt, she slid a bit further from her former life.

A part of her was gone forever. She'd been a good mouser in her day, but she would not stand a chance in the wilds of London now. Not without a protector. Somewhere in the transformation from cat to woman, she had lost her edge.

The viscount's deep voice jolted her from her reverie. "In future, if it is discovered that there exists an impediment to this marriage, an annulment can be obtained."

"And if there exists no impediment?" Georgiana hardly dared ask the question. Would she be bound to this man for life? She could hardly fathom such an arrangement! Why, she'd never pledged herself to a single tom, and she hadn't the least confidence that it was wise to do so now.

He hesitated, a cloud darkening his expression. "I shall not force you to live under this roof if, after your memory has returned and you are sensible enough to make your own decisions, you choose to leave. After a time, it will not matter to me what the *ton* think of my disreputable personal life. And then you will be free to go. I have some influence among the members of Parliament and the Church authorities. I will see to it that an annulment is granted, or that you are pensioned off at a generous sum.''

"How kind of you,'' Georgiana replied, more tartly than she'd intended.

Without warning, the viscount's gaze went icy. "You have no choice, my dear.''

"A lady always has a choice.''

The corners of his lips lifted almost imperceptibly, drawing Georgiana's gaze to them. With a deferential nod, he said, *"Touché.* Your choice is to marry me and accept my offer of protection, or leave here with whatever clothing my saintly aunt might lend you. Sir Hester's killer will track you down in no time. Are you prepared to confront him alone?''

Georgiana turned her head. "My lord, for all that you are being kind and generous in offering to marry me, I must confess, I do not think I am well suited to be your wife.'' She heard the tremble in her voice and marveled at this sudden inability to conceal her emotions. Was this part of being human, too?

The viscount's voice lowered to a husky whisper, a deep masculine tone that sent chill bumps racing up Georgiana's spine. "Are you afraid of me, my lady?''

"A little.''

"You needn't be, minx.'' His gaze, so cold a moment before, was as inviting as a bed of clover.

Oh, the impossibility of it all! Shutting her eyes tightly, Georgiana was appalled that a hot tear squeezed from beneath her lashes and streamed down her cheek. A tear! She'd never cried before, never felt a moment's remorse or regret, never experienced any of these strange emotions washing over her. When the viscount reached out and wiped that single tear from her cheek, she shivered with emotion. Where had her characteristic aloofness flown? Where had her diffident manner gone?

With shocking clarity, she realized that her new life as a lady was going to be terrifying. She couldn't control her emotions as readily as she could before. She was no longer the cool sphinx she once was, content with or without human company. And worse, she sensed that Viscount Seybourne was not going to be as easily tamed as the affable Sir Hester. With the baronet, a simple purr or a plaintive meow produced anything from a tickle beneath the chin to a generous helping of salty haddock or a saucer of cream. A lift of Georgiana's tail signaled her interest in play; a haughty turn of her head put the old man off.

But *this* man—this handsome, wolfish creature whose touch filled her with terror and pleasure at the same time—was a different animal. Unlike Sir Hester, she could not bend him to her will with a purr or a growl. She couldn't put him off with a shake of her head or a well-placed bite to the finger. This man was crowding her, cajoling her, toying with her own emotions the way she had always toyed with those of the humans she condescended to live with. It was a frightening shock to think her emotions were no longer within her total control. It was a jolt to her senses to realize how transparent she was. Good heavens, no wonder humans were always getting themselves into so much trouble!

And then another thought amplified her panic.

What would she do when Lord Seybourne, soon to be her husband, turned that hungry look on her with the expectation of being satisfied? Would she fight him off, or leap into his arms?

She had no idea. Certainly, she had fended off many a prospective suitor with claws and fangs. But, she had wooed a few, too, when she was hungry and needed a little help in catching dinner. To a cat in the streets, survival was of paramount concern; sex was something necessarily snatched in an alley. And romance was as rare as caviar. To a woman who had never experienced a *sexual* touch that was loving, too, Lord Seybourne's allure was hopelessly confusing.

"I am waiting for an answer," he reminded her gently. "Shall we marry? Or shall you return to the wilds of London, without my protection?"

"All right, my lord—"

"Call me Lawrence, or Lawrie, please, if we are about to be married."

"I will marry you, then. But on one condition. After I recover my memory and am sensible enough to fend for myself, you must devise a way to release me from my marital obligation. I shan't be troubled if my reputation is ruined into the bargain. I will leave London, and no one in this city will ever see hide nor hair of me again.''

''Are you from the country, then?''

Georgiana shook her head. ''No, I don't think so.''

A puzzled look creased the viscount's brow. ''What do you mean, you don't think so?''

Touching her fingers lightly to her temple, Georgiana feigned a pensive expression. ''I'm afraid I cannot remember anything of my past, my lo—I mean, Lawrence. I took quite a bump on the head, you know.''

''Aye, I am aware. Do you not remember anything about your identity or your past?''

''Only my Christian name, I'm afraid.''

''Can you not recall the name of any relatives who might be in a position to help you or offer you a roof over your head?''

''No, I am certain there is no one.''

He seemed oddly pleased to hear this. Standing, he flashed Georgiana a grin and said, ''Well, then, there is no known impediment to our marrying. I shall use my influence to obtain a special license right away, and tomorrow I shall send for the Reverend Smallpage. Aunt Inez will be thrilled to hear that I've inaugurated her pet cause by marrying you, by the way.''

''Because I am a wanton woman?'' Georgiana asked, the trace of a deep-throated trill in her voice.

Her tone brought a frown to the viscount's face. ''I didn't mean to say that. Please forgive me, Georgiana. I suppose I shouldn't make light of Aunt Inez's cause—nor should I presume anything about your past—but you see I really have never been given to spend time fretting over a woman's history. Why should a woman be held to any higher standard of conduct than a man?''

''Why, indeed?'' Georgiana dipped lower in the bed, pulling the counterpane to her chin. With the viscount's dark eyes trained on her face and shoulders, she felt naked and vulnerable. The man had a way of igniting little brush fires on her skin, wherever he looked at her. And his lack of regard for her past relaxed her. A little.

Georgiana dreaded the moment when the viscount's feral, lust-filled hunger matched her own. She was vulnerable to his charms, that much was certain. She would have to be on her guard if she intended to protect herself. And she did. Silently, she consoled herself with the thought that she didn't need anyone, much less a man, to make her happy. She would get out of this marriage soon enough—when it no longer held any advantage for her. And then she'd be on her own again. A survivor. That's what she'd always been, and still was.

The urge to sleep was still strong and primal, overwhelming her in an instant. Georgiana's eyelids drooped heavily and she yawned, this time remembering belatedly to cover her gaping mouth.

The viscount's voice echoed in her ears as she slipped into a deep, velvety slumber. "Good heavens, minx. You certainly do sleep a lot. Perhaps it is the result of that bump on your head. . . ."

Chapter Three

At Carlton House, the corpulent King George IV, clad in skintight gold satin knee pants, immaculate white stockings, and gleaming black slippers, reclined on an Oriental-inspired divan and let out a resounding belch. A footman decked out in pale-blue livery lifted the monarch's gouty leg and gently positioned it atop a tufted, tasseled foot-cushion. Once settled with a glass of port within his reach, and a branch of grapes balanced on his huge belly, the king turned his attention to the man seated opposite him.

"Sorry to keep you waiting, Seybourne, but this damned leg of mine is driving me mad! Between my gout and the vexations of that fool woman I am married to—who, by the way, was recently reported to have been seen making love to a mustachioed Italian on the deck of a frigate headed for Genoa—I am driven to distraction!" The king popped a grape into his mouth and chewed thoughtfully.

Seybourne sat on a crocodile-legged chair, which was obviously designed for fashion as opposed to comfort. Crossing his long legs, he suppressed a grin and said, "I understand you are bedeviled by troubles within and without the boundaries of England, sire. Thank God that Boney has been safely interred at Saint Helena these past five years.''

The king rolled his eyes theatrically. "But, my spies tell me that Puss'n Boots has delusions of grandeur. Despite his infirmities, he persists in plotting an escape from his luxurious prison island. And there are those who would abet his plans to upset everything accomplished at Vienna. Which is precisely why my silly wife should cease courting the favors of every silly Italian who invites her to the opera. Good God, does the woman not realize how great a prize she would be to Boney's sympathizers, both foreign and domestic? Why, they could kidnap her and hold her hostage in exchange for Napolean's release.''

"Perhaps Your Highness should insist that the queen return home,'' Seybourne suggested.

"Oh-ho! But that is the rub! I do not want the wretched woman back in England!''

The viscount allowed himself a sympathetic chuckle. It was well known about London that King George despised his uncouth, ill-mannered, reputedly *dirty* Brunswick wife. And it was equally well known that he had treated her rudely from the day she arrived on English shores, even to the point of calling for a strong drink the moment he laid eyes on her.

In fact, the king's callousness toward his wife was a source of contention among both Town *and* country factions, aristocrats and common folk. While the Tory ministers deplored Caroline's conduct, they desperately counseled the king to avoid the spectacle of divorce proceedings. Opportunistic Whigs, on the other hand, portrayed the king's rejection of his wife as symbolic of His Highness's antipathy toward the common people. Suffice it to say, the domestic squabbles of Caroline and George had taken on gigantic political proportions.

"I do not believe you have come here to discuss my wife, however.'' The king tossed a naked grape-branch onto a silver platter, then, grunting, reached for his glass of port. "You said the matter was of some urgency, and so I assume it has something to do with your infiltration of the Kit-Kat Club. Pray, what new intelligence do you have for me?''

"I am afraid that I have rather disturbing news to report, sire. I believe that there's a plot underfoot to destroy your government, perhaps even to assassinate you."

A violent spray erupted from the king's mouth and stained his satin breeches with a mist of purple splotches. Muttering a series of oaths, he kicked his good leg in the air and slammed his glass of port on the table beside him. Then, returning his gaze to Seybourne, he banged his fist on the satin cushion beside him, and cried, "Who the devil is plotting to kill me *now?* Are you telling me, man, that there is another Cato Street Conspiracy brewing?"

After calmly describing the circumstances of Sir Hester's death, Seybourne recited the pertinent parts of the note he had discovered. Omitted from his report was any mention of the naked woman named Georgiana.

Sighing, the king closed his eyes. After a moment, he looked at Seybourne, his expression full of bitter resignation. "Just a sennight ago, Lawrence, you told me that the members of the Kit-Kat Club were not so radical as I had feared, that my paranoia after Thistlewood's arrest was unjustified, and that it was Henry Hunt I should concern myself with."

"The plot being hatched, sire, may not include every member of the Club. Certainly, it has never been discussed in my presence. Perhaps a lone anarchist has taken cover within the Club."

"But the note you read to me," the king pointed out, "implies that there exists a conspiracy of at least two."

"That is true," the viscount conceded. "But rest assured, I will expose these conspirators and I will apprehend them before they have had an opportunity to harm a hair on your head."

"The note did not precisely say they meant to kill me, did it?" The king's voice wavered as he intensely scrutinized Seybourne's face for reassurance.

"No, it did not." But the viscount wasn't at all certain the king's person was safe from an assassination attempt. He fully intended to treat the note as a threat to George's life.

With a groan, the monarch reached for his bottle of port, poured himself another healthy measure and threw it back with one gulp. "Refresh my memory, Lawrence. Tell me more about this Kit-Kat Club."

"As you know, sire, it is a small, select organization, numbering nine in members. It was named after an eighteenth-century drinking club."

"Did you have any difficulty obtaining membership in the club?"

"None," the viscount replied. "Upon my return from Australia, which I owe to Your Highness's mercy—"

The king gave a short, nervous burst of laughter. "Now you surprise me, speaking in such euphemistic tones. I would hardly call it mercy, my friend. After all, I merely offered you a royal pardon in exchange for your agreement to spy on this Whig organization for me. Considering your lifelong friendship with Lord Turner Pigott, you were the ideal man for the job. The fact you are spearheading his election campaign, by the way, is a perfect ruse!"

With a grin, Seybourne said, "No offense, sire, but I do hope the old boy wins."

King George laughed heartily at Seybourne's plain speaking. But he could not be long distracted from thoughts of his own predicament. "Away with you, then. Go and find out who killed Sir Hester, and who in the Kit-Kat Club is conspiring to murder me."

Seybourne stood and made a low elegant leg before the king's divan. "Yes, sire. I will return when I have further information concerning this unpleasant matter." After a slight hesitation, he added, "By the way, I am getting married this afternoon."

That brought a gasp of surprise from the king. "Married? To Lady Spraddlin? What in the hell for? Dear God, man, why marry the baker when you are getting the bread for free?"

The viscount felt a wave of heat beneath his cravat. " 'Tis not Lady Spraddlin, sire, that I am engaged to. I am marrying a young woman unfamiliar to London society. Her name is, ah, Lady Georgiana deWulff. She is a distant cousin that I recently met for the first time. Love at first sight, you understand."

"Oh, yes. Know all about that! Well, off with you, then. And have a happy wedding. I wish you all the connubial joy that I have failed to experience with that hideous cow from Brunswick!"

Laughing, Lord Seybourne made a quick exit. Truth be known, he was quite anxious to return home and see how his pretty minx was faring under the capable hands of his Aunt Inez.

Georgiana stood in the center of Lord Seybourne's Tenterden Street drawing room, her head spinning as a hubbub of activity swarmed around her. She could hardly believe that she was getting married today. The rapidity with which her life had altered amazed her.

But what amazed her even more was that, after hours spent contemplating her dilemma, she could think of no better solution than to marry the viscount. That the notion held a scant amount of wicked appeal irritated her further. She was enormously troubled not only by her increasing dependence, but also by her feelings of alternating resentment and attraction toward Lord Seybourne.

Despite her jumbled emotions, however, Georgiana's survival instinct prevailed. In a strange, new world that included endless cups of tea and constant impingements on her nap time, she needed a protector. As much as she hated to admit it, she needed Lord Seybourne. *If only temporarily.*

Just as Sir Hester once had been her protector, now Viscount Seybourne assumed that role. With one profound difference: Whereas Sir Hester had offered her sanctuary from the animal kingdom, Lord Seybourne aroused every feline instinct she'd ever possessed. The irony wasn't lost on Georgiana, but she was helpless to extricate herself from the situation.

And when she heard the front door of the town house slam shut, and the servants outside the drawing room greet their master with friendly hellos, her knees wobbled so badly that she nearly collapsed.

The viscount stood for a moment in the threshold, his gaze

scanning the crowded room. When his stare at last locked on her, Georgiana felt like a school of minnows had been released in her stomach. The crooked smile that played across his lips was oddly endearing. Just looking at the man filled her with jittery anticipation.

"So there is my bride." The low growl of his voice was undetectable to all but Georgiana's sensitive ears. Without taking his gaze from hers, the viscount crossed the room in long, wolfish strides.

Georgiana tensed, her nerves clanging as wildly as if she'd found herself in the predatorial sights of a sex-hungry tom. Pivoting, she bolted in the opposite direction and plowed directly into the formidable figure of Aunt Inez.

The impact shocked them both. Expelling a whoosh of sherry-laden breath, Lady Twitchett rocked back on her heels. Had it not been for the viscount's quick reaction, she would have tumbled over.

Grasping his aunt's arms, Lord Seybourne said, "Are you all right?"

The plump dowager disengaged herself from her nephew's embrace and fanned her face with an intricately carved ivory fan. "I am fine, boy, but see to Georgiana. 'Tis she who appears to be frightened out of her wits!"

The viscount's pale-blue gaze slid to Georgiana. Nervousness attacked her; liquid heat flooded her stomach and filtered outward through her limbs. Strangely, a chill swept across her shoulders at the same time. "I was just going to fetch a shawl," she stammered. "This gown is incredibly flimsy, and I cannot seem to find a sunny spot in this entire drawing room."

Lady Twitchett took her hand and held it between her own pudgy ones. "Good heavens, you are the oddest creature I have ever seen. Sleep all day, and then all you want is to find a warm, sunny spot and curl up in it and be left alone. Do you know, Lawrie, that I have had to pull her away from that front windowsill three times in the last fifteen minutes. I thought the girl's fascination with the passing carriages a bit dotty till I realized she was probably waiting for your arrival!"

"Is that so." The viscount appeared skeptical of Georgiana's motive for standing beside the window all morning.

As well he should be. Contrary to Lady Inez's speculations, Georgiana had dreaded the viscount's arrival. She only hoped that she could get through this charade of a wedding ceremony without clawing someone's face to shreds. Cornered, she'd always put up a good fight.

Inhaling a deep breath, she clenched her teeth together in what she hoped passed for a friendly smile. "Your aunt is right. I have been terribly nervous about the wedding, but your presence is reassuring. Does my gown suit?"

She turned in a half pirouette, holding between her fingers the skirt of her white wedding gown, an Empress-waisted confection with dotted Swiss bodice, lacey neckline and feminine puffed sleeves. Detecting the frankly admiring masculine gaze of her husband-to-be, a tingle of pleasure flowed through her body. By the time she relaxed her clenched teeth, her jaw ached.

Seybourne could have sworn he heard his bride-to-be *purr* as she dropped her skirt and locked gazes with him. A sense of unreality swept over him as Inez fussed over Georgiana's dress, picked at her fluffy sleeves and rearranged a tiny row of bows along the hem of her neckline. Staring into Georgiana's eyes, he felt an intense flash of recognition. Something in their kindred souls connected. Seybourne had the sudden urge to reach out and draw Georgiana into his arms, press his lips to her mouth and never let her go.

But before he acted on the impulse, the warmth of her gaze faded to an icy hardness. Georgiana quickly fixed her attention on Aunt Inez, as if the older woman were the most fascinating creature on earth.

Seybourne felt as if he'd taken a fiver in his nose. Was he stark-raving mad to marry a woman whose moods altered in an instant? Was he insane for wedding a minx whose gaze burned fiery-hot one second, then flickered ice-cold the next, all without the least apparent provocation?

He consoled himself with the reminder that when a decent period of time had passed and Sir Hester's killer was brought to justice, he would orchestrate a way to release Georgiana from the bonds of matrimony. It would not be easy, but he was not without influence, and he was confident he could do it. Life would return to normal; Georgiana would continue with her previous life, whatever that was; and he would be free to resume his comfortable arrangement with Lady Mercy Mary Spraddlin.

Turning to survey the crowded room, he was only slightly relieved to see one of his friends, Sir Morton Drysdale, approaching with two glasses of sherry.

"Here you go, old man. You look like you need a douse of something to restore your mettle." Under his breath, Sir Morton added, "Hardly surprising, given the impromptu nature of this wedding. Don't think I've ever seen such a hurried affair. And why didn't you tell your friends about this beautiful cousin of yours? Of course, now that I see her, I quite understand your reasons for hiding her from us."

"I told you, I hadn't seen the girl in years. Then, it was love at first glance. I would thank you not to mention the subject again."

"Not regretting your decision, are you?" Sir Morton whispered.

"Of course not!" Catching Georgiana's inquisitive gaze, Seybourne quickly introduced her to Sir Morton, the bluff towheaded young man who'd latched onto him when he joined the Kit-Kat Club.

When Sir Morton had politely bowed over Georgiana's hand and said his hellos to Lady Twitchett, the viscount said tersely, "Are the others here?"

The Kit-Kat Club was never mentioned by name in public, but Sir Morton didn't feign ignorance of Seybourne's meaning.

"Aye, all but Sir Douglas and he'll be here shortly, I suspect. Had an appointment at Tattersall's last I heard, but he's not one to miss a fancy party, not if he can help it." All this was said while the young man eyed Georgiana from the top of her head to the tip of her toes.

Which irritated the devil out of Seybourne. Suppressing the urge to grasp Sir Morton by the shoulders and shake him, Seybourne said, "I am certain Georgiana has matters to discuss with Aunt Inez. Shall we adjourn to the other side of the room for a moment, Morton? I wish to greet some of my guests.''

To his credit, the younger man took the hint, and with polite demurrals, made his adieu to Georgiana and Inez. Seybourne threw his bride-to-be a bleak, inscrutable gaze before crossing the room to join Mr. Jack Craven and the other Kit-Kat Club members, including the latecomer, Sir Douglas Babworth, a pale, portly man with mousy-brown hair who always seemed to be sweating.

"Sorry to be running a bit behind, Lawrie." Babworth mopped his face with a handkerchief. "What's this I hear about Sir Hester's being killed? The bruit about Tattersall's was that someone shot him, and the Bow Street Runners believe the motive was robbery."

Higgenbotham, a glass of whiskey in his hand, inclined his head toward Seybourne. "Damned bloody mess, this is! Though I must admit the matter seems to be wholly unrelated to Abercorn's writings. Even so, there's bound to be an extra bit of attention brought to our clandestine group. Servants talk, you know, and it is only a matter of time before the authorities begin asking questions. That kind of publicity, we do not need!"

"Why?" Lord Seybourne asked. "Since when must a political *salon* exist in utter secrecy?"

"We are not just a political *salon*," Sir Douglas replied primly. "We have got an agenda—one that the king would not cotton to, I swear!"

Smiling coolly, Seybourne sipped his sherry. "An agenda? Something I am not privy to? Come on, boys, what is this all about? I have been a member for very nearly two years now, and you are making me feel like an outsider."

Jack Craven's craggy long face appeared behind Higgenbotham's shoulder. "Two years is hardly any time at all, Lawrie."

Seybourne stiffened. "I suggest you apprise me of this organization's secret agenda—if there is one! Or is this some child's game that you are playing? Better tell me now, or I will notify the Bow Street Runners that the members of the Kit-Kat Club require some looking into!''

Craven smiled. His tone was conciliatory as he stood shoulder to shoulder between Higgenbotham and Babworth. ''Come now, Lawrie. You said when you joined the club that you were one of us. Lord Pigott vouched for you, said you had every reason to be angered by the king's frivolous, wasteful policies. Was Pigott mistaken, perhaps? Are you not committed to working diligently for Parliamentary reform, recision of the Sixteen Acts, and repeal of the corn tariffs?''

''I have yet to see this club do anything toward that end,'' Seybourne replied tightly. ''All we do when we meet is eat and drink and tell dirty jokes about King George and Mrs. Fitzherbert.''

''Stick with us, Lawrie,'' Craven said mildly. ''Douglas didn't mean to imply the Kit-Kat Club has a revolutionary agenda, did you, Doug? No, I didn't think so. In truth, we are an innocuous group, just a drinking club whose primary source of entertainment is the king's tawdry affairs. What could be more harmless than that?''

Seybourne clamped his lips together as Aunt Inez approached.

'' 'Tis time, boy,'' she said, laying a strong hand on his arm.

He drained his sherry, gave his acquaintances a curt nod, then turned his back on the men. Across the room, his bride awaited. The weight of the world settled on his shoulders as he strode toward her. The eyes trained on his back felt like hot lances pricking at him, reminding him that there were sinister forces at work in London. Moreover, he had a strong gut-feeling that there was something profound about Georgiana he didn't know.

But when he stood beside her and faced Reverend Smallpage, he was engulfed by the equally strange premonition that he was marrying the one woman in London who might actually penetrate his defenses. To Seybourne, that was a far more terrifying threat than a Whig conspiracy upsetting King George's Tory applecart.

* * *

"You may kiss the bride."

Georgiana shuddered as Reverend Smallpage recited the words. A hush fell over the drawing room while every person in it stared at the newly wedded couple.

The air between Georgiana and the viscount crackled with tension, enough to ruffle the hair on her back and set her to growling, if she were still a cat. His touch on her arm startled her. Though she was never afraid to look into his eyes, panicky sensations roiled through her each time she met his pale-blue, wolfish gaze. Her instincts told her to flee, but common sense reminded her that there was nowhere else to go.

"Do not be frightened." Lord Seybourne's whisper was inaudible, except to Georgiana.

He lowered his head and pressed his lips to hers.

It was an undemanding kiss, yet it knocked Georgiana's world off its axis. Whatever feline instincts remained in her body were in an instant subjugated to her more primal feminine ones. Suddenly, Georgiana's femininity conquered every aspect of her physical being. Conflicting feelings of desire and apprehension coursed through her veins. Lord Seybourne suddenly was more terrifying to her than he was before—yet more attractive, too.

How could that be? Was this what it meant to be human, to be female? If so, Georgiana thought she'd combust with the warring emotions welling up inside her. It simply wasn't possible to reconcile her terror with her urge to kiss her husband back!

Kiss him back? Had she completely lost her senses?

Half aware that everyone in the room was watching, Georgiana stared into Lord Seybourne's gaze. It had gone from pale, icy blue to the most heated, hungry color she'd ever seen.

And she could still feel the warmth of the viscount's lips— long removed from her own— burning on her own mouth. A mounting hunger swelled inside her even as her body shivered with nervousness.

The wedding party pressed in around the couple, men clapping Seybourne on the back, ladies squeezing Georgiana's arm and issuing vague future invitations to tea.

Lady Inez gently led Georgiana to a small group of women on the other side of the room. Turning from her husband, Georgiana caught his eye. The corners of the viscount's lips turned up and, as always, his gaze tracked her as an animal tracked its prey.

Strange, how a man's presence could be felt even when not seen. These females possessed a far greater arsenal of hidden talents and perceptions than Georgiana had ever imagined. Evidently, they were as sensitive to men as cats were to mice. Georgiana felt the viscount's gaze upon her as palpably as if he'd touched her skin.

A pretty redhead, rather buxom and clad elegantly in a morning suit of pale lavender with matching gloves and slippers, bared her teeth in what Georgiana supposed was meant to be a smile. Standing beside her were two other ladies, their features surprisingly similar to one another, with thick brown hair parted in the center and coiled in muffs above their ears. With their matching big noses and droopy eyes, they resembled basset hound pups from the same litter. Georgiana could have sworn they sniffed the air as Aunt Inez pressed her into their exclusive huddle.

"Ladies, I trust that you will welcome Georgiana warmly into your clique. She is a newcomer to London ... ah, after spending her youth in the Kentish countryside with some of Seybourne's distant relatives."

The redhead offered her lilac-gloved hand. "I wish you much happiness, dear. My name is Lady Mercy Mary Spraddlin, and these are Misses Julia and Henrietta, the Doggett sisters. I have been a friend of your husband's for years. Dear Lawrence, he always said he was dead set against getting married. But I suppose it took the right girl to convince him of the bliss that married life can offer." She ended this remark with an arch of her brows and a knowing smirk.

Georgiana rankled. Clearly Lady Spraddlin knew something of the circumstances under which Lord Seybourne came to be obligated to marry her. Not one to run from a challenge, she opened her mouth to speak but was quickly cut off by Lady Inez.

"Mercy Mary!" Lady Twitchett cried. "You promised!"

"Oh, very well." The lavender-scented woman cast Inez a martyred look, then patted Georgiana's arm. "Would you have tea with me and my friends, Henrietta and Julia, tomorrow afternoon, around three o'clock? We should be most pleased to acquaint ourselves with you more thoroughly, dear. And I promise, we won't bite."

Perhaps not, thought Georgiana, but she didn't think the three women were beyond scratching her eyes out. Mindful of the need to fit into the viscount's world, as least temporarily, however, she said, "Thank you ever so much. I should be happy to join you for tea tomorrow afternoon."

"Lovely," the three women simpered all at once.

"There now, that wasn't so hard," Lady Twitchett whispered, as she led Georgiana toward the far end of the room. A narrow balcony ran the length of the back of the house, overlooking the beautiful gardens tended by dozens of workers. People stood in clusters along the cast-iron rail of the balcony, admiring the view of the walled-in garden, drinking tea or sherry, socializing happily beneath the unseasonable warmth of the spring sun.

Georgiana stepped through the French doors and stood against the railing, her ear half tuned to Lady Twitchett's constant stream of instructive chatter. The older woman pointed out various people in the room, attempting to acquaint Georgiana with the viscount's friends, trying desperately to integrate her into a class of people destined to reject her.

"That grinning tow-haired man talking to your husband is Sir Morton Drysdale. Better remember him, he visits frequently, along with Mr. Sam Higgenbotham—he's the tall, skinny man on the other side of Lawrie."

Stifling a yawn, Georgiana glanced in the direction Inez indicated. "And who is the thin-faced man with the black eyes, who keeps looking at me as if he'd like to eat me?"

Inez shot her an admonishing look. "Don't be so vulgar, dear. That is Mr. Jack Craven, another acquaintance of your husband's. I suppose Lawrie met them at Brooks's or another of those damnable gaming-hells. Do try to keep your husband at home more often, dear. He spends entirely too much time roaming about the city at night. God knows doing what.''

"Lady Twitchett, what is my husband's relationship to Lady Mercy Mary Spraddlin, the creature in that incredibly ugly purple getup?''

"The color is lavender, dear. And why do you suppose there is anything between them?''

"I am not blind, my lady. Are you telling me I am wrong?''

"You're a shrewd miss, aren't you? But, you needn't worry about her, dear. Lawrie never had any serious interest in her. I would not have allowed him to marry a woman of her ilk.''

"Isn't that a bit archaic coming from the president of the Society for the Rehabilitation of Wanton Women? I overheard the Doggett sisters discussing your passion for that organization.''

"Oh, believe me, dear, I am all for salvaging the reputation of any woman that desires redemption and is willing to work for it. I abhor the double standard as much as anyone. But I am afraid it exists, and there is nothing we can do about it. Men are physically incapable of the virtues we women can attain. It is due to their biological makeup, you see. *Men have certain urges they cannot control.* Oh, it's all been scientifically documented, my dear. You needn't look so shocked.''

Georgiana smiled. "Men are animals. Is that what you are telling me, aunt?''

Sighing, the older woman nodded. "I regret to say the poor dears cannot even aspire to the feminine virtue of monogamy and chastity.''

Touching the older woman on the sleeve, Georgiana suppressed her laughter. "I think I should enjoy a saucer of cre— I mean, a spot of tea.''

"I will fetch it for you, dear.'' Inez turned just as an older handsome man approached. "If Lord Chumley will entertain you in my absence, that is.''

Introductions were politely made, and Georgiana smiled warmly as Hughes, Viscount Chumley, bent low over her hand.

When he straightened, she could see that he was a tall man of
elegant bearing, clad in black serge trousers and an immaculately tailored cutaway coat. His wide smile revealed perfect
white teeth and sparkling eyes above a patrician nose. Georgiana thought he was the epitome of neatness and expert groom-
ing. However, in comparison to her shaggy-haired husband
on the other side of the room, he was a wan reflection of
masculinity.

How odd, she thought, that this man's presence did nothing
to jangle her nerves or set her senses to tingling. She thought this
business of being a female strange indeed—when her intellect
registered a handsome man but her body did not respond, what
did that mean?

Lord Chumley stood against the railing, glancing admiringly
at the garden below. "Lovely, is it not? Do you favor gardens,
my lady?"

"Certain of them," Georgiana answered. "Although I have
found that many flowers cause acute indigestion. I ate a flow-
ering heliotrope once that very nearly killed me!"

"Excuse me?" Lord Chumley cupped his ear and leaned
closer to Georgiana.

Realizing her mistake, she said, "Never mind, Lord Chumley. Just a private joke between . . . ah, my husband and me.
It really isn't worth explaining."

He nodded skeptically. "Your husband confides in you,
then—about everything?"

"I should think so," Georgiana replied tartly, uncertain why
she lied, except that the man's challenging expression seemed to
call for a spirited defense of her otherwise fraudulent marriage.

The man changed the subject without ever taking his eyes
off her. "I see you surveying the garden. Have you an eye
toward relandscaping it? The roses bordering the brick wall
are particularly lovely, I think."

"Oh, yes," Georgiana said, looking down dutifully. Her
eyes were suddenly drawn to a patch of verdant herbs beneath
the overhang of an olive tree in the rear of the garden. A passing
breeze carried the unmistakable odor of catmint to her nose.
The thrill that passed through her was a familiar ripple of

excitement, almost as pleasurable as the viscount's touch—without the fright, of course.

"Are you all right?" Lord Chumley asked.

Georgiana realized she'd been standing with her eyes closed, her nose lifted to the breeze. Exhaling, she turned and smiled at the handsome viscount. "Oh, yes, I'm fine. It's my wedding day and I'm just happy. I've turned silly, I suppose. Please forgive me."

Aunt Inez appeared with a cup of tea, affording Lord Chumley the excuse to bid his adieu. When he'd escaped, Georgiana sighed and sipped her tea—tasteless, watery stuff. She could barely choke it down. A servant appeared and in *sotto voce* confided that the watercress sandwiches were soon to be depleted. A decision was called for, and Inez went off to consult with the cook. "I shall return in a trice, dear," she said.

But Georgiana was all too happy to have a moment to herself. She turned and walked idly down the length of the balcony, stopping at the far end to stare wistfully at the patch of catmint. She was only vaguely aware that the air had suddenly turned colder, and the other guests had returned to the study, where a low fire and the body heat of a crowd provided almost sweltering heat.

She preferred the bite of the chill spring air. Not to mention the tantalizing minty scent of the herbs below. She held her cup and saucer and leaned against the railing. Oh, if only she could return to the uncomplicated life she'd led.

But it hadn't really been that uncomplicated, had it? She'd done things to survive that would turn Aunt Inez's ears purple if she heard them. If the viscount knew what she was truly about, he'd toss her out on her ear. Which further deepened her resentment toward him. Because she knew that her marriage was a sham. As soon as Lord Pigott's campaign ended, and the viscount's stringent regard for his reputation abated, Georgiana would be disposed of. And then she'd be worse off than she was now—in the long run, this brief sojourn in the lap of luxury would only dull her senses and make her less capable of getting along in the world.

Damme, but she was tired of being abandoned each time

she grew comfortable in some human's home. She shivered, glancing over her shoulder at the huddle of modish women whispering behind their fans. With her sensitive ears, Georgiana caught much of what was said. She heard them gossip about her icy manners, her cool demeanor. Labeling her common, they even wondered whether Inez had foisted one of her wanton women upon her nephew as some sort of social experiment.

Anger ruffled the nape of Georgiana's neck. Those high-minded witches in lavender gloves thought they were better than she! Lady Spraddlin and her dog-faced friends considered her a wanton woman, who should be grateful for the charity of a wealthy man like Lord Seybourne.

The tiny knot of resentment in Georgiana's stomach soon grew to a burning ball of rage.

Her feline senses returned with a vengeance. A movement on the flagstones below snagged Georgiana's gaze. Darting from stone to stone along the dank earth was a little gray mouse, beady eyes alert, tiny pink-lined ears twitching. The urge to leap from the balcony and give chase was strong. Georgiana could almost feel the tiny animal squirming in her claws.

But, what happened next was the fulfillment of her worst nightmare.

Suddenly, Georgiana tumbled over the railing of the balcony. Her cup and saucer slipped from her fingers and shattered on the bricks beneath her. One part of her mind registered the firm push at the small of her back, which sent her headlong over the cast-iron railing. Another part of her brain controlled the twist of her body, the windmill action of her arms.

The bricks came up fast, threatening to smash every bone in her body. Georgiana succumbed to her instincts while, up above, a sinister chuckle carried faintly on the wind.

With a squeak, the mouse below dove for the cover of a mossy rock. The smell of catmint was strong in Georgiana's nostrils as her slippers touched on the stones and bricks of the garden path.

Chapter Four

A high-pitched shriek tore through the drawing room. Pivoting toward the open French doors that led onto the balcony, Lord Seybourne saw Lady Spraddlin lean over the railing and fling out her arms as if to grab hold of something. His pulse soared as he realized his former mistress was standing where, just a moment before, his wife had been. Lady Spraddlin's horrified expression as she stared down into the garden could only mean that Georgiana had fallen over the railing.

With Drysdale, Higgenbotham, Babworth, and Chumley on his heels, Lord Seybourne rushed toward the balcony. The four men crowded along the railing as the wedding party converged behind them. Peering down, they beheld the most incredible sight.

Thirty feet below, standing on the garden flagstones and staring up at them with the roundest, greenest eyes Seybourne had ever seen, was the newly married Lady Georgiana Seybourne. Her ebony hair was in sensual disarray. But, other than the look of stunned bewilderment she wore, she appeared none the worse for her tumble off the balcony.

"What in the devil happened?" Seybourne blurted.

Georgiana opened her mouth to speak, but before she could

answer, Lady Spraddlin cried, "She fell over the railing. Head-first, I saw it! How on earth she managed to land on her feet, I will never know. 'Tis a miracle, I swear it!"

"She fell over the balcony?" Sir Morton echoed.

"Are you all right?" Seybourne called down.

Georgiana's tentative nod filled him with relief. Her cheeks remained as pale as alabaster, however; he feared there might be internal injuries the lady wasn't aware of. Pushing off from the railing, he addressed his guests. "Everything is all right, my friends. Just an unfortunate accident, but it appears Lady Seybourne is uninjured. Please go on enjoying yourselves while I tend to my wife."

He walked calmly through the drawing room, smiling affably at the sea of perplexed faces pressing in on him. Then, he flew down the stairs and out the back door, bolting into the garden to gather Georgiana in his arms. Inside the house, he took the steps two at a time to her bedchamber. When he laid her on the bed, Aunt Inez and Lady Spraddlin quickly appeared at his elbow.

Georgiana stared silently at the three of them. She appeared to have lost her ability to speak again, and Seybourne thought with chagrin that the shock of her accident might undo the scant progress he'd made since he first scooped her up in his arms at Sir Hester's house.

"Whatever happened to the poor chit?" his aunt warbled.

"She must have thrown herself over," Lady Spraddlin drawled.

The thought made Seybourne's blood boil. Was his new wife so repelled by him that she attempted to kill herself? Even though he promised to let her out of their sham marriage once Lord Pigott's campaign ended, was the notion of a temporary marriage to him so repugnant that she preferred death?

Or was there something more sinister at work in Lord Seybourne's house than a woman's attempt to escape a loveless marriage?

Mentally cursing himself for taking his eyes off his wife, if only for an instant, Seybourne bent over and laid his palm on Georgiana's cheek.

Eyes round and unblinking, she flinched beneath his touch.

Seybourne straightened, humiliation flooding his neck and face. The fact that Lady Spraddlin witnessed Georgiana's reaction stung like an arrow through his heart.

"La! It seems you have a skittish bride on your hands, Lawrie." The redhead stood disturbingly close to him. "Perhaps she was so afraid of her wedding night, she dove off the balcony in order to avoid fulfilling her wifely obligation to her new husband."

"Hush your mouth, Mercy! I'll not countenance your rapier tongue when it comes to criticizing my wife. She is my wife, you know. Whether you approve or not, makes no difference to me."

Aunt Inez, issuing orders willy-nilly for the production of cold compresses, hartshorn, and a pot of tea, was oblivious to the quick, venomous exchange that took place between Seybourne and his former mistress. Georgiana stared wordlessly, apparently in a state of shock. Seybourne hoped she did not hear his conversation with Lady Spraddlin.

"And I'll thank you not to overset *Viscountess* Seybourne," he added tightly, stressing his wife's new title.

Lady Spraddlin flushed, her lips pursing in an unattractive frown. "There's something peculiar about that girl, Lawrie. You would be well advised to conduct a thorough investigation of her background. If I were you, I would hire a Bow Street Runner to find out whether there is some riverfront trollop gone missing—"

Lady Twitchett, inserting her ample figure between the feuding couple, laid a damp rag across Georgiana's forehead. "I daresay, no one keeps records of missing prostitutes, dear. No one really cares, is why."

"All right, you two!" Lord Seybourne's temper snapped. "I can handle this matter. Please leave Georgiana and myself alone for a time, would you? Inez, you shall explain to my guests that I am unable to rejoin the party. Everyone will understand. And Mercy Mary, you shall convey my apologies to them."

His aunt nodded and obediently waddled from the room, but

Lady Spraddlin stayed behind. She stood very close to him and spoke in a harsh, excited whisper. "You'll be wishing soon enough you hadn't married the chit, Lawrie."

He grasped her arm and roughly set her away from him.

Tossing back her shoulders, she patted her hair into place. "I do not take lightly your mistreatment of me, *my lord.*"

The threat in Lady Spraddlin's voice rasped like a drawn sword. Moving away from Georgiana's bed, Lord Seybourne ushered his former mistress through the door and into the deserted corridor. He struggled hard against the impulse to shake her.

"What in God's name has come over you, Mercy? For two years, you have regarded me as your own personal pet rehabilitation project. Well, you have accomplished your goal! I am no longer the social pariah I once was. Did you expect me to pay for your friendship by offering marriage? Was that the unspoken price of our mutually convenient affair?"

"I admit I was disappointed in your decision to marry this chit, Lawrie. But I am no green girl. Do not flatter yourself. My wounded heart healed faster than you might have thought possible. I merely believe you have committed a terrible mistake by bringing this girl into your home. Get rid of her, Lawrie, before it is too late!"

"I cannot rid myself of her before Lord Pigott's campaign is ended. Only then, will I consider allowing her an annulment. Or, she can live in the country if she likes."

"Why not just export her to Italy and pretend she is dead?" Lady Spraddlin shot back.

"Would you have me toss her into the streets naked? Turn her over to the Bow Street Runners and watch her dance in the wind for a murder she could not have committed?"

"How do you know she didn't kill Sir Hester?"

"There was no gun in the room, and yet the baron was killed by a gunshot wound to his chest. Had Georgiana shot the man, wouldn't there have been a weapon close at hand?"

Lady Spraddlin tossed her head so that her coppery ringlets danced angrily. At length, she returned Seybourne's salvo with a cruel non sequitur. "Be that as it may, you've made me a laughingstock, Lawrie! All my friends believe that you have turned me out for that raven-haired minx in there. Society is watching with bated breath to see how I will react.''

"Damn Society!"

"I have no intention of being made a fool, dear. I shall make a public show of my friendship toward your new wife. Then everyone will know that your marriage means nothing to me. And to that end, I have invited your sweet Georgiana to tea tomorrow, along with Henrietta and Julia. Have her delivered to my home at three, will you, Lawrie?''

"Bloody hell! You have invited my wife for tea? What a foolish notion—''

Lady Spraddlin cut him off with a fingertip pressed to his lips. "Have her there at three, dear. Or I shall bring Henrietta and Julia here. Do you understand?''

The viscount nodded. "Georgiana will be there.''

"Good.'' With a flirtatious backward glance over her shoulder, Lady Spraddlin turned and descended the stairs.

Lord Seybourne's stomach clenched as he watched her go. He could not, at the moment, afford to alienate the dubious affections of Lady Spraddlin. Her disapprobation could expel him from every Whig drawing room in London, a complication that would seriously hinder his investigation into Sir Hester's death. And if he failed to capture the murderous traitor, the king's life might be endangered. With sinking heart, he realized he had no choice but to send Georgiana to Lady Spraddlin's home for tea.

Yet, he dreaded subjecting his wife to his former mistress's caustic tongue. Which further befuddled and amazed him, because he had sworn that he would not become emotionally entangled with a woman to whom he was only temporarily married.

Why, then, was he obsessed with concerns for Georgiana's welfare and happiness? Why did he care whether Lady Spraddlin and the hideous Doggett sisters offended her? She was just the bait he used to trap a killer. Wasn't she?

Scratching his chin, Lord Seybourne stood for a moment in the chill, dimly lit hallway, trying in vain to comprehend the hold that Lady Georgiana had on his imagination. Her silence intrigued him; it seemed as if she trusted no one's counsel other than her own. Her icy demeanor bespoke a woman of cold nature, an aloof creature determined never to depend on another soul for survival, succor, or even companionship. And yet there were moments when the woman turned such a warm stare on him that his body ached with desire, and his heart thundered in his chest. He felt like a ball of string beneath a cat's paw, and he didn't know what to do about it.

Exhaling a long-held breath, he ruefully reminded himself that falling in love with Georgiana was not only foolish, but possibly dangerous. Any emotion, any tenderness, that he felt for her could jeopardize his ultimate mission: to find Sir Hester's killer and expose the conspirators who plotted to overthrow the Tory government.

Never in his life had Lawrence deWulff, Viscount Seybourne, felt so alone. And that included the weeks he'd spent chained to a rowing bench in the dark, fetid galley of a ship transporting convicted criminals to Australia.

Georgiana rubbed her eyes with the back of her hand and yawned. Someone had pushed her over the balcony's railing, but who? She mentally recounted the minutes leading up to her dive into the garden, but she couldn't recall there being another person on the balcony beside her. She'd thought she was alone, breathing in the scent of catnip and enjoying the solitude of a moment away from the discordant bustle of the party.

The next thing she knew, she'd gone headlong over the balcony. Luckily, enough of her feline instincts remained to enable her to right herself before she landed on the bricks. Though her muscles ached, she suffered no serious injuries as a result of the incident. Just a little shaken, that was all. But when Georgiana was overset, her natural tendency was to withdraw into herself.

Suppressing a smile, she recalled the viscount's concerned expression when he laid her in the bed and leaned over her.

Her silence obviously unnerved him; well, he would get used to it just as Sir Hester had grown accustomed to her aloofness and her inexplicable mood swings. Georgiana was simply unable to feign affability. Sometimes, she went days without uttering a word or showing one sign of affection. Why should she alter her behavior for a temporary husband?

Temporary! The word stuck in her throat like a hair ball. Though it shouldn't disturb her, the thought that Lord Seybourne was so quick to provide an exit from this fraudulent union made the hair on her nape bristle. Woefully unprepared for the conflicting emotions that engulfed her, Georgiana considered her options. She could run away and risk life in the dangerous streets of London, without her natural predatorial skills and defense mechanisms. Or she could remain beneath Lord Seybourne's roof, playing the part of a mysterious woman whose memory was lost due to a bump on her head.

She threw one arm over her eyes to shield them from the sun. With a sigh, she realized she had much rather remain within the viscount's protection. And with a characteristic surge of honesty, she admitted to herself that she was inexplicably attracted to him.

The thought was frightening and dizzily exciting at the same time. In a strange way, the viscount was more a threat to her tattered virtue than one of those randy toms who sprang on her without warning and satisfied his carnal needs in an ear-splitting moment of raw passion. She had certainly never enjoyed such random couplings; yet she had been prey to them throughout her past.

If Seybourne wanted her, would their coupling be the same? Would it be painful and unpleasant? Would the viscount leave her afterward without a word of apology or affection?

Probably. Nothing in her experience had led her to believe that a sex act could be anything other than violent and quick.

But in the depths of her imagination, a kernel of hope was planted. Lord Seybourne's touch was different from any she had ever known. Gentle, yet firm. Hungry and tender. When he gathered her in his arms, heat spread through her body and flowed through her limbs like a liquid fire. When, in the drawing room, their gazes had locked, the need in his eyes was more a warm embrace than the prelude to an angry mauling.

Perhaps with the viscount, sex will be loving and tender, Georgiana mused. Perhaps the strange mixture of fear and pleasure she experienced each time he looked at her presaged an entirely different sort of physical experience.

Sighing, she slipped further beneath the covers, pulling them to her chin and closing her eyes. Unaccustomed to this barrage of strong emotions, she was easily fatigued. A nap was what she needed to chase away the doldrums. A nap was always welcome. As her eyes grew heavy and her breathing slowed, she recalled Lord Seybourne's comment that she slept for uncommonly long periods of time.

Well, that was something he'd have to get used to, also. Because no matter what other feline traits evaporated when she was transformed into a human lady, Georgiana didn't think she'd ever learn to function properly on less than twenty hours of sleep a day.

The crash of her bedroom door startled her awake. Her eyes flew open, and her senses soared to full alertness in an instant.

Filling the doorway was the viscount, tall and broad-shouldered, his pale eyes burning with desire. He kicked the door shut behind him, then stalked toward the bed, his lean muscular legs moving in long, graceful strides. Standing over her, he stared down. A shudder of fear and confusion shimmied through Georgiana. Had her husband come to possess her at last? Had he burst into her room with the intent of claiming his marital rights?

It was what she had expected, after all. Her heart hammered relentlessly as she appraised the raw animal need in Lord Seybourne's tightened expression. Any unweaned kitten could have recognized the animal lust that glowed behind those eyes. She had been wrong to think he would treat her any more tenderly than the scroungy, scraggly tomcats who pounced on her in back alleys. She should have known better. Men were all the same, no matter the species, no matter the breed.

But, she would not be taken without a fight. With an angry hiss, Georgiana reared up from the bed and flung herself at

Lord Seybourne. She lunged, arms outstretched, and raked his cheek with her fingernails. Then she leapt from the bed, flying through the air with every intent of making for the door, escaping the bedroom and fleeing the viscount's household.

The arms that wrapped around her middle held her as tightly as an iron harness. For a moment, Georgiana thought her ribs would crack. Gasping for breath, she felt the viscount's hard body beneath her struggling, flailing limbs. There was no escape from his embrace, or from the thrall in which he held her.

He tossed her on the bed. She landed on her back, breathless, stunned and frightened, amid a bank of pillows and mounds of soft quilts. Hissing, she cowered against the headboard, her body tensed for battle, her nerves steeled for the painful jointure she anticipated.

He stood beside the bed, fists clenched at his sides. The moment stretched into an interminable yaw of tense silence. Lord Seybourne's gaze pinned Georgiana against the elaborately carved headboard. Repressed violence radiated from him, charging the air between them so thickly that Georgiana's hair bristled. Holding her breath, she stared at Lord Seybourne in utter bewilderment. What on earth was he waiting for?

Then, his features tightened into an impenetrable, indecipherable mask. "Bloody hell," he muttered. Turning on his heel, he crossed the room with silent strides, broad shoulders rippling beneath the black superfine of his coat.

For a long time, Georgiana stared at the door that closed behind him. The quietude following his departure was more unsettling than his explosive entrance. What had he meant to do to her? What had restrained him from having his way with her? What kind of man burst into a woman's room with nothing but animal lust burning in his eyes, only to do a French turn at the first sign of her resistance?

Not any kind of male Georgiana had known, that was certain. It was nearly nightfall before her breathing normalized and her nerves calmed sufficiently for her to sleep.

And when she did, her mind gave over to riotous, erotic dreams filled with images of her mysterious husband. Her sleep was haunted by the sensations she'd experienced when he held her hand, kissed her, and held her close against his hard, warm body.

Tossing restlessly, she dreamed of being possessed by the viscount—possessed in every sense of the word. Dark fantasies filled her with desire, as well as fear. But, her dreams were a mere shadow of her waking trepidation. In Georgiana's conscious mind, she remained terrified of the strong emotions Lord Seybourne inspired in her. Above all, he threatened to undermine her indifference and selfishness, the traits that had helped her survive in a cruel world.

In his darkened study, Lord Seybourne sat behind his desk, elbows propped on the arms of his chair, fingers steepled beneath his chin. The silence which followed the dispersal of his wedding party was suffocating; the loneliness which overshadowed the viscount was oppressive. And the foul, thunderous mood he'd been in when he descended from Georgiana's bedchamber had caused Aunt Inez and the servants to flee him, abandoning him to a bitter solitude. Alone, he contemplated what a fool he'd been for marrying the wild woman-child above stairs, an enigmatic chit whose moods shifted like the clouds and who, in less than forty-eight hours, had nearly driven him insane.

Clearly, she hated him. He had gone to her chambers for talk, not for bed play. But before he could open his mouth, she flew at him like a cornered animal, scratching and clawing as if she wished to murder him.

Touching his cheek, he winced. Her fingernails, amazingly sharp, had drawn blood down the side of his face. Examining the bloody tips of his fingers, he wondered if the king's life were really worth the trouble he had gone to. It was a transient thought—he would have married Atilla the Hun if it meant saving England's monarch—but a rueful smile tugged at his lips nonetheless.

A brisk knock interrupted his thoughts. Calling permission to enter, Seybourne was surprised to see several members of the Kit-Kat Club file into his study. They crowded around his desk, and slouched into the few chairs that graced his small sanctuary.

Standing opposite Seybourne's desk, Jack Craven stared intently at him. "Has she got her claws in you already, Lawrence?" His thin face split in a devilish smile.

Seybourne extracted a white linen kerchief from his inside breast-pocket and pressed it to his bleeding skin. "The cat scratched me," he lied.

Craven nodded skeptically. "Never was a cat-man, myself. I prefer hunting dogs, if you really want to know."

Lord Hughes Chumley, seated opposite Seybourne's desk, one leg crossed negligently over the other, spoke up. "In a roundabout way, that brings us to the object of our visit, Lawrence."

"I should hope you'd have an excellent reason to visit a man on his wedding day," Seybourne said. "From the looks of you, I would think you had come as a vigilante lynch mob, if I did not know better."

On the opposite side of the room, lining the camelback sofa, sat Lord Anderson Whitney and Mr. Sam Higgenbotham. Both longtime members of the secret Kit-Kat Club, they laughed easily. Still attired in the formal dress they had worn to Seybourne's wedding, they were elegant models of Society despite their reformist sentiments.

Sir Morton Drysdale and Lord Turner Pigott lounged aimlessly, postures relaxed and faces flushed from drink and revelry.

At length, Seybourne broke the silence with an explosive oath. "Is any one of you blasted idiots going to tell me what you're here for?"

Striding toward the desk, Sir Morton patted the air. "Do not overset yourself, Lawrie. We have come to give you a bit of good news! After your wife's unfortunate incident, we thought you would like a spot of good news to cheer you up!"

Mr. Higgenbotham spoke from across the room. "How is your wife faring, anyway? Was she injured in the fall?"

Seybourne forced himself to appear relaxed. "No, she suffered not a scratch. But, she is quite shaken up, as I'm sure you understand.''

Lord Chumley leaned forward. ''I was with her just moments before she fell. Egad, I cannot understand how it happened!''

''Could someone have pushed her?'' Lord Turner Pigott asked.

Seybourne studied the diminutive man who had sponsored his entry into the Kit-Kat Club. The same man whose campaign for a seat in the Commons he was orchestrating. He would have liked to tell the man to go jump in the Thames, but he could ill afford to cut his ties with the Kit-Kat Club now. ''Pushed? Why would you ask such a question, Pigott?''

Mr. Higgenbotham said, ''I didn't see anyone with her.''

Sir Douglas Babworth, rounding on the man, said curtly, ''Were you really watching, Sam? Did you have your eyes on her the moment she went over the railing?''

Lord Chumley said, ''Why would anyone want to kill Lady Seybourne?''

''Why, indeed?'' Sir Morton asked.

''Did anyone in this room observe the accident?'' Lord Seybourne said. Good God, why hadn't he realized it before? The bait he had used to attract Sir Hester's killer, indeed, had drawn the villain out. Just as Seybourne had planned.

But, he had failed to protect his wife from a killer's hands! A sickening wave of remorse washed over him as he realized how close Georgiana had come to being murdered. And how little he had done to shield her from danger.

''Did any of you see anything?'' Seybourne demanded, clutching the edge of his desk.

Mr. Higgenbotham and Lord Whitney shook their heads. Sir Douglas Babworth and Lord Chumley said, ''No,'' in unison. Jack Craven heaved a huff of exasperation, as if he thought the entire matter tedious. Sir Morton, his bland face a picture of bewilderment, answered in the negative, also. And Lord Turner Pigott, whose word was about as valuable as Spanish coin, said in his usually oily manner, ''How could I have seen her? I was on the other side of the room.''

Shifting in his chair, Seybourne threw his booted feet atop

his desk. "Well, she is not injured, and so I am to be thankful for that."

The men in the room murmured their general agreement.

Mr. Craven said, "Please give my best regards to your wife and tell her that I, for one, am most relieved to hear that she suffered no harm. I hope in future I shall have the opportunity to know your lovely bride better. I shall certainly look forward to dancing with her at your country-house ball."

"Country-house ball? What the devil are you talking about?"

"The one you are hosting on behalf of Queen Caroline," Craven replied smoothly.

"Queen Caroline? Are you mad?"

There was a nervous brief outburst of laughter among the other members of the Kit-Kat Club. Seybourne quelled the jollity, however, with a dark, threatening expression.

Sir Morton Drysdale spoke excitedly. "That is what we came here to discuss with you, my lord. 'Tis the matter of Caroline's return to England and the gala receptions the Whig party is planning for her. She is in the midst of negotiating a divorce settlement with her husband, as you know."

Sir Douglas Babworth chimed in. "The King is more than willing to increase her income—"

"—provided that she remain on the Continent," Lord Chumley drawled.

"But this is a matter between the king and queen," Seybourne said. "We are a political club, interested in Parliamentary reform, not the royal family's domestic squabbles. Why should we waste our time attempting to curry favor with the queen?"

Craven, folding his arms across his chest, glanced at the others, as if to assure himself of their support before turning to Seybourne with a stern gaze. "The queen has been treated so shabbily by the king that the people have rallied round her as if she were Joan of Arc. The commoners love Caroline! Mark my words, upon her return, there will be dancing in the streets. *And when Caroline speaks out in favor of Parliamentary reform, the people will demand it.* There will be no stopping us once we have the support of Caroline and the common people."

Inwardly seething, Seybourne chose his words carefully and spoke in a low, even voice. "So you plan to exploit Caroline's popularity for your own uses?"

"*Our* uses," Sir Morton said. "You are on our side, are you not, Lawrie?"

The viscount forced a tight smile. "Do not be foolish, of course I am. The notion of entertaining the queen at my country home merely took me by surprise, that is all."

Craven chuckled. "Sorry old boy. I suppose we should have eased the idea on you rather than springing it on you like this."

"Has Caroline agreed to attend a dinner at my estate in Kent?" Seybourne could only imagine the eruption of profanities that would occur when he told the king what the Kit-Kat Club had planned.

Lord Turner Pigott stepped forward. "Aye, her chamberlain, Pergami, has sent word ahead that the queen will arrive at Dover in a sennight. Then her entourage will proceed through Canterbury and toward Wrotham, eventually stopping at your manor house, my lord."

Seybourne sighed. "I shall have to write my steward at Wolfharden Manor immediately and instruct him to begin preparations for this rather unusual gathering."

Sir Morton cleared his throat. "The queen likes to dance, my lord."

Rolling his eyes to the ceiling, Seybourne replied, "Yes, I am afraid that is common knowledge from here to Moscow. Do not worry, I shall see to it that Caroline of Brunswick has all the entertainment she requires."

"*Queen Caroline,*" Craven corrected. "How fortunate that you are newly married. This will give your bride an opportunity to be introduced to Whig society. I think I speak for all the members of the Kit-Kat Club when I say that we are looking forward to meeting her when she is in . . . ah, better spirits."

"I'll drink to that!" Sir Morton leaned over Seybourne's desk to shake hands warmly. "What say we all adjourn to

Brooks's and douse ourselves in brandy to celebrate Seybourne's nuptials and the queen's arrival in England!''

Seybourne stood, signaling the end of this impromptu meeting. His visitors gathered around him, offering their congratulations again, slapping his back and pumping his hand vigorously. There was an atmosphere of comradery and good cheer, but underneath it lay an undertone of impending disaster.

Things were moving too quickly, spinning out of control. In less than forty-eight hours, Sir Hester had been killed and a conspiracy to overthrow the government discovered. In a daring scheme to draw out the traitorous murderer, Lord Seybourne had married the beautiful naked woman found beside Sir Hester's corpse. But when someone pushed her over the balcony railing, Seybourne had been helpless to protect her. His sense of failure was just slightly overwhelmed by the growing suspicion that he had made an enormous mistake in marrying a woman who hated him.

And now the members of the Kit-Kat Club were insisting that the viscount host a party for the scandalous Queen Caroline.

As his Whig acquaintances filed out of his study, a chill dread enveloped Lord Seybourne. Surrounded by political intrigue and shadowy murder plots, all he could think of was how foolish he had been to marry Georgiana. His decision to use her as bait for a killer filled him with self-loathing. Her evident hatred of him rankled like a thorn wedged deeply in his paw. The fact that he wanted her, even now, bewildered him.

He crossed the room to a sideboard laden with liquor bottles and glasses. Pouring himself a generous shot of brandy, he shivered with emotion.

Admit it to yourself, Seybourne! You are obsessed with the woman. You cannot stop thinking about her. You cannot stop wanting her!

The single kiss they shared in the drawing room had burned an indelible memory on his mind. Draining his glass, Seybourne tried valiantly to erase the memories of Georgiana's sweet breath, her soft, fragrant hair, her luscious, lithe little body.

But it was impossible.

He wanted the very thing he couldn't have—a woman who feared him and was repelled by him. A woman who thought he married her for decorum sake. A woman he dangled as bait to lure a killer into the open.

Pacing the Aubusson carpet of his study, crystal decanter in one hand, glass in another, the viscount pondered his dilemma until his vision blurred and his gait was unsteady. Yet there was no ready answer to his problems, and there was no one to whom he could turn for advice or compassion. At last, he fell onto the sofa, exhausted by his own anguished meditations.

As he sank into a deep sleep, his glass slipped from his hand and hit the floor. A violent jerk of his body brought him to full alertness in the middle of the night. He thought he heard the plaintive cry of a cat.

Head throbbing, stomach roiling, he struggled to his elbows, searching the dark shadows of the study for signs of a cat. Cursing, he slumped back on the sofa. He would have to remember to lecture the housekeeper about her penchant for allowing cats to roam the house freely. He knew they were indispensable mousers, but he had never established a rapport with one of the mercurial creatures. They were fickle, uncommunicative animals, who possessed no sense of loyalty. And loyalty, above all things, was the trait Lawrence deWulff, Viscount Seybourne, most admired.

Chapter Five

Georgiana awoke the next morning with a long, languid stretch and an openmouthed yawn. Considering the short amount of time she slept—less than ten hours—she felt amazingly rested. The white muslin night rail Aunt Inez had provided was soft and cool against her skin. Gradually, she was becoming accustomed to sleeping on her back with her long, slender limbs strewn about the bed. As hunger rumbled in her stomach, she realized too that she was looking forward to a cup of tea, rather than the saucer of cream Sir Hester used to greet her with each morning.

Arms above her head, eyes squeezed tightly shut against the morning sun which peeped through her window, she froze. Her nose tickled and she lifted it to sniff the air. The aroma of a man, tinted with dusky cologne, overlaid with alcohol and spiced with a trace of perspiration, filled her nostrils.

Her eyes flew open. Turning her head, she was surprised to see Lord Seybourne seated in a chair beside her bed. His pale-blue eyes, a trifle pink around the rims and bracketed in finely etched lines, stared back at her. With one leg crossed over the other, arms folded across his chest, he sat as still as a statue, his unblinking gaze full of wary appraisal.

Georgiana's body tensed for battle, or for flight. She pushed herself to a sitting position and drew her knees to her chest. She would have flung herself at the viscount again had it not been for his smooth, soothing voice.

"Come now, Lady Georgiana, must we repeat that unseemly episode?" Touching the red jagged line that marred his complexion, he added, "Trust me when I tell you that I have no intentions of forcing myself upon you. You are quite safe from me, dear. My tastes do not run to violent lovemaking."

It took a moment for Georgiana to absorb the impact of his words. Slowly, she relaxed and leaned against the headboard. When she noticed the viscount's gaze flicker to her bare shoulders, she yanked at her disheveled night rail and pulled the counterpane to her chin.

Another stretch of silence spanned the short distance between them. Georgiana found it odd that Seybourne was not discomfited by the quiet; in her experience, most humans were eager to fill up gaps of silence.

At last, Lord Seybourne stretched his own long legs in front of him and sighed. "Sleep well?"

She nodded.

"Are you hungry? Shall I ring for some tea and toast?"

"Yes, thank you."

He stood and pulled a bell rope. Within minutes, a maid poked her head in the door and accepted the viscount's breakfast order.

The sounds of carriages rattling down Tenterden Street filtered through the thick glass of the bedchamber window. Fishmongers hawked their inventory; climbing boys chirped a litany of services; and knife-sharpeners sang ditties extolling their skills. Life proceeded apace outside the small bedchamber where Georgiana and Lawrence, like two big jungle animals, cagily appraised one another.

Startled by the sudden reentry of the maid bearing a tray, Georgiana welcomed an interruption to the disturbing staring contest. With the servant's exit, however, came the prickly silence once again, made all the more uncomfortable by Lord Seybourne's intense scrutiny while she ate.

"Do you always tear your toast to shreds before you eat it?" he asked.

Didn't everyone? Suddenly conscious of her mannerisms, Georgiana daintily touched a linen serviette to the corner of her lips. Thank heavens she hadn't had the urge to bat her toast around on the floor and chase it.

"I am sorry, my lord," she said. "I suppose my nervousness has caused me to act strangely. I hope you will forgive my temporary lapse of manners; perhaps when my memory returns, so will my sense of decorum."

He smiled easily, unnerving her.

She tensed, ever ready for any sudden movement her predator might make. When she noted his look of surprise—or was it consternation?—she realized her jumpy reactions were entirely inappropriate to the situation. Forcing a weak smile, she raised her teacup to her lips.

Before she could sip the tepid liquid, Lord Seybourne interposed another question. "Someone pushed you off the balcony yesterday, didn't they?"

The cup clanked against the saucer as she set it down. "Yes, my lord."

Seybourne rose from his chair and sat on the edge of her bed, his body leaning toward hers, his smell surrounding her. "Who pushed you, dear? You must tell me!"

Shakily lifting the tray from her lap, she said, "I don't know!"

Lord Seybourne took the tray from her hands and placed it on the bed table nearby. Then he scooted closer to her, his hands clasping hers, his face so near that Georgiana could see the stubble shadowing his strong jaw.

Her nerve endings tingled. New sensations flowed through her veins and pooled in the most sensitive parts of her body. With her back pressed to the headboard, she fleetingly considered hissing and clawing the viscount's face again.

But when her eyes fastened on the ugly red scar across his cheek and the cord of muscles flinching beneath it, she discovered she was unable to maul her new husband again. In fact, she realized with terrifying insight that she had no impulse to jump over his head or beneath his arm. Though his nearness overwhelmed and frightened her, she actually *enjoyed* this deliciously strange sensation.

He lightly touched her face. "Why are you so frightened, minx?"

"I am not frightened of you, my lord. 'Tis my memory loss that frightens me."

Warmth darkened his gaze. "You mustn't allow yourself to become overset, Georgiana. In time, your memory will return, perhaps in dribs and drabs, perhaps all at once. Till then, you are safe here. I will not let anyone harm you."

She tilted her head so that it was cupped in his open palm. Relief and gratitude poured through her. Unable to resist the urge to clasp the viscount's hand, she pressed it against her cheek and rubbed her skin against his calloused flesh. Her scent mingled with his, marking him as hers. For a brief moment, she allowed her breathing to slow and her muscles to relax. The deep rumble that sounded in her throat jolted her back to reality.

Her chin jerked up and she roughly batted the viscount's hand from her cheek. Their eyes met—his wide with bewilderment, hers blinking with embarrassed astonishment.

"That noise you made," he stammered. "It sounded like a cat . . . purring."

"Don't be ridiculous," she said in clipped tones.

His expression faded to one of incredulous amusement. With a friendly pat on her arm, he rose to his full height and stared down at her. "You are a strange little woman, Georgiana. I hope that your memory returns anon. I should like to know more about you."

Georgiana turned her head, unwilling to meet his gaze. Then she yawned and burrowed deep beneath her bedcovers, signaling their discourse was over. As her lids grew heavy, she was vaguely aware of the viscount's departure.

His words as he closed the door behind him barely penetrated her slumber. "Good heavens, but that minx surely does sleep a lot!"

* * *

The king spat the seed of an apricot from his mouth. A hollow ring sounded from the brass pot positioned beside his ottoman. With the juice of a plump hothouse fruit running down his chin, he reached for the glass of pale straw-colored wine sitting on the small ormolu table beside his sofa.

"Have some, Seybourne? 'Tis an excellent sauternes, unavailable while Boney was ripping the Continent apart. I pray that we have seen the last of that maniac."

Declining the proffered wine, with a shake of his head, Seybourne sat stiffly in a claw-footed armchair.

"What have you to report to me?" the king asked.

"As you know, Sir Hester's murderer has not yet been revealed. However, I am certain the killer was at my wedding party yesterday."

The rotund monarch arched his brows. "How so?"

"Someone pushed Georgiana over the railing on the second-floor balcony. I believe it was the same villain who killed Sir Hester. My wife fell two stories onto the brick pavement of the garden below."

The king choked on his fruit, coughing phlegmatically and clutching his huge belly as he struggled to get his breath. Then, he violently spit a seed into his hand before tossing it negligently into his spittoon. "Good God! Is she dead?"

"No," Seybourne replied hesitantly, hardly certain how to explain her miraculous survival. "In fact, she had not a scratch on her. Not a single broken bone or sprained limb. She landed on her feet like a . . ."

"Cat?" George IV was on the verge of laughing, his fleshy lips quirking in irrepressible mirth. "Egad, did you marry a cat, Lawrie?"

"I hope not." Seybourne's tone was bleak.

For a moment, the king stared at him in stunned disbelief. Then, shrugging as if to dispel some ridiculous thought that had buzzed through his head, he returned abruptly to his original question. "Let's get back to the Kit-Kat Club. How does all this relate to their malevolent purposes?"

"I am not yet certain. But, there is one new development, sire." Seybourne leaned forward. "The other members of the club have decided to entertain Caroline of Brunswick when she returns to England. They've set a date, less than a sennight from today, and they've also received word from her chamberlain that she will attend the dinner and dance they have planned in her honor."

As Seybourne had expected, the king erupted with indignation and apricot pits. His howling could be heard through the north wing of Carlton House, and his one good foot stomped the floor like an angry bull's. A frightened valet was quick to open the drawing-room door and inquire whether a doctor should be summoned.

George, his aim surprisingly good, threw a half-eaten apricot at the liveried servant, who just managed to close the door before the fruit exploded against it with a juicy splat.

Stammering with rage, the king turned his reddened face to Seybourne. "What? God's blood, I must be as daft as my poor mad father was! I thought you said the Kit-Kat Club was hosting a dinner and dance for that she-devil cow, my wife!"

"Aye, sire, 'tis precisely what I said." Seybourne knew the king well enough to know that once he vented his spleen, he'd calm down and listen rationally. After a few moments, George did just that, allowing the viscount to continue. "What's worse is that my fellow Whig sympathizers have offered my country manor, Wolfharden in Kent, near the town of Wrotham, as the site for this *soirée.*"

"The party is going to be held at your home, Seybourne?"

"Aye, my lordship. I haven't much choice in the matter. If I refuse to host the dinner dance, my allegiance to the Whig party will be suspect."

The king rubbed his glistening lower lip and donned a pensive expression. At length, he said, "At least we can keep a closer surveillance on this wanton Jezebel who calls herself the 'Queen of England' if she and her entourage are camped out at your home."

Seybourne nodded. "I have been informed that the Kit-Kat Club members intend to lobby Caroline for support of their own pet causes, Parliamentary reform, for example, and restriction of the king's household budget.''

"Bloody poppycock, that's what that is! Whose bloody idea was that? Babworth's? That idiot with the sweaty upper lip! Or was it that chinless cake named Higgenbotham?''

Seybourne thought back to the confrontation he'd had with the men in his study after the disastrous wedding party. He'd been preoccupied and hadn't paid sufficient attention to who exactly broached the subject, or who seemed most eager to win the queen's political affections. Frowning, he admitted, "I honestly can't say, sire. It seems to me all the members of the Club had made this decision jointly and presented it to me after the fact, so to speak. As the newest member of the club, I am apparently not included in every high-level policy discussion that takes place.''

The king was silent a moment longer, apparently in deep contemplation. When he spoke, it was in a low, conspiratorial tone. His complexion had a pasty-white cast that bespoke of years of overindulgence and dissipation. Still, there was a limpid sparkle to his blue eyes hinting of the handsome, charming man he'd once been.

"Lord Seybourne, I hesitate to burden you with this worry, but given this recent bit of intelligence, I believe you should be aware of what is at stake.''

The viscount leaned forward, listening intently.

"I have it on good authority—don't ask me to name my sources, for I shan't—that a revolution is brewing in Italy. Some of the most radical reactionaries are calling for Boney's release from St. Helena. Can you fathom it?''

Seybourne gasped. "Traitorous fools!''

George sighed, and leaned his head against the curved back of the plush red sofa. "Aye, but what if Caroline fell into the clutches of these maniacs? She has long expressed a reverence for Napolean, silly woman that she is. Think of the embarrassment England would suffer if she lent her support to some crazy band of Italian anarchists. Which she might do if Lord Sidmouth refuses an increase in her allowance.''

" 'Tis beyond belief,'' Seybourne muttered.

"Your Whig friends might even plant a seed of sedition in her silly head . . . just to embarrass me. She has aroused some sympathy among the common folk, you know, those who think it cruel of me to have taken lovers during my marriage."

Seybourne discreetly held his tongue.

And then, with a wave of his plump hand, the king dismissed him. "Keep me posted, Lawrie," he said without rising.

Seybourne stood, made a leg in obeisance to the monarch, then saw himself to the door. When his hand was on the knob, he was halted by the king's commanding voice.

"Don't fail me, Lord Seybourne. I wouldn't want to have to send you back to those gauche Australians!"

The fat man's hearty guffaws followed him down the long corridor that led to the main staircase. Seybourne's booted heels clicked furiously on the polished Italian marble as he stalked toward freedom. Temporary freedom, that is. If he failed to apprehend Sir Hester's killer and expose the men who threatened to destroy the king, soon he'd be living in Australia.

But if he didn't reconcile his increasing attraction toward his wife with the fact he was using her as bait, he wouldn't be able to live with himself, no matter where he was exiled.

Lady Mercy Mary Spraddlin, perched on the edge of a Queen Anne chair, smiled as the newlywed Lady Georgiana Seybourne entered her drawing room. Her companions, Misses Julia and Henrietta Doggett, sat on a sofa perpendicular to an ornate marble mantelpiece topped by basaltware urns and pale-blue Wedgwood vases filled with fresh flowers. The Doggett sisters, both of them fair complected and blessed with gobs of thick brown hair and incongruously bushy black eyebrows, scanned Georgiana from head to toe as she approached.

Georgiana paused in the middle of the pale-blue carpet, busily patterned with rows of squares and columns of dainty floral designs. Studying her surroundings, she mentally noted all avenues of escape.

The room was altogether too bright for her tastes; the walls beneath the chair-rails were painted a pale blue while above they were covered with exquisite hand-painted paper boasting an aviary of nightingales, hummingbirds, and all sorts of enticing winged creatures.

The effect on Georgiana's senses was one of startlement. With no ready hiding place in sight, she was impaled by the portrait-stares of somber-looking ancestors imprisoned in heavy gilt frames. The veiled animosity she sensed in Lady Spraddlin's teeth-baring smile heightened her discomfort. Muscles tense, hands clasped at her waist, Georgiana stood still as a statue, her gaze finally alighting on her hostess. Aware that she was a stranger to the protocol of house calls, she imitated Lady Spraddlin's smile and glided toward the vacant chair across from her.

The grouping of the drawing-room furniture had obviously been designed so that a small party such as this could carry on an intimate, cozy chat before the fireplace. Yet to Georgiana, the room for all its glinting ormolu, warm oil paintings, harps, and pianofortes, seemed as cold as ice.

Shivering, she drew her lace-edged shawl tighter around her shoulders.

"Why, Lady Seybourne, are you cold, dear?" Lady Spraddlin stared at her with a moue of feigned concern.

" 'Tis merely a chill," Georgiana replied. "A spot of hot tea will be just the thing, I'm sure."

As if on cue, a maid servant entered bearing a tea tray laden with an exquisite gold-rimmed porcelain tea service. Lady Spraddlin demonstrated her skill at the art of pouring tea, and after all four ladies were furnished with cups of steaming tea, she pushed back in her chair and commenced what could only be termed a polite interrogation of Lady Georgiana.

"How are you taking to Lord Seybourne's town house?" she inquired nonchalantly, her eyes cutting from the Doggett sisters to her guest.

Lady Seybourne suddenly knew what it felt to be a cornered mouse. Carefully balancing her untouched tea, she replied, "It will take a bit of getting use to, my lady. But the staff and servants are most accommodating, and Lord Seybourne has been nothing but kind."

Lowering her cup to her saucer with an unladylike clang, Julia Doggett spoke up. "How long have you known Lord Seybourne? If you don't mind my asking, that is?"

Henrietta slanted her sister a look of mildly amused admonishment. "Julia! Now that's a rude question. 'Tis none of our business how Lady Seybourne came to know her husband."

Georgiana flashed them all a shy, knowing smile. An irrepressible craving to do mischief suddenly overwhelmed her. "I'm afraid I cannot divulge the details of my past life. Unfortunately, it is an unsavory story of a penniless girl forced to fend for herself on the cruel streets of London."

Lady Spraddlin's smile broadened while the Doggett sisters fairly panted with anticipation.

Julia, dark brown eyes gleaming, wet her lips and leaned forward on the sofa. "Tell me, did you have many male protectors before you met your husband?"

"Julia!" cried Henrietta and Lady Spraddlin in unison.

" 'Tis quite all right," Georgiana assured them. "There is nothing about my past, other than the identities of the men who patronized me, that I wish to keep in the dark. I suppose, after all, that it is no secret when and where Lord Seybourne and I met. Indeed, had it not been for the urgings of his aunt—that saint!—I would probably be wool-gathering in some desultory little cell in Newgate."

"How positively awful!" Lady Spraddlin clutched her throat and gaped.

Julia and Henrietta shook their heads and clucked their tongues. "Are you simply ecstatic to have been rescued by the viscount?" Julia gushed.

Georgiana, in the process of lifting her cup to her lips, froze. She lowered the cup and pinned her gaze on each woman in turn. For a long moment, the only sound in the drawing room was the ticking of a huge glass-encased clock gracing the top of a pedestal table in a corner. Lady Spraddlin's features hardened beneath Georgiana's stare. But the Doggett sisters looked like whipped pups, their chins drooping and their large red-rimmed eyes blinking furiously.

"To say that Lord Seybourne rescued me is to suggest that

I *required* rescuing.'' Georgiana paused, struggling to speak without hissing. "I am, and have always been, quite capable of taking care of myself."

A grudging look of admiration sparkled in Mercy Mary's eyes. "A most excellent quality, my dear. I dare say, we women have to look after ourselves, do we not?"

"If a ca—creature does not fend for herself, no one else will," Georgiana said.

"Just so," Lady Spraddlin replied.

Lady Julia cut in after an awkward moment of silence. "You haven't tasted your tea, Georgiana!"

"So I haven't." Lady Seybourne lifted the cup and tasted it. As usual, the brew was so bland she wrinkled her nose in distaste.

The next half hour passed torturously slow while Georgiana listened to an endless recital of silly gossip about people who sounded dreadfully boring. At last, the hands on the clock signaled the time for a polite departure.

"I should very much like to return your kind invitation, Lady Spraddlin," she said smoothly, rising. "When I have adjusted to my new surroundings, of course. And you, Julia and Henrietta, would be most welcome in my drawing room anytime. I hope I shall see all of you again soon. Good day."

And with that, she strode from the room and toward the stairwell with supreme confidence, and not a little trepidation that the Doggett sisters and Lady Mercy Mary Spraddlin would indeed make an appearance in her drawing room.

Chapter Six

Georgiana kneeled at the edge of the brick path that intersected the garden in the rear of Lord Seybourne's town house. With a small wicker basket hooked over her elbow, she grasped a handful of the minty herbs that had previously captured her imagination. Raising the clump of unearthed greens to her nose, she inhaled deeply, savoring the damp grassy smell and the luxurious feeling of crisp leaves against her cheek.

Tossing the herbs into her basket, she sniffed the air. Though her sense of smell was not nearly so acute as it once was, she detected Lord Seybourne's scent the moment he stepped through the French doors that opened from the downstairs parlor into the garden. His footsteps on the flagstones filled her with anticipation, and when he stood beside her, she was nervously aware of his masculine presence. Her urge to rub her face against his legs was strong, but she managed to tamp it down.

Dusting her hands on her apron, she rose and faced him. She was accustomed now to his usual reticence. What his eyes said to her could never be expressed in words.

His chest expanded as he inhaled. Georgiana stood very close to him and watched his gaze darken. Suddenly, the garden wilted in the background, and all that she could see and hear and smell was Lord Seybourne. Only her sense of touch remained unfulfilled; she ached to run her fingers through his shaggy hair.

Was this what humans felt when they mated? Was this the seedling of love unfolding in her belly, or was it simply animal lust? Never had she been so frustrated or so fascinated with a game of cat and mouse.

"I presume you are feeling much better, my lady," he said in a honeyed drawl. "I hear from my aunt that you had quite a bit of fun with Lady Spraddlin and the Doggett sisters this afternoon."

Georgiana arched her brows. "They were exceedingly rude, Lawrence. I couldn't resist toying with them. I hope I have not caused you any embarrassment, however."

He chuckled. "Nothing that Inez couldn't clear up. She spent the afternoon with Henrietta and Julia, explaining to them that your fall off the balcony muddled your thinking a bit more than the doctor had originally thought. According to Inez, you had just finished reading *Pamela* when you sustained this fall. Seems you got your own background commingled with a fictional character's."

"That is quite a tall tale for your aunt to have told."

"It was enough that the Doggett sisters agreed to keep quiet." After a pause, Seybourne said, "As long as we are discussing this topic, have you been able to remember anything of your past, Georgiana?"

"Oh, no!"

The viscount looked disappointed, but he took Georgiana's arm and guided her toward the open French doors. "Why don't you come in and sit with me a while? I could use the company, and perhaps a bit of conversation would stimulate your memory."

The weight and warmth of his hand on her arm threatened to truly muddle her thinking. Again, she had the silly urge to rub up against the man, and mark him with her own perfume. She wasn't at all sure whether her impulses emanated from the remaining vestiges of her feline characteristics, or from her emerging human nature.

Either way, the strong attraction she felt toward the viscount weakened her determination to maintain her independence and an emotionally safe amount of distance. Pulse quickening, she shook her head and pulled away from Lord Seybourne's touch.

"Thank you, my lord, but I was going into the kitchens to brew a pot of tea."

"I am not surprised. Aunt Inez told me you have been turning your pretty nose up at our tea for the past three days."

Georgiana smiled, aware as she descended the brick steps that led to the basement kitchen, that the viscount followed close behind. Heads turned when they entered the uncomfortably warm cooking area, but the head cook discreetly returned to the onion he was chopping. The two assistant cooks and three scullery wenches quickly busied themselves, too.

"Hilda, do you mind if I put on a pot of water to boil?" Georgiana had already befriended the kitchen staff. Hilda, a plump red-faced woman who served as second assistant cook, was particularly affectionate and quick to offer pastry treats and savory morsels.

Hilda left the capon she was trussing, wiped her hands on her apron, and said, "I'll do it for ye, m'lady." After filling a pot with water and hanging it over the fire, she said, "Anything else I can do far ye, miss?"

Carefully avoiding Chef's pile of chopped onion, Georgiana laid her herbs on the huge scarred butcher block that occupied the center of the brick-floored kitchen. "Let's see, I will need some cinnamon and cardamom, heavy cream and sugar."

"What sort of tea are you planning to brew?" Lord Seybourne asked, settling on a wooden stool beside the butcher block. Crossing his arms over his chest, he watched in amusement as Hilda gathered the ingredients requested and set them before Georgiana.

She could hardly tell him she was making the spiced tea Sir Hester had so loved. It was the old man's secret recipe, but she'd heard him mumble it under his breath a hundred times. And though it wasn't the sort of concoction most house cats craved, Georgiana had eventually acquired a taste for it. Recalling the baronet's delight when she first dipped her nose into the saucer of spiced tea he prepared for her, Georgiana smiled wistfully.

"If I had known this strange brew would make you happy, I would have ordered it done days ago."

"I am afraid I only just remembered the recipe this morning," Georgiana replied.

Hilda soon set a pot of hot water before her, along with a silver tea strainer and two cups. Georgiana added her catmint leaves and the other ingredients to the pot, then waited for it to brew.

Lord Seybourne used the interval to resume his gentle interrogation of her. "Can you remember when and where you used to drink tea brewed like this?"

"No," she lied.

"Well, have you been able to remember who pushed you off the balcony, my lady?"

"I saw no one." *Which was the appalling truth.* Whoever had pushed her must be exceedingly well schooled in the art of stealth. No one had ever sneaked up on Georgiana before. "Nor did I hear anyone."

"It is all very puzzling. Have you not been able to recall anything about Sir Hester's death? Why you were in his study? Why you were . . ." He paused, looked around the kitchens and lowered his voice. "Naked?"

"No." Modesty was certainly a new emotion for Georgiana, but heat flooded her cheeks at the thought of Lord Seybourne seeing her nude. And not only that, he had picked her up, covered her with his cloak and transported her home in his carriage. Why, he'd already had the opportunity to study every inch of her body. With equal parts titillation and embarrassment, she shivered.

He chuckled. "You are certainly not cold, my lady. The temperature must be near a hundred degrees in here. I suggest we take our tea into my study. Hilda, would you prepare a tray, please?"

Georgiana followed the viscount out of the kitchen, down the corridor, and up a flight of stairs to his private study. It was a distinctly masculine room, smaller than Sir Hester's, but more forbidding. The paneled mahogany walls and crimson carpets lent the room a closed-in, somber feel.

Her attention was drawn to a portrait of Lawrence hanging above the mantelpiece. Standing before it, she stared, startled by the malevolent expression the painter had attributed to her husband.

"Why, you must have been in a black mood when that portrait was painted!"

Seybourne waved his hand dismissively at the portrait and gave a bleak chuckle. "I would rather not discuss that portrait's model, my lady. Wouldn't you be more comfortable on the sofa, there?"

Lord Seybourne gestured toward a small leather sofa in the corner of the room. Beside it was a table laden with books and a multibranched candelabrum situated to provide reading light. Sinking into the well-worn soft cushions, Georgiana was once again assaulted by the aroma of the viscount's body. She knew instinctively that this room was where he spent a great deal of his time. For that reason, she was intrigued by every inch of it, the bookshelves lining the back wall, the heavy velvet curtains draping the front windows, and the exotic display of artifacts gracing the mantelpiece.

The viscount stood before the mantelpiece, one arm resting casually on the heavy oaken ledge.

Georgiana was relieved when Hilda entered with the tea tray. Upon the servant's departure, the viscount shoved away from the mantel, crossed the room, and expertly poured two cups of tea, adding sugar at Georgiana's instruction.

"For a man, you are amazingly adept at the art of serving tea," Georgiana commented, raising her cup to her lips.

Standing, he lifted his cup in a mock salute. "My brother and I were raised by my Aunt Inez, who as you may have noticed, has certain very strong opinions about how men and women should behave toward one another."

The sweet, spicy aroma of the cream-thickened tea swirled beneath Georgiana's nostrils. As she sipped, a soft, guttural sound escaped her lips. She only just managed to keep from purring.

The viscount took a drink, his eyes fastened on Georgiana. Then, he took another, and before he spoke, he'd drained half his cup. " 'Tis excellent, not like any tea I have ever tasted. You are to be commended, my lady. Now if you can only remember who taught you how to make this tea."

His approbation pleased Georgiana almost as much as the familiar aroma and comforting taste of the tea. Eyes closed, she continued to drink until her cup was empty. Returning her cup and saucer to the tray, she sighed contentedly. But as she pushed back into the leather sofa, she sensed an alteration in the atmosphere that made her hackles rise. Her eyes popped open as the viscount set his cup and saucer on the tea table and came to sit beside her on the sofa.

Leaning toward her, he grasped her hand. "I do adore it when you make those little noises, Georgiana."

"What noises?" she squeaked.

"I dare say, I cannot describe them. No other woman I know has ever made them." With a self-deprecating chuckle, he added, "Perhaps that is a reflection on my ruinous experiences with women."

"I find it exceedingly difficult to believe that you have been anything less than wildly successful with the female species."

Seybourne's eyes widened a bit at Georgiana's odd choice of words. He scooted closer to her, his body so near she could feel the muscular tension of his thighs. "I have always valued solitude—up till now, that is."

"You are a loner," she remarked baldly.

He said nothing, merely tightened his grip on her fingers and stared into her eyes.

Disarmed, Georgiana clutched for a conversational lifeline. Never had silence disturbed her, but suddenly she felt the need to babble. Yet her throat felt like a skein of yarn had been forced down it, and her heart thundered so violently she doubted she could eke out another word. She leaned back as Lord Seybourne leaned forward.

"My lord," she started, appalled by the husky sound of her own voice, and the emotion it conveyed. "You have asked me myriad questions concerning myself—"

''None of which you've answered.''

''Nonetheless, I've not yet had the opportunity to ask you some pertinent questions. Despite the fact we've both agreed this marriage will end at some indeterminate future time, 'twould be wise if I knew something of your background. La! I almost exposed our little charade at Lady Spraddlin's when it was painfully clear I knew next to nothing about you.''

''I don't want to talk about my past, Georgiana.'' He lowered his head and dipped his nose to the crook of her neck. He nuzzled her throat, gently rubbing his bristly jaw against her skin. His harsh involuntary sigh fanned Georgiana's flesh with moist heat.

The sensation was nearly more than she could bear. She drew a jagged deep breath, amazed by the wanton urges the viscount's touch induced. When his lips pressed against her throbbing pulse-point, pleasure burst through her body with such explosive force that she gasped. Little waves of urgent need radiated through her body.

Half turning, she leaned into him and pressed her palms against his chest. She should have pushed him away; instead, she gripped his lapels and clung to him. As his arms encircled her waist, she melted into him, suddenly desperate for his protection. For a moment, she forgot completely her determination to remain emotionally detached from her temporary husband. All she cared about now was that he held her, possessed her, and *loved her*.

His kisses, alternatingly urgent and tender, scrubbed her sensitive neck with gooseflesh. He suckled the delicate lobe of her ear and grazed her shoulder with his teeth. Everywhere Lord Seybourne's lips found vulnerable bare skin, they warmed her flesh expertly. Instinctively, Georgiana arched her back, exposing her *decolletage* to the viscount's brazen mouth.

His fingers toyed with the facing of her neckline. With his head resting on her shoulder, he looked up at her, his gaze questioning. Georgiana, unable to speak, gave him a barely perceptible nod. Her assent was reflected in the darkening of his eyes. Then, his breathing deepened and he scooped his fingers inside the neckline of her dress.

His fingertips—calloused from handling the leather ribbons of his equipage—skimmed her skin. Georgiana, her own breath coming in shallow gusts, was shocked by the powerful feelings his touch provoked.

A faint mewling sound escaped her lips, exposing the intensity of her need. A twinge of embarrassment raised her anxiety level; then, she realized her sounds of pleasure heightened the viscount's excitement. When he nestled closer against her breast and buried his face in the bend of her neck, his kisses were hot and passionate. Along with Georgiana's defenses, a wall of inhibitions came crashing down.

Heat pooled and throbbed in intimate places of her body. She tangled her fingers in Seybourne's thick, shaggy hair and held him close to her bosom. Her heart hammered beneath his cheek. If this was what men and women experienced each time they made love, Georgiana didn't know why they ever did anything else.

The viscount lifted his head and gazed at her, his eyes drunk with hunger. "Let me make love to you, Georgiana. Right now, right here!"

Woefully unprepared to cope with her husband's urgent request, Georgiana panicked. She wanted him more than anything in the world, but she was frightened.

"No!" She hated herself for doing it, but she pushed him away.

He drew back, his expression full of stunned disappointment.

Terror coursed through Georgiana's body. What did she know about men? What did she know about making love to one? She could only imagine a furtive, violent coupling—having no reference point for the viscount's brand of intimacy, she had no idea how to react to it.

Folding her arms across her chest, she scooted to the corner of the sofa, where she huddled warily and stared back at Lord Seybourne. Between them, raged a wordless flood of emotion: His confusion clashed violently with her fright and ambivalence.

Slowly, he rose from the sofa to his full height. He ran his fingers through his tousled hair and shot his cuffs. "Very well, my lady," he said curtly. "Though we are legally husband and wife, I must honor your decision on this matter."

"You said the marriage was only temporary," Georgiana reminded him. "When the threat of a scandal abates and Lord Pigott's campaign has ended victoriously, you intend to obtain an annulment, or banish me to the country, or feign my death and send me packing to the Continent with a forged identity!"

"Where did you hear such nonsense?"

"I have a keen sense of hearing, my lord."

"I suppose you do," Seybourne muttered. After a brief hesitation, he added gruffly, "Well, I suppose your virtuous restraint is wise, given your inability to remember who you are. God forbid you should remember you are Lady So-and-So, the wife of some country MP, or Lord Wellington's niece!"

"You needn't fear such exalted connections on my part," Georgiana remarked drily.

"Why? Do you remember something that you are not telling—"

"No!" Georgiana pounced to her feet. Smoothing her skirts, she brushed past the viscount and strode toward the door. Over her shoulder, she said, "I am going to take a nap now, if you do not object."

"Would it matter if I did?" As she flounced through the door, he added under his breath, "Bloody hell, the woman sleeps more than an opium eater!"

Like a wolf in his lair, the viscount remained cloistered in his study. He sat behind the desk, palpably aware of Georgiana's presence above stairs. His attempts to study the accounting ledgers stacked on his desk were wholly ineffectual. His wife's perfume surrounded him; he still felt the throbbing of her pulse beneath his fingers. The taste of her cool, tender white skin remained fresh on his lips. Numbers blurred into columns of fuzzy black ink as his body throbbed with repressed desire.

The shadows lengthened. With a pull of the bell cord, Seybourne summoned a footman, who quickly lit several branches of candles and an oil lamp, then exited discreetly. Content to brood in solitude, the viscount paced the study floor, perused books he'd long meant to read, and made far too many trips to the sideboard, where the brandy was kept.

At last, he slumped in a heavy leather club chair, where he tried in vain to read a few verses of Byron's *Manfred*. But the lines faded into gibberish before his bleary eyes. On the page appeared the ghostly image of Georgiana, her retroussé nose taunting him. Slamming shut the book, Seybourne tossed it aside. He leaned back his head and sighed. Never had his sexual yearning contained such poignancy and pain; never had his conscience been so laden with guilt. Never had his solitude been so lonely.

Shoving off from the chair, the viscount took three long strides to the sofa and collapsed onto it. Without bothering to take off his boots, he stretched out, threw one arm across his eyes and tried to sleep.

But it was no good. Despite his constant mental analysis of his dilemma, he could see no way out of his betrayal of Georgiana. Frustration seethed in him like boiling tar, filling him with silent anger and better recriminations. Even the ignominy of his criminal convictions hadn't caused him such pain. His decisions then had been easy ones.

His mind flashed on the face of his twin brother Francis, older than he by mere minutes. Yet, Francis had been as different from Lawrence as night from day. That their facial features were identical had resulted in Lawrence being charged with smuggling and murder, not Francis. The truth was, Lawrence deWulff had never smuggled contraband, much less fired the shot that killed a Bow Street Runner.

But Lawrence had harbored no reservations about his actions then. His sense of loyalty had been his guide, and despite the horrendous consequences of his decisions—and the ultimate futility of it—he had never regretted his decision.

Now, there was no clear-cut answer to his conundrum. His recent interview with the king had galvanized his determination to see this investigation through to the end. With the Kit-Kat Club's decision to host a party for Caroline of Brunswick, the stakes had raised exponentially.

No one could help Lord Seybourne. No one could ever understand the reasons why his betrayal of Georgiana was necessary. With the fomenting of an Italian revolution, and rumors of Boney's support of a group of woefully misguided nationalists, it was imperative that the Kit-Kat Club conspiracy be exposed and Sir Hester's killer apprehended.

Still, the viscount muttered a sanguine oath as he shifted restlessly on the sofa, aching for sleep. His physical need for Georgiana, coupled with the guilty knowledge that he was betraying her, precluded relaxation. If he didn't rest soon, he'd have to drown himself in liquor just to pass into a state of blissful oblivion.

Heavy footsteps trod the stairs and brought him fully alert. The study door creaked open; holding his breath, Seybourne lifted his head and prayed to see Georgiana in the threshold.

Instead, Sir Morton Drysdale, his boyish face split in a smile, strode into the room. "Wake up, man! We told your butler we needed no escort. Knew you'd be happy to receive us."

In Sir Morton's wake, appeared Mr. Jack Craven and Hughes, Lord Chumley. The three men entered the study as if they owned the place, Chumley heading toward the sideboard for a drink, while Craven hitched one buttock on the huge mahogany desk strewn with Seybourne's books and papers.

The viscount swung his boots to the carpet and sat up. His head was foggy from drink and worry, but some part of him was relieved that a distraction had materialized. Scratching his head, he yawned and accepted the glass of brandy Chumley offered him.

"Haven't any of you a proper sense of decorum? I'm on my honeymoon, for Christ's sake," he said grimly.

Craven extracted a meerschaum pipe from his inner coat-pocket. Pinching some of Seybourne's finest tobacco from a silver box on the desk, he tamped it into the bowl. "Doesn't look like any honeymoon I've ever seen. Or don't you know that you are entitled to sleep with your wife after the nuptials?"

"I was merely taking a nap," Seybourne said.

Chumley, decanter in one hand and glass in another, laughed.

"Are we, then, to presume you have worn yourself out exercising your connubial rights?"

"Presume what you like, but don't be impertinent," Seybourne replied.

Sir Morton flopped down on the sofa next to him. "We have all heard the story by now, Lawrie. No need to hide it from us. You were forced to marry Georgiana by that meddling aunt of yours."

Seybourne rubbed his hand down the back of his head, hesitating. "Who told you that?" he asked quietly.

Craven interjected. "Lady Spraddlin and those insipid Doggett sisters are bruiting it all over Mayfair that your bride was a wanton woman in desperate need of some rehabilitation."

"Damned honorable of you to take the wench in." Sir Morton's grin was quickly wiped away by the sharp gaze Seybourne turned on him.

"I will not have any of you speaking ill of Georgiana," the viscount said. "No matter what she was prior to our wedding, she is the Viscountess Seybourne now, and she is my wife. Anyone who disparages her will be attacking my honor, and I shall call out the first man who dares to do so."

Chumley leaned against the mahogany desk and looked at Seybourne over the rim of his glass. "I think we all understand now, Lawrie. Sorry if you took offense with our levity. We only meant to cheer you up, old man. After all, we are your friends."

Craven nodded, his face obscured by a cloud of smoke. "You need your friends at a time like this, my lord. You shouldn't drown your sorrows in drink, or cool your heels down here on your study sofa. Why not get out of this house for a while?"

"It seems like someone died in here!" Sir Morton added.

Chumley set down his drink, crossed the room and clapped Seybourne's shoulder. "Come out to Brooks's with us for a bit. Forget about all of this, at least for a few hours. Things will be better when you have returned."

"Absence makes the heart grow fonder, Lawrie." Craven's smile was one of the most unpleasant Seybourne had ever seen. "When you return, perhaps your new bride will allow you into her bedchamber. I swear, it breaks my heart to find you sleeping down here in your study!''

''Come with us!'' Sir Morton cried.

Seybourne started to object, but Chumley's hand on his shoulder was a mighty inducement. Slowly, he rose to full height, only to experience a wave of dizziness which almost knocked his brandy glass from his hand.

Sir Morton leapt to his feet and grasped Seybourne's arm, while Chumley returned the brandy glass to the sideboard.

''So, it is decided,'' Craven said, tapping his pipe against the side of a heavy crystal ashtray. ''But before we hit the gaming tables, I strongly suggest we get our friend a thick, bloody slab of beef to fortify himself. Looks a bit puny to me, he does.''

''Yes, some food would do me good.'' The thought of sinking his teeth into a steak strengthened Seybourne's nerve. With a scant uplift of his spirits, he accompanied the men down the stairs.

As he left out the front door of his house and clambered into Craven's gleaming black equipage, he had a strange feeling that he was being watched. Seated on the leather-covered squabs, he looked through the glass window of the coach and saw the dim flicker of a candle behind the curtains in Georgiana's bedchamber.

But if she watched him as he left the house, she had no wish to see any more of him. The curtains swung to, and remained still. Gritting his teeth, Lord Seybourne turned his attention toward his acquaintances. And a lump formed in his throat as he realized he would soon betray them, as well.

Chapter Seven

Craven's expert driver quickly transported the men south, crossing Piccadilly to arrive at 60 St. James's Street in less than a quarter of an hour. Emerging from the carriage, Lord Seybourne drew an uneasy breath, shot his cuffs, and nodded coolly at a pair of passing cyprians, strolling past arm in arm.

"Why not take one of them for your pleasure, Lawrie?" Craven asked, alighting beside him. " 'Twould be a passing good way to spend the evening, and the three of us would not resent your change of heart one whit."

"Were I actually on the prowl, I should take them *both*," Seybourne said. "However, I am a married man now, no matter how miserably, and I do not wish to engage in such scandalous conduct."

"Well, I am certainly unattached and game for a bout of bedplay," Sir Morton said, disappearing after the strolling women.

Seybourne rolled his eyes and the men—minus Sir Morton—entered Brooks's. After checking their cloaks and hats at the front door, they ascended a grand staircase to the club's dining room where beefsteaks, oyster pie and two bottles of the house's finest claret were quickly produced. They ate heartily while discussing the latest *on-dits* concerning the king's Bill of Pains and Penalties against Caroline, and Henry Brougham's spirited defense in Parliament of the much maligned queen. Strengthened by the repast, Seybourne then accompanied his companions into the main gaming room.

He was not at all surprised to notice the rest of the members of the Kit-Kat Club—Whitney, Higgenbotham, Babworth and Pigott —circumnavigating the room, laughing it up with sympathetic Whig politicians and journalists. His friends seemed particularly interested in hobnobbing with the most rabid, radical element of the Whig party. He made a mental note to investigate these men and the Club's outside ties with them before going to Wolfharden Manor to prepare for Caroline's dinner dance.

For a moment, he stood in the center of the room, thoroughly miserable. He wanted to go home, sit beside Georgiana's bed and watch her sleep. He had concluded that her head trauma had produced not only acute memory loss, but also a sort of sleeping sickness. In a way, he regretted that she would eventually recover from this particular malady. He loved to watch her breathe through slightly parted lips, her lovely breasts rising and falling, her long black hair strewn across the pillow.

She made a little noise when she slept—a low trill deep in her throat—that completely captivated his imagination. When he'd kept a vigil by her bed the night before, it had taken a herculean effort not to touch her. Though he knew nothing about her past, he finally admitted to himself, as he wandered aimlessly round the gaming tables, that he was thoroughly smitten with her.

Sir Douglas Babworth appeared out of nowhere to give him a playful jab on his arm. "Come on, Lawrie. Join us in a bit of faro, why don't you?"

"Oh, all right," Lord Seybourne agreed, with a sigh. At least it would distract him from thoughts of Georgiana. If he didn't get his mind off her, he would drive himself stark-raving mad.

The next few hours passed in a blur, until Seybourne's winning streak became boring, and Sir Douglas's dismal luck turned dangerous.

The dealer called for new bets, and Sir Douglas rummaged through his pockets. He tossed ten notes on the green baize and placed his marker on the ten of diamonds.

Seybourne groaned. "For God's sake, man, the dealer's almost at the end of his deck."

"So what?" the younger man asked irritably.

"He has drawn eight tens out of that two-deck stack of cards already," Seybourne persisted, retrieving Babworth's marker.

The table boss standing behind the dealer pointed his finger at Seybourne and cried, "Too late! The wager is good!"

At the same instant, the dealer drew a card from the black leather shoe in front of him, and tossed it face up on the table. Several of the other gamblers moaned at the sight of the face card; one man who'd placed his marker on the king of diamonds whooped and cheered loudly as stacks of chips representing varying denominations of currency were swept toward him on the end of a long bamboo stick.

"Sorry, lad, but you've lost your money!" The table boss moved his bamboo rake toward Sir Douglas's pound notes.

Seybourne quickly scooped them up and handed them to his young friend. "His bet was off the table before the card was drawn, I am afraid. The house has no claim to his money."

Play stopped immediately. The dealer relaxed in his chair and watched while the table boss summoned two men whose faces looked like pig bladders, and whose grotesque muscles strained the expensive fabric of their coats.

The table boss skirted the table and, flanked by the two surly-faced bouncers, stood in front of Seybourne. "Tell the young punk to give over those pound notes," he demanded, his lip curling in an ugly sneer.

An icy calmness fell over the viscount. "I won't do it. I withdrew his marker before the king was dealt. He doesn't owe you a farthing."

"The game was in play when you snatched up his bet!"

"No card had been drawn. Several players put down markers and laid down chips or money at the same time I withdrew my friend's wager. If the house was willing to accept bets at that point, then it should be willing to allow a man to pick up his marker.''

''Says who?'' the table boss jeered.

Lord Seybourne spoke through gritted teeth. ''I am Lawrence deWulff, Viscount Seybourne. Now if you please, my friend and I will leave.''

''If you please,'' the man mocked him, ''my two friends will see you out.''

''That is fine with me.'' Seybourne plucked Sir Douglas's sleeve and drew him along as the two strode through the room. Men glanced up curiously as the two Goliaths followed closely, trailing them as they descended the stairs, dogging their heels as they exited the club.

Passing through the doors, Sir Douglas gulped. ''Lawrie, perhaps I should simply give the men my money. 'Tis not worth losing our lives over.''

''Have no fear, Douglas,'' the viscount said, glancing over his shoulder. He hesitated a moment, looking up and down the street for Craven's carriage. There was a line of coaches parked along the street awaiting the gentlemen inside, but Craven's rig was nowhere in sight. ''Damned curious,'' muttered Seybourne, acutely aware of the two hulking men who hovered behind him.

One of them grasped his arm and said, ''Step into the alley, won't you, Lord High-and-Mighty?''

Sir Douglas pivoted and started to flee in the opposite direction, but the second bouncer reached out with surprising alacrity and caught him by the tail of his cutaway coat. ''Why you're as sweaty as a greased pig! Well, you won't slip away from me!'' he said, pulling the young man toward the nearest alley running off St. James's Street.

''I'll pay the money!'' Sir Douglas babbled as the giant grabbed him by the scruff of his neck and lifted him off his feet.

Seybourne shrugged out of his coat and rolled up his sleeves as he walked toward the alley. Had Craven's coach been easily accessible, he'd intended to toss Sir Douglas into it and take these two bouncers all for himself. Frankly, he'd been spoiling for a good set-to ever since his encounter with Georgiana on his sofa in his study. His body craved release, if not with a woman, than in hand-to-hand combat with a ruthless pugilist. Had the two bouncers only known how ready he was to fight—or how well trained as a pugilist he was—they might have thought twice about disappearing down a dark alley with him.

As he stepped into the dark alley, Lord Seybourne drew away from his opponents and lifted his fists to his chest. One of the bouncers held Sir Douglas captive, while the other raised his fists to Seybourne. The viscount circled the bigger man warily appraising his height, his strength, his potential weak spots.

When the man tilted his shoulders, Seybourne instantly recognized a vulnerable spot. Lightning quick, his arm shot out and his rock-hard fist crashed into the man's left jaw, shattering teeth and breaking bones in one powerful blow.

"Oooh! You bloody ass!" The man bellowed, blood streaming from his mouth. Doubled over, he held his face and swore colorfully.

Seybourne turned toward the other man, his fists readied.

Sir Douglas, suddenly released, turned and fled, leaving Seybourne alone with the bouncers. The viscount gave a grim smile, just as happy to finish this unpleasant business himself. Maybe his young friend had at least learned a lesson that would curtail his extravagant gambling habits.

However, Seybourne's odds of surviving this skirmish quickly plummeted. The injured bouncer produced a knife from his inside coat-pocket, a long, sinister-looking weapon whose blade flashed in the moonlight. The one who had just released Sir Douglas pulled a small pistol from the back waistband of his pants.

Seybourne could hardly defend himself against a gun and a pistol, not with his bare fists. He froze, muscles taut, gaze locked on the man wielding the pistol. His only chance for survival was to talk the man out of shooting him—an unlikely prospect, given the circumstances—or to turn and flee, perhaps losing himself in darkness before his pursuer was able to get off a well-aimed shot.

The gunman spoke out of the side of his mouth. "Stay where you are," he told his partner. "I'll finish off this stiff-rumped aristocrat meself!"

The murderous glee in the gunman's voice was evident. He slowly advanced on Lord Seybourne, the metallic snout of his pistol glinting in the dim light reflected off dank-smelling puddles. The viscount instinctively inched backward, his boots sliding carefully over the rough bricks of the alley. Waiting for an opportunity to distract the gunman, he stared at the man, constantly assessing the level of violence in his eyes, waiting for the opportunity to turn and flee, judging the situation second by second.

The viscount's senses tingled with awareness. In the distance, he heard the raucous cheers of gamblers inside Brooks's, the clip-clop of horses' hooves and the rumble of coaches on St. James's Street. The greasy smell of cooking beefsteaks mingled with the sweet decay of trash loaded in bins that dotted the alley. Coal burning in fireplaces tinged the crisp night air with a sooty flavor, while the prospect of rain creaked in Seybourne's joints.

He froze, his mind devoid of panic or fear, his ears pricking. For a moment, he was all animal, acting on instinct and reflex only, unafraid, vicious in his will to survive.

The gunman's eyes widened, and a crude smile split his face. "So, you ain't afraid of dyin', are ye, Lord High-and-Mighty?"

A chill deepened the night air, altering the atmosphere. Seybourne's nape prickled and his fingers coiled at his sides. Aware of another presence in the alley, he held his breath.

A movement drew the gunman's attention; foolishly, he turned his head to look at his partner.

The man whose jaw had been cracked crumpled to the ground in a heap of black superfine. His knife fell to the bricks with a clang.

That was all the distraction Seybourne needed. He moved forward in a flash, his leg shooting outward to knock the pistol from the gunman's hand. Then he shifted his weight and laid

TREAT YOURSELF TO 4 FREE REGENCY ROMANCES.

A
$19.96
VALUE...
FREE!

No
obligation
to buy
anything,
ever!

into the man with a roundhouse punch to his jaw. Stunned, the huge man wavered on his feet, but didn't fall. Seybourne finished him off with a swift uppercut to his chin. When the man doubled over, he delivered a chop to the back of the man's neck, which sent him sprawling facedown on the bricks.

Chafing his palms, he peered into the darkness.

"Nice work, old man," said a familiar voice. The gaunt face of a fellow Kit-Kat Club member soon emerged from the shadows, smiling.

Seybourne exhaled, relieved. "I never thought I would be so happy to see you, Craven. You showed up in the nick of time. I was just about to do a French turn and risk taking a bullet in my back."

"I own you are a fast runner, but you would never have outdistanced a bullet."

"Well, then, I am doubly indebted to you for your intervention," Seybourne replied. "Thank you." After an uncomfortable pause, he said, "By the way, where is young Douglas?"

"Cowering in my coach, I'm afraid."

"But I didn't see your rig—"

Craven cut in, surveying the two fallen club bouncers with obvious distaste. " 'Fraid my driver fell in at the end of the line. What shall we do with these reprobates, eh? Leave them where they are, or return them to their rightful owner?"

Seybourne stepped over the body of the gunman. Eager to return home, he said, "I think we owe them the courtesy of informing the doorman of their whereabouts. After all, I believe they both could benefit from some medical attention."

Craven agreed, and the two men walked briskly down the alley, emerging onto St. James's a mere half block from the entrance to Brooks's. After informing the doorman of the bouncers' whereabouts and sorry conditions, they climbed into Craven's rig, now conveniently parked beneath a gaslight at the corner. Slumped in a corner, Sir Douglas greeted them with a rather sheepish expression.

"Sorry to leave you back there, my lord," Sir Douglas said, as the carriage took off with a jolt. "But I thought it best to run for assistance. Lucky I did, too, for I nearly ran headlong into Craven here just as he was leaving the club.''

"Yes, when I realized the two of you had left the faro table," Craven said, "I thought you had gone out to summon my driver for a lift home. Thinking that I'd quite had enough, too, I followed you out. Imagine my surprise when Sir Douglas nearly knocked me down. Egad, I thought for a moment the lad had seen a ghost, he was so white!"

"Damme! I did the honorable thing!" Sir Douglas cried. "If I hadn't summoned help, those two oafs would have beaten Lord Seybourne to a pulp."

Seybourne chuckled, leaning over to slap the younger man on the knee. "Very little chance of that, my friend, not as long as it was hand-to-hand combat. But when my adversaries produced a pistol and a knife, well then, I admit I was a trifle uncomfortable."

Jack Craven let out a sharp bark of laughter. "A trifle, you say? Why, I wish I could have seen your face when that monster pulled a pistol from his pants! I would have fainted from fright, I'm sure!"

Sir Douglas laughed, too, at first a bit nervously, then, with hearty gusto. Seybourne forced a smile to his lips, unable to articulate exactly what about the young man's behavior, other than his cowardice, alarmed him.

By the time the laughter died down, the carriage was slowing to a stop in front of Seybourne's Tenterden Street town house. Craven's tiger swung open the door, while Seybourne said his good-nights, thanking Craven again for his fortuitous appearance in the alleyway.

He jumped to the ground, but as he did, a thought occurred to him. Turning, he grabbed the door as the tiger started to push it shut. Holding it open, he leaned inside and said, "For God's sake, Jack, how did you manage to sneak down that alleyway without making a sound? I am quite sure my sense of hearing is keener than the average man's! But, I never knew you were there until that sharp with the knife fell to the ground."

Craven's expression, lit by the glow of the carriage lamps, momentarily went blank. Then, he smiled and replied, "When

I was young, I spent some time in the Orient. Remind me to tell you about it some day. I learned a smattering of martial artistry, in particular, the ability to move as silently as a cat.''

''You learned well,'' Seybourne answered.

The carriage rumbled off, and the viscount stood for a moment, pondering Craven's response. Then, Georgiana's image popped into his mind, dispelling all thoughts of the evening's unpleasant confrontation. He turned and ascended the steps to his front door, eager for the sanctuary of his home.

But he found that his house was in a tumult, the likes of which would make an angry swarm of bees look placid.

Servants scurried about the place, lighting lamps and candles even though it was long since the household's normal bedtime. A footman, cotton towels thrown over his shoulder, emerged from the kitchens bearing an ewer and basin. Dashing through the entrance hall, he sprinted up the stairs two at a time.

Aunt Inez stood at the top of the steps, her dumpling-shaped face pale without its usual wash of cheek rouge. Wearing a flannel mobcap and a chenille wrap pulled tight around her nightclothes, she looked as if she'd just rolled from her bed. ''Oh, Lawrie, thank heavens you're home!'' she cried, wringing her hands.

He bounded up the steps and stood beside her on the landing. ''What is the matter, Aunt? For God's sake, why all the commotion?''

'' 'Tis Georgiana! She thought someone was in her room.''

Seybourne's heart dropped like an anchor. He grasped his aunt's shoulders and spoke very deliberately to her, as if she were hard of hearing. ''Tell me. What happened? Is my wife all right?''

The old woman's head bobbed up and down. Sniffling, she managed to eke out the story of the night's events. '' 'Twas well past midnight when I heard footsteps running down the corridor. La! I thought the house was on fire, what with all the running around I heard. I tumbled out of bed and opened my door and nearly plowed straight into Lady Georgiana!''

"What in the bloody devil was she doing at your door?"

Aunt Inez was not too rattled to take notice of her nephew's strong language. Slanting him a harsh gaze, she replied tartly, "She awoke from a bad dream and thought someone was in her room. Lord, she screamed like a cat whose tail had been stomped on! But the servants have searched her chambers and the rest of the house thoroughly, my lord, and there is no one here. Nevertheless, Georgiana was frightened out of her wits."

"Are you saying she only *dreamed* someone was in her room?"

"Yes! No! Oh, I don't know!"

"There was no one found in her room, or elsewhere in the house?" Seybourne demanded.

"The servants found no one!"

The viscount sighed, pinching the bridge of his nose against a pounding headache that had just begun. "Thank God she wasn't hurt. And I hope that it was just a bad dream, as you said, Aunt."

"Oh, dear," his aunt said, twisting her fingers. "I fear I've made a dreadful mistake by promoting this marriage, Lawrie. 'Struth, I thought I was killing two birds with one stone by marrying you off to this unknown girl. After all, she is very beautiful, any jackanapes with eyes can see that. And I thought . . . well, I thought—"

"Yes, Aunt?" Despite the crisis being over, Georgiana needed Lawrence; he was eager to go to her. Resisting the urge to shake his aunt by the shoulders, he repeated, "Yes?"

"I never have liked that Lady Mercy Mary Spraddlin!"

Shaking his head, he said, "This is no time to discuss my former mistress, Aunt. I must see to my wife." He took two long strides toward Lady Seybourne's closed bedchamber door.

Aunt Inez plucked his sleeve. "Don't go! There is no urgency now, for Georgiana is already asleep."

He halted and turned toward his aunt. "Hardly surprising."

"Especially after the sleeping drought I gave her."

"Then why is the household swarming?" the viscount asked, as a footman bearing a tea tray ascended the stairs and headed toward his aunt's bedchamber.

"The servants are in a state of frenzy due to my histrionics, not hers! And I must speak to you while I have got the courage. Now, before I lose my resolve."

"Speak, then."

"I owe you an apology," his aunt said, her chin up yet quavering ever so slightly. "I didn't want you to marry Lady Spraddlin, boy. And I thought if you were married to someone else, you might escape an unfortunate connection with her. That is why I went along so readily with the notion of your marrying Georgiana."

"Well, this is quite a surprise. I knew you and Mercy Mary were not the greatest of friends, but I always believed you held her in the highest esteem. She is, after all, the second in command of the Society for the Rehabilitation of Wanton Women, is she not? And one of your most generous contributors?"

" 'Twas her late husband, actually."

The implications of that remark sank into Seybourne's brain rather slowly. "The Earl of Spraddlin was a patron of the Society? Why didn't I know of this?"

"Dear boy, you must remember that it was while you were in Australia for those five years that I founded the Society. I can't have told you everything that happened during that time. Besides, by the time you met Lady Spraddlin, she was completely reformed."

"Reformed?" The viscount's blood ran cold. "You mean to say that she was a—"

"Not even a high-class one, I'm afraid."

"And the earl?"

"Sponsored her rehabilitation when the Society was in its infancy. Apparently met her one night when he was in his cups and made an uncharacteristic visit to a bawdy house. To his credit, he felt sorry for her. Contributed quite a large sum of money to my newly founded Society. And in exchange, I took the young lady into my care and personally saw to it that she was properly turned out, educated in the feminine arts and taught proper table manners. You should have seen her wielding a fork and knife when she first came to me! La! 'Twas a horrid sight! But, as you can see, she is now completely transformed."

"And the earl married her when you were through."

"Yes, dear. I don't think it was what he had in mind when he first sponsored her. But when he saw what a lovely young thing she was, he proposed marriage. Sweet, really."

"And how is it that no one in London knows of this unusual situation?" Seybourne frowned. "Or am I the only cat's paw who *doesn't* know? Is that it? Am I a laughingstock because I first squired a rehabilitated cyprian all over Mayfair, then got rooked into marrying another?"

Aunt Inez smiled. "Oh, no, dear. No one ever knew Lady Mercy Mary's true lineage—or lack thereof. When it was time for her to come out into Society, I simply created a fictitious background for her, secured vouchers for Almack's, and allowed the earl to introduce himself to her properly. All for appearances' sake, you see. Worked quite well, if I say so myself. It would have, that is, if the earl hadn't died so, er, precipitously."

"Just before I returned from Australia?"

"Just after, I'm afraid," his aunt corrected him. "You met him, Lawrie, you just don't remember."

He frowned. "I was in quite a fog the first six months after my return. You dragged me to a hundred hothouse routs and I dare say, I remember few of the people I met."

"You also met Lady Spraddlin at one of those parties."

"Well, I cannot say whom I admire the most, Aunt. You, for opening your heart to a woman less fortunate than yourself. The earl for his kindness, his egalitarianism, and his generosity. Or Lady Mercy Mary, for her astounding good sense, ambition, and enterprise. I think I like her better than before, knowing this."

"Oh, my. Perhaps I should have kept my mouth shut."

Seybourne thought back to his aunt's earlier comment about wishing to prevent a marriage between him and Lady Spraddlin. "Why on earth did you think Georgiana a preferable bride to Mercy Mary?"

The old woman gulped convulsively, her hand fluttering near

her throat. "Just a feeling, Lawrie. Call it woman's intuition. I just don't think Mercy Mary is the right woman for you. And I feared you were about to marry her. That is why I acted so impulsively when I caught you with a naked woman in your arms."

"And why are you disclosing Mercy Mary's background to me now? Is it not a violation of the trust she has placed in you?"

"I suppose so, but I thought you should know. With all the strange goings-on around here, lately, Lawrie, I just thought you should know."

"Strange goings-on? Do you mean tonight? But, I thought you said Georgiana had a bad dream."

His aunt sniffed. "That is what she said. And there was no one found in the entire house; nor was there any sign that someone entered the house forcibly. However, I did hear someone running down the corridor and I don't think it was Georgiana. You know how quietly she treads."

"Like a kitten," the viscount agreed. "But surely you aren't suggesting that Lady Spraddlin has something to do with tonight's incident. Even if there was an intruder, it couldn't have possibly been her." The viscount coolly dismissed his aunt's concerns as they related to his former mistress. Had she any inkling of the depth of intrigue he was involved in, she wouldn't cast her suspicions on a widowed countess.

In fact, his aunt's suspicions were proof to Seybourne of the woman's veiled snobbishness. For all that she was a fountain of progressive dogma, she maintained a deeply ingrained belief that men were scoundrels and women fell into one of two categories: whore or Madonna.

"Aunt, I am ashamed of you," he gently chided her. "You of all people, suggesting that Mercy Mary has anything to do with what occurred here tonight."

His aunt's smile faltered on her lips. "But, Lawrie, someone pushed Georgiana off the balcony. Or so she said! And then, the incident tonight—"

"But, Georgiana did not see anyone, you told me that yourself."

"Oh, Lawrie, it is too strange. But suppose Lady Spraddlin . . . well, what if she was not quite as thoroughly rehabilitated as I thought?"

"Nonsense! She is no threat to Georgiana's safety, Aunt. I assure you. Just the same, I promise to keep a closer eye on my bride. I was negligent in leaving the house for such a long time this evening and it won't happen again."

"Oh, Lawrie, I fear I have stirred up a recipe for danger. Perhaps I was too eager to marry you off to Georgiana. I should not have foisted you on this strange little minx who cannot remember who she is. 'Twas cruelly selfish of me."

"Yes, it was," Seybourne said, laughing. "But, there is something rather comic in the notion that my bachelorhood was sacrificed for the greater good of a wanton woman's redemption."

"Well, you needn't fear anyone finding out the truth, that's for certain! The only person who knows the circumstances of your meeting Georgiana—other than myself—is Mercy Mary. And I can assure you, she will be discreet on that point, if nothing else. She has her own skin to protect and she knows I would flay her if she ever told! After all, I have kept her confidence *completely*. Didn't even tell you until now, God forgive me!"

"I believe He does, Aunt. And so do I. Let us hope for Georgiana's sake that Mercy Mary keeps her lips sealed." Seybourne kissed his aunt's forehead beneath the ruffled edge of her mobcap. After giving her a warm hug, he escorted her to her bedchamber, said his good-night, and pulled the door shut behind her.

Then, he walked toward his wife's room, pausing at the door to consider whether he should knock and risk awakening her. In the end, he softly opened the door and crept to the chair beside her bed. It was the third night he spent in that chair, raptly watching her sleep, fascinated by every catch in her breath. There was something incredibly peaceful about the rhythm of her breathing. Not for the first time, he thought it was like the soothing sound of a cat's purr.

Slouching in the chair, he threw his long legs out before him and folded his arms across his chest. Within minutes, his eyes were shut and he fell asleep. Perhaps Georgiana's penchant for deep slumbers was infectious.

Chapter Eight

On the fourth day of Georgiana's new life, she awakened to the usual sounds of carriages rattling down Tenterden Street and milk vendors shouting their prices. But there was something distinctly different about the morning, a warm vibrance that streamed through the window along with the sunlight. Her eyes blinked open and she stretched, yawning while she scanned the room.

Unfamiliar muscles tingled with pent-up energy. The urge to bound out of bed and down the stairs was irrepressible. Tossing off her bedcovers, Georgiana wondered what had caused this radical change in the atmosphere surrounding her. What had jolted her from her slumbers? With her stomach growling, she stepped out of her night rail and quickly dressed herself in a gray muslin smock with long fitted sleeves, scooped neckline, and white apron.

The clothes Aunt Inez had chosen for her were serviceable, but hardly worthy of her figure. Still, she was glad for the fact that she was limber enough to fasten the row of buttons down her back without the need for an abigail's assistance. She wasn't certain she'd ever be accustomed to depending on a maid or servant for help in her toilet. Though she abhorred untidiness, she preferred to dress and bathe herself.

Sitting at the Sheraton vanity, she studied her reflection while brushing her long black hair. There was new color in her cheekbones and a subtle definition to her features that she hadn't noticed before.

But she had little time to admire herself. The scare she'd suffered during the night provoked a hundred new questions concerning the viscount. She felt the need to find him and subject him to a friendly interrogation. Lord, but she was losing her old instincts, she thought, as she crossed the floor to her bedchamber door.

Her old instincts, especially her inclination to find a dark corner and watch the world go by, were definitely on the wane. Suddenly, she craved company and conversation. The prospect of meeting new people was inexplicably as intriguing to her as a big eight-legged bug had once been.

Georgiana paused at the door, her fingers clutching the handle. Frozen, her nerve endings sang like a swarm of cicadas in the summer night. Well, all her feline instincts had not deserted her. She turned slowly, lifting her nose and sniffing. From the scent, she could detect who had been in a room, even after he was long gone. Lord Seybourne's scent hung heavy in the air, redolent with musk, expensive French cologne, leather, a trifle too much brandy, and the pungent, sweet odor of tobacco.

Inhaling deeply, she stood for a moment and thought how strange that this man's scent caused such a strong reaction. She knew, then, that her husband had spent the night in her room. Her gaze traveled to the chair beside her bed. He'd kept his vigil once more, watching her while she slept, *protecting her*. The thought filled her with a warmth quite unlike anything she'd ever felt.

Sir Hester had been a protector, but not in the sense that Lord Seybourne was. No man—no male creature of any species—had watched over her so intently or so determinedly. Georgiana felt a purr emanating from deep within her body; she liked being surrounded by the viscount's aroma. Being surrounded by his arms had been even more thrilling. But what she liked best was being surrounded by *him.*

At the time in her life when she should have felt most vulnerable, she was infused with confidence and a sense of safety. Turning on her heel, she flounced from her bedchamber with a painfully happy heart.

Even the servants looked aghast when she sauntered into the breakfast room. She nodded to Aunt Inez, who had speared a sausage on her fork and was working tenaciously on one end of it with her tiny teeth. Seated catty-corner to the viscount, the old woman's eyes widened as Georgiana breezed past her toward the sideboard. Working her jaws vigorously in an effort to finish off the sausage, she managed to grunt, "Gund mum-um."

With a crash, the viscount lowered his morning newspaper instantly. "What was that you said, Aunt—"

Dishing a healthy portion of baked apples, beef hash, sausage, and buttered toast onto her plate, Georgiana turned and met the viscount's gaze. "Why does everyone look so surprised?"

Carefully folding his paper beside his plate, he stood. Then, he pulled out the chair opposite Aunt Inez, and returned to his seat only after Georgiana was in hers. Smiling, he at last replied, "It is just that we have grown accustomed to your sleeping well into the day."

Aunt Inez was more precise. "We were getting used to your sleeping like a lazy cat. *All the time,* in other words."

Georgiana chuckled. "You should have realized my excessive sleeping was a symptom of the trauma I suffered. But I am feeling much better this morning. In fact, I could not wait to spring out of bed once the sun awakened me."

"I am glad to hear it," the viscount answered. "Does this mean that you have regained your memory?"

"No." Georgiana tucked into her breakfast with a single-mindedness borne of her past experiences. The room fell silent as she ate, but she didn't notice the curious stares directed at her until her plate was clean. Indeed, had she not sensed the discomfort thickening the air, she might have lowered her head to her plate and licked it spotless.

"Is something the matter?" she asked, sipping a cup of spiced tea brought from the kitchen by a conscientious maidservant. Georgiana's tea was now a staple in the cook's repertoire and made available to her whenever she wanted it.

Lord Seybourne glanced at his aunt before answering. "You were hungry," he said, his pale eyes twinkling.

Georgiana caught the look of disapproval and concern on the older woman's face. That Aunt Inez would expect such delicate manners struck her as a bit unfair, since just a few minutes earlier, the old woman had been gnawing on a sausage the way a hungry dog gnawed on a bone. But Georgiana could hardly defend her poor manners by pointing out Inez's faults. Nor could she admit that she had learned to eat fast before her food scampered away or was stolen from beneath her nose.

"Indeed, I was exceptionally hungry." Georgiana prudently changed the subject. "I suppose you have been made aware of last night's disturbance, my lord."

"Of course. I am relieved beyond all measure that you were unharmed."

"She said it was a dream, Lawrie!" Aunt Inez studied Georgiana. "Was it, gel? Or was there someone in your bedchamber?"

Georgiana appraised the older woman's skeptical, critical stare. "I thought I was certain that someone was in my room, standing over my bed and staring at me. It was a man—"

"How could you be sure?" Aunt Inez asked. "It was dark."

"There was sufficient moonlight to silhouette his form. I'm quite certain it was a man. Anyway, I awakened and he was standing there, staring down at me. I was terrified!" *She had hissed and spat at the intruder, probably startling him of out his wits.* "I screamed, and the man shot out of my room like a bullet."

"Well, I did hear footsteps," Inez confessed. "But they could have been yours. When I opened my door, you practically fell on top of me."

"I rushed out of the room behind the man. I suppose I was

in a blind panic," Georgiana said. "I am sorry if I frightened you, Lady Twitchett."

The older lady simpered her forgiveness and sipped her tea.

The viscount leaned toward Georgiana, a look of genuine concern on his handsome features. "Did you get a close look at the intruder?"

"No. It was too dark for that." Which was true. Georgiana's night vision had diminished in the past few days, and though she knew her night visitor was a man, she could say little else about his identity.

Lord Seybourne turned to his aunt. "I believe her. Someone *was* in this house last night."

"Lawrie, the servants checked every inch of this house, and there was no one here! And no broken windows or forced locks!"

"The front door was unlocked when I arrived home," he reminded his aunt gently. "The intruder could have run from Georgiana's room, down the stairs and straight out the front door!"

"Pish-posh! It wasn't half an hour after Georgiana screamed that you returned home, Lawrie! And I happen to know your valet was waiting up for you. Surely, he would have seen a stranger pounding down the stairs."

"Perhaps not," Seybourne replied. "At any rate, I shall investigate the matter further."

Georgiana, having drained her teacup, felt refreshed and rejuvenated. Her faith in Seybourne's ability to protect her allayed her previous night's fears.

"Aunt Inez, I was wondering if you would accompany me to Piccadilly this morning? I should like to visit a new modiste and have some clothes tailored specially for me."

The viscount's brows shot up. "An excellent idea. I will see to it that the carriage is ready whenever you would like to go."

"And perhaps we could visit the shoemaker and the milliner and the reticule maker and that little market on Glasshouse Street where they sell the most remarkable fresh herrings and sardines!"

"Sardines!" Aunt Inez turned a look of chinless wonder on

the viscount. "You see what I mean, Lawrie! Truly, she is a trifle strange! Oh, I fear I have made a dreadful mistake—"

The viscount laughed heartily. "Do not worry, Aunt. I prefer to think that my new wife is *unique*. Strange is such a harsh stigma for a pretty lady to bear."

Georgiana smiled. *My wife is unique.* She liked the sound of that. The viscount's voice—his slow smile, his ability to make her feel safe—was more soothing than a bowl of warm milk on a cold winter's day. Her smile widened as Lord Seybourne met her gaze, reached across the table, and squeezed her hand. Georgiana was surprised by her own reaction. Rather than flinching, withdrawing, or bolting from this unexpected touch, she nearly melted with emotion.

Aunt Inez made a little cry of surprise, abruptly stood and headed for the door. "I shall get my cloak and hat, Georgiana. Meet me in the foyer."

Seybourne's gaze never left Georgiana's face. He rose, skirted the edge of the table, and leaned down. Gently, he kissed her cheek, lightly clasping her elbow. Georgiana wished desperately that he would take her in his arms and hold her tightly against his body. Instead, he raised her hand and lightly grazed his lips over her knuckles. Pleasure curled Georgiana's toes, then snaked up her limbs and spread thoughout her body.

"Buy whatever you fancy, Georgiana," he said, his voice low and husky. "It delights me to see a smile on your face."

"Thank you, my lord—"

"Never call me that, Georgiana. I am your husband."

Her husband, her protector. The idea was both daunting and thrilling. Withdrawing her hand from his embrace, Georgiana walked beside him out of the breakfast room. A servant had already fetched her a coat, gloves, and hat. Inez was heard in the foyer below, instructing the staff as to their duties while she was out.

At the landing, Seybourne hesitated, his expression unsure. "Would you like to . . . oh, no, never mind."

"Would I like to what?" Georgiana asked.

"Last night, my friend Sir Morton Drysdale mentioned he and a lady companion were heading out to Astley's Amphitheatre this afternoon. I was wondering . . . would you care to join them?''

''Yes!'' Georgiana clapped her hands in glee. She had no idea what to expect at such a place, but she was delighted with the opportunity to go anywhere, to get out of this house where she had been shut up for four days, to spend some time with Lord Seybourne, getting to know him—and his friends.

A look of relief spread over his features. ''Wonderful. We shall depart here at five o'clock. I will send word to Sir Morton that we will stop by his lady friend's house and collect the two of them. Be sure to buy something new to wear, dear. And above all else, have a wonderful time.''

''I will.'' Georgiana descended the steps with renewed optimism. It was good to be alive. She always had been a cat who could land on her feet. *Lucky, that's what she was.* For Lawrence, Lord Seybourne, was undoubtedly a kind and generous husband. And his kisses were sweeter than butter. What more could a cat—or a woman—ask for?

The viscount quickly called for his horse. The meeting of the Kit-Kat Club was scheduled to begin in a quarter of an hour, and he had almost made himself late by dawdling in the breakfast room with Georgiana.

Nudging his horse's sides, he urged the animal to a healthy trot. Today's meeting was at Lord Chumley's Cleveland Street address and, as the traffic was light, he could still appear at the appointed hour with little difficulty. As he turned into Oxford Street, heading east, however, his mind centered on Georgiana. He couldn't get her off his mind, and the phenomenon disturbed him. What use was there in entertaining romantic thoughts of her? The relationship was doomed from inception, limited by the constraints of their unique situations.

He was using her as bait, and thereby betraying her. She was biding her time until her memory reappeared, and accepting his generous offer of room and board until a better arrangement manifested itself. They were both withholding their true identities from one another (although Georgiana couldn't be blamed for failure to reveal hers, the viscount mused). And they were both counting the days, hours, and minutes till they were released from the chafing restrictions of their sham marriage.

Still, Lord Seybourne couldn't help but be attracted to Georgiana. Aside from her obvious beauty, she possessed a feral quality that fascinated him. Behind her green eyes was the promise of many secrets. Even the scent of her, slightly sweet and slightly musky, drove him to near insanity. Whenever she was around, he struggled to control his animal urge to hold her, kiss her, bury his nose in her silky mane.

Why, then, was he tossing her to the wolves, so to speak? Even as he turned north onto Cleveland Street, the realization that he was betraying her impaled him like a flaming arrow. Yet, his options were as limited as they had been the day his brother was charged with smuggling and murder. And, a man had nothing if not his honor. Seybourne had no choice but to obey his sovereign.

For his country, then, and perhaps to save the life of the English king, the viscount had to continue in his investigation. King George's life was far more important than the viscount's love life. If and when Georgiana realized he'd used her to attract Sir Hester's killer, then she would leave him, and rightly so. The thought made his stomach roil. But what kind of man was he if he allowed his affection for a woman to interfere with the duty his king had thrust on him?

A gentle tug of the ribbons was all it required to bring his trusted mount to a halt. Lord Seybourne slid from the horse and tossed the reins to a waiting stable boy, then quickly ascended the stone steps to Lord Chumley's elegant town house. The gray stone Georgian structure matched the midmorning sky; its gleaming crimson door, bracketed by elaborate Coade stone carvings, opened the moment he stepped beneath the porte cochere.

A stuffy butler ushered Lord Seybourne into the house and up a broad winding staircase of Italian marble. At the landing, the uncommunicative servant turned right, proceeded halfway down a long, dimly lit hall, and paused before a pair of shiny mahogany doors. After a brisk knock, the man pushed open the doors and gestured Lord Seybourne into the room.

He was surprised to find all the other members of the club present in Chumley's drawing room. Scanning the perfectly appointed room in one side-to-side glance, he noticed Sir Morton slouched in a wingback chair, one trousered leg thrown negligently over the arm. Higgenbotham and Whitney bracketed the sideboard, where decanters of liquor and wine appeared plentiful, while Pigott paced before the street-front window, and Chumley leaned against an elaborately carved Jacobean mantelpiece.

Sir Douglas Babworth was in the far corner of the room, seated on the bench of a French rococo pianoforte, pecking on its keys while Jack Craven stood behind him, whispering in the younger man's ear.

At Seybourne's entrance, the low buzz of conversation evaporated. Heads snapped up, and everyone in the drawing room stared at the viscount. Then, as if on cue, they unanimously greeted him with clubbish salutations and polite inquiries about the health of his new wife, Lady Seybourne.

The viscount strode toward the sideboard and poured himself a glass of brandy, neat. The liquor burned his throat, roughening his voice and heightening his awareness of the prickly atmosphere in the drawing room.

There was more polite conversation while men tightened their small circle, pulling up chairs and rearranging sofas to make Lord Chumley the center of attention. After inquiring whether everyone had the drink they wanted, however, Chumley gave over his place at the mantel to Mr. Jack Craven.

"Queen Caroline's triumphant return to England will be a turning point in the Radical movement, gentlemen and lords," the thin, craggy-faced man began. He and Seybourne were the only men in the room who stood, rather than sat.

Sir Douglas, face shining pink and glowing eagerly, half stood and waved his hand to attract Craven's attention. "When will Her Majesty be arriving?"

"The middle of next week," Craven answered.

Exclamations of surprise erupted.

"Isn't that earlier than expected?" Sir Morton asked.

"Her entourage is eager to cross the Channel while the weather is pleasant," Craven replied. "So the date of the dinner dance has been changed. The gala event will now take place on Friday, a week from tomorrow."

Seybourne nearly choked. "I cannot possibly arrange a dinner party for an entourage as large as Caroline of Brunswick's on such short notice."

"She is *Queen* Caroline," Mr. Higgenbotham corrected.

"Well, whoever the hell she is, you cannot expect me to have Wolfharden ready on a week's notice! Another of you will have to host the party!"

"Impossible, Lord Seybourne," Craven replied coolly. "Your home is on the queen's parade route, so to speak. It is perfectly situated for her to make her way from Dover to Canterbury and then to your family manor house near Wrotham. 'Tis the best possible plan that the party be held at your home."

Seybourne fairly quivered with anger. He was being used for the convenience of his country home. For a fleeting instant, he wondered if Lord Pigott had some foreknowledge of the queen's spectacular return to England when he recruited him into the Kit-Kat Club. But he dismissed that idea when he remembered that it was he, nearly two years ago, who approached Pigott.

He turned to the man who had sponsored his introduction to the Club. "Look, Pigott, you must see how foolish this notion is. Why, the queen will only be offended if she is not entertained in the style to which she is accustomed. What of the guest list? What of the preparations required? I cannot possibly get Wolfharden presentable in one week."

"No need to worry about the guest list," Lord Chumley said. "My secretary has already prepared the list, and my staff has spent the entire day writing out the invitations. The Londoners who are invited will receive their invitations tomorrow. The rest of the cards will be sent via the mail coaches or by private courier."

Pigott stood and began pacing again. As he walked, he looked as if he were washing his hands with invisible soap and water. "Undoubtedly, we are subjecting our visitors to short notice."

Sir Douglas, seemingly unable to contain his excitement, leapt to his feet. "But who would turn down an invitation to meet the queen?"

Seybourne could think of many people who might, beginning with the king on down, but he bit back a caustic retort and took another swig of brandy. He thought of Georgiana and the incredible toll this ambitious party would take on her. And he thought of the dangers of putting her on public display at such a large gathering. It was very likely that Sir Hester's killer would be among the crowd and would seize upon an opportunity to harm the only witness to his crime.

"If you are worried about your new bride," Craven said, as if he could read Seybourne's thoughts, "you needn't be. Lords Chumley and Whitney have generously volunteered to make their entire staffs available to you. Beginning tomorrow, herds of servants will be transported to your home. Those who cannot be fitted into your servants' quarters will be ensconced in various countryside inns. By the time you arrive at Wolfharden yourself, Lawrie, the house will be in perfect order. Silver polished, paintings straightened, carpets aired."

"I will arrange for a marvelous orchestra," chimed in Sir Morton Drysdale. "I hear the queen loves to dance."

There was general agreement around the room that the queen loved to dance, and not a few remarks about her propensity to dance barefooted with vast amounts of dimply white flesh and mud-caked toes exposed.

Seybourne drained his glass. The warmth that oozed through his veins did little to mitigate the anger coursing ahead of it. "All right, I shall leave within three days' time for Wrotham and Wolfharden Manor. If this party is a fiasco, however, don't blame me. I have said my piece. I think this gala event a bad idea. Too risky by half. The queen is not a stable woman, if the reports coming from the Continent are true. We should not exploit someone of diminished mental capacity! For all that we may win a mouthpiece for our policies, in the long run, we will lose out. The people of England will not find Caroline so sympathetic a figure when they get to know her, mark my words!''

The viscount's outburst was met with icy silence. He sensed the stiffening of muscles and the hard scrutiny his fellow Kit-Kat Club members were turning on him. He had to tread carefully here, because to react too violently to the notion of entertaining the queen might make suspect his Whig allegiance. However, some indignation was entirely appropriate; after all, no man in his right mind would welcome that woman's entourage into his home on such short notice. She and her merry band of expatriates, poets, and social outcasts were notorious for moving into guest quarters and practically destroying them.

''I quite appreciate your concern, Lawrie,'' Lord Chumley said. The older man, his patrician features schooled in a handsome expression of concern, rose slowly from a velvet-covered club chair. He crossed his arms, resting his chin on his fist in a pensive pose. ''You make a valid point, to boot. We must not lose sight of our goals, gentlemen. One of the Kit-Kat Club's most pressing concerns is revocation of the Six Acts, particularly the ban on freedom of the press and the law forbidding the congregation of political dissenters. We must not allow the frivolity of Caroline's court to overshadow the seriousness of our endeavors. To that purpose, we must not allow this party to deteriorate into an orgy.''

''An orgy?'' Seybourne pivoted and headed toward the sideboard, where he refilled his glass while the others discussed in subdued tones the importance of maintaining a modicum of decorum at the upcoming Wolfharden *soirée*.

When he returned to the huddle, he stood slightly apart from it, distancing himself in order to study the men. He wondered which among them were impostors, murderers, traitors.

Not a single man appeared edgy; no one behaved guiltily, or drew Seybourne's critical attention. Only Lord Pigott paced the floor and wrung his hands, but he had always had an agitated manner.

''It is settled, then. Eh, Lawrie?'' Chumley slapped him on the back. ''Anything I can do to help, just let me know.''

The rest of the men stood, stretching their legs and preparing to leave. Jack Craven shook Seybourne's hand and promised to arrive at Wolfharden early in the day a week from Friday. "I can help you with any last-minute preparations," he told Lawrie.

Sir Morton laughed and playfully punched Seybourne's upper arm. "Preparations? With all the servants Chumley and Whitney are sending you, old man, you and your wife won't have to lift a finger."

Craven and Babworth were discussing the possibility of returning to Brooks's for another try at faro as they exited the drawing room. Lord Pigott merely cast Seybourne a rueful glance and said, "Good night," before slipping out behind them. That left Seybourne alone with Sir Morton Drysdale and Lord Hughes Chumley.

"Have you any reservations, Lawrie?" Chumley said, rolling a glass of brandy in his palms.

"About the party, you mean? A hundred." Seybourne sighed heavily. "I resent being called upon to host this ill-fated event. God knows Caroline will not be happy till she has torn my house down and frightened my cattle."

Chumley smiled crookedly and met Seybourne's gaze with a sparkling, inquisitive stare of his own. "Is it the ill timing of the party you object to? Or is it the fact that we intend to use the queen to espouse our political beliefs?"

Setting his glass on the nearest table, Seybourne responded carefully. "Our objectives are too important to this country to be jeopardized by a risky collusion with a woman whose mental stability is tenuous, at best. Claiming Caroline as a Whig sympathizer has many appealing virtues. But suppose the common man loses his infatuation for her? Supposing she falls out of favor with the public? What then? She might, in the long run, do our cause more harm than good."

"You have a valid point," Chumley said. "That is why it is so important to control and restrain the flighty queen."

"Control and restrain her? What the devil are you talking about? If the king couldn't curb her insouciant mannerisms, how do you expect a nine-member debating society to do so?"

Sir Morton gulped noisily, then set his glass on the table next to Seybourne's. "Eight."

"Excuse me?" Seybourne stared quizzically at the pudgy young man who of all the members of the Kit-Kat Club had become his favorite.

"There are now eight members of the Kit-Kat Club," he said. "Don't forget, Sir Hester is dead."

How could he forget? A strange silence befell the three men, and then the sound of the front door slamming dispelled the uncomfortable moment. Seybourne turned abruptly and shook Chumley's hand. "Thanks for your hospitality," he told him, suddenly eager to leave. "No need to see us to the door. I will see you next at Wolfharden."

"Right. You've nothing to worry about, Lawrie. All the arrangements for the party will be tended to, and it will be a spectacular event that you will not forget soon. You'll see."

"Want to go to Brooks's for a bit of cards and a beefsteak?" Sir Morton asked as they descended the stairs.

"Have you forgotten?" Seybourne replied. "Georgiana has accepted your invitation to Astley's this afternoon."

"What great fun! Madge will be delighted." The young man's exuberance was a welcome relief to the serious mood of the meeting from which they'd just emerged.

At the bottom landing, servants handed them cloaks and hats. Outside, Seybourne and Sir Morton swung themselves on their horses.

"We will come round to Madge's house at a quarter past five and collect the two of you," Seybourne said. "Sound all right?"

The younger man smiled and tapped the brim of his hat. As he nudged his horse into a gentle trot, he called out, "See you tonight, then!"

Wondering why a strange feeling of unease was coiling around the base of his spine, Seybourne smiled back and waved. Then he turned his horse south and headed toward home. He wanted to be there when Georgiana returned from her shopping trip. He wanted to be there to see her face light up with pleasure and her lips part in that slow, knowing smile of hers. Most of all, he wanted to be there to draw her into his arms and hold her tight against his body.

She might not be his wife for much longer. When his investigation was complete, or when her memory returned, whichever came first, she'd most likely vanish from his life. But, while she was his, he could pretend that she was never going away. *There wasn't any harm in dreaming, was there?*

Chapter Nine

Astley's was packed. Georgiana sat between Lord Seybourne and Madge, a pretty freckle-faced girl who from all appearances had set her cap for Sir Morton Drysdale. Though the couples had some of the best seats in the house, in boxes on the second level just above the rowdy groundlings, they were crammed so tightly together in their rickety chairs that their shoulders and legs touched.

Georgiana found herself in closer physical proximity to her husband and Madge than she had ever been to two human beings. Her old instinct would have been to bolt from the chair and flee for fresh air and space. But her increasing control over her feline reflexes kept her pinned to her seat—that and the oddly pleasurable feel of the viscount's long, lean leg flush against her own.

Hundreds of candles cast a warm, glittering light over the theater's interior, bathing the stage and the circular arena below in an otherworldly glow. Gobs of wax dripped from huge chandeliers, bombarding the heads of elegantly coifed ladies, occasionally interrupting the orchestra's performance by landing in the conductor's eyes or between the strings of a violin or cello.

Young boys carrying trays of boiled peanuts, or waving

souvenir pennants for sale, circulated among the groundlings, shouting their prices over the roar of the crowd. Sometimes, the vendor made a sale to someone in an upper box. Then small pouches filled with peanuts flew through the air, and pennies rained down in exchange.

Georgiana reveled in the gaiety of it all. She couldn't help but be entranced by the spectacle unfolding in the ring below.

A man wearing white tights and a crimson cutaway jacket stood at the center of the dirt-packed ring. Addressing the crowd in a booming voice, he announced each act with all the pomp and puffery of a mountebank touting snake-oil elixirs at a carnival. Each time a new animal was released into the ring, the crowd cheered, whistled, and hooted. When a huge black stallion roared from the tented stables into the arena, the audience went wild.

The horse, wearing only a red blanket on its back, galloped round the ring with snorting nostrils, and ears laid flat against its head. The man in white tights slapped his leather whip on the ground and yelled, "Ladies and gentlemen, my name is Grisaldi. And this is Iago the Trained Stallion!"

As if the horse could understand English, it tossed its head, reared up on its hind legs, and let out an enormously loud whinny. The animal's eyes flashed yellow and rolled back in its head. It eyed the crowd with hostility and deep distrust. And sure enough, just as it lowered its front feet to the ground, the diminutive Grisaldi sauntered to ringside and retrieved a small monkey from another white-and-red-clad handler.

Madge inhaled sharply, her mouth rounding in an exclamation of wonder as the horse resumed its mad race around the paddock-shaped arena. "Oh, what a frightening creature!"

Its hooves pounded the earth so ferociously that waves of thunder vibrated right up through the row of spectators and rattled Georgiana's bones.

"Iago is upset," Georgiana said, eyeing the animal. Her pulse quickened as she watched the horse gallop in circles, its mane flying, its tightly braided tail held straight out behind.

Lord Seybourne leaned closer to her, his body nudging hers, his leathery masculine scent subdued by the strong, earthy animal odors that thickened the air. "Dear, 'tis only a circus animal. What causes you to say the horse is upset?"

"Oh, Lawrie, she is only joking," Madge said. "Everyone knows that animals, horses especially, don't have feelings! Iago isn't upset. He just needs a bit of the whip, that's all."

Georgiana shuddered, her gaze fixed on the horse. "Look at his ears, the set of his tail. Something has happened to upset the poor animal. Grisaldi would be wise to call off this silly performance. He will only injure Iago if he permits the animal to perform tonight."

Madge elbowed her. "You are too serious, Lady Seybourne. Iago isn't a human being. He's just an animal! It isn't as if the stupid creature has feelings or emotions."

"How do you know?" Georgiana instantly regretted that she'd used such a sharp tone with Madge. Reminding herself that Madge was, after all, just a stupid creature, she gently squeezed the other woman's arm and said, "Oh, I'm sorry, Madge. I don't know what came over me. It's just that I hate to see any animal suffer." Then, she returned her gaze to Iago and Grisaldi.

Sir Morton leaned across Madge and said, "What are you two ladies gabbling about?"

"Nothing to concern you," Lord Seybourne replied. In a quieter voice, he said to Georgiana, "You are getting yourself overset about this, minx. Are you sure you are all right?"

She quickly threw him a half smile. His look of tender concern moved her, but her attention was riveted to the sight below.

Iago had picked up speed as Grisaldi strutted toward the center of the ring. The monkey, dressed in a colorful costume with frills at the neck, clung to the man's shoulders as if he sensed the horse's agitation. Disaster brewed in the ring; of that, Georgiana was sure. Iago gave off waves of anger while the monkey radiated fear.

The viscount pressed himself closer to her side. "Georgiana, you look positively frightened out of your mind. Please, dear, tell me what I can do to help—"

Georgiana shook her head. Her chest squeezed painfully as

she watched Grisaldi lash at Iago's flanks with his tasseled whip.

She gripped Seybourne's arm, digging her fingernails into the sleeve of his black superfine coat. His arm slid around her back, and he tried to draw her closer to him, but she was too overwrought to snuggle into his embrace. Her mind was numb with outrage.

"How can that man be so stupid, Lawrence? You must stop this cruelty! Stop it, Lawrie, please!"

"Stop the performance?"

Was she serious? Did she really want him to call a halt to the nightly performance at Astley's?

The viscount couldn't believe his ears. He stared in wonder at his wife's profile. Her eyes were wide, her lips parted, her entire body stiff as a poker. If he hadn't known better, he would have thought her silky black hair, piled loosely on top of her head with tendrils framing her heart-shaped face, was thicker and bristlier than it had been a moment before.

But that was impossible. There had to be some logical explanation for Georgiana's odd behavior.

"Darling, listen to me," he implored her. He was surprised to find that her discomfort actually pained him. "There is nothing to fear. The animals will not be harmed, I promise you. I have seen this performance before."

"Heavens, it isn't a bearbaiting!" Madge chimed.

Georgiana's green eyes snapped like Grisaldi's leather whip. Her nails dug so deeply into Seybourne's arm that he winced. "Lawrence, stop this," she said. "Iago is . . . he is hurt! 'Tis cruel to subject him to this abuse!"

"Hurt?" Seybourne looked at the animal thundering around the ring. Perhaps Georgiana didn't understand what Grisaldi intended with the monkey. Wishing to allay her apprehension, he patted her hand and said, "The monkey is merely going to mount Iago's back and ride around the ring. It's a well-rehearsed act, I assure you. No danger will come to the horse or the monkey."

Although the same could not with certainty be said of Grisaldi. The man in white tights struggled to uncoil the nervous monkey from his neck. With each pass Iago made around the ring, the monkey seemed more determined to wrap himself around Grisaldi's head.

"I am convinced Iago is in pain," Georgiana said.

The viscount, struck by her insistence, wondered if she possessed some preternatural ability to communicate with the beast. Bewildered, he covered her hand and pried her nails from his arm. "Georgiana, calm yourself."

Her head whipped around. Her voice was a low hiss. "I cannot calm myself! I will not!"

"What is the matter?" Sir Morton asked, leaning over.

"She thinks the horse is hurtin'!" Madge replied, shrugging and theatrically rolling her eyes.

Georgiana pressed her eyes tightly shut for a moment. The crowd was growing restless, its catcalls getting louder and more caustic. Iago literally raced around the ring, refusing to slow long enough for Grisaldi to untangle the monkey and toss it on the horse's back.

The monkey shrieked and yelled, clinging like ivy to Grisaldi's head. The animals simply refused to perform their act. And the crowd knew Grisaldi had lost control.

Someone in an upper box tossed a ripe tomato into the ring. The fruit landed just in front of Iago, splattering pulp and red meat all over his hooves and heaving chest.

Iago, skidding to a halt, pawed the ground. His teeth flashed, and white foam dripped from his chin as he snorted and tossed his head wildly.

"Good God, I think she's right, Lawrie," Sir Morton said. "Something is wrong with that animal."

"I ain't seen no one hurt the beast," Madge said.

"There's no visible wound or injury," Lord Seybourne agreed, perplexed. "But it is obvious the horse has no intentions of letting that monkey ride on its back."

Georgiana's eyes flew open. "That's it! It must be his back. Iago doesn't want the monkey to mount him."

"A monkey can't hurt a horse!" Sir Morton cried.

For a long moment, Lord Seybourne stared at Georgiana. He had admitted to himself that he wasn't looking forward to the day she was no longer his wife. He had admitted to himself that she was different from any woman he'd ever met. He had even admitted to himself that he loved her.

But could he admit that she might be right about Iago?

Did he love her enough to make a fool of himself in front of a crowd of rowdy London theatergoers?

Without a second thought, he leapt to his feet. Scrambling over the knees of Georgiana, Madge, and Sir Morton, he made it to the narrow aisle separating the rows of crowded chairs, then ran toward the edge of the box. Leaning over it, he cupped his hands around his mouth. "Stop the performance!" he yelled at the top of his lungs.

At first, his voice was lost amid the jeering and yelling of the crowd. But he continued to scream and wave his arms at Grisaldi.

The man with the monkey around his neck suddenly caught sight of Lord Seybourne. He stared up, straining to hear.

Seybourne leaned farther over the side of the box. "Stop the performance! Iago is injured!"

Grisaldi screwed his face into a knot of confusion. Then, the little man's mouth fell open and his eyes rounded. He clutched at the squirming monkey, dropping his whip as he did so.

Seybourne turned and looked at Georgiana. Her eyes were gleaming with tears. She mouthed the words, "Iago's back!"

Facing the arena again, Seybourne shouted down "Look at the horse's back!"

Comprehension dawned on Grisaldi. At last, he rushed to the side of the ring and handed the monkey to a waiting animal trainer. Then, he turned and walked slowly toward the prancing Iago.

The horse's muscled flesh gleamed from his exertion. The louder the crowd roared, the louder the beast snorted. Rearing up on his hind legs, Iago clawed the air. Then his hooves hit the ground with a dull crash, and he trampled the packed earth like a bull preparing to charge.

Grisaldi approached slowly, his lips moving steadily, his hands held out before him patting the air. Seybourne watched in amazement as the horse calmed. Grisaldi ran his hands along the animal's neck and withers, placating him. The crowd fell strangely silent, watching with bated breath this unusual spectacle. When Grisaldi gently lifted the animal's red satin blanket, the slightest whisper could have been heard.

The hair on Seybourne's neck prickled. He gripped the edge of the balcony with white knuckles and felt the blood coursing through his veins.

Grisaldi whipped off the blanket, exposing an ugly gash down the center of Iago's back. Seybourne exhaled, his stomach clenching at the sight of the animal's wound. So Georgiana had been right all along. The horse was in terrible pain. Anticipating the monkey's climbing on his back, Iago must have been frightened out of his wits and angered that he should be subjected to such torture.

Grisaldi's face contorted with emotion. He wrapped his arms around the animal's neck and pressed his face into the horse's thick mane. Finally, he led Iago from the ring amid an enormous roar of approval from the crowd.

Seybourne returned to his seat, picked up Georgiana's hand and pressed it to his cheek. "How did you know that the horse was hurt, minx?"

"God! I have never seen anything like it!" cried Sir Morton.

"Passing odd, that's what it is," Madge said. " 'Twas as she could read the horse's mind."

Georgiana's face was pale, but when she smiled, the color slowly returned to her cheeks. "Just a woman's intuition," she said.

Pinned beneath the warmth of her gaze, Lord Seybourne wondered how much of his own thoughts she could detect. It troubled him to think he was as transparent as Iago in her eyes.

And then—as if to confirm his gravest suspicions—she turned her hand over and pressed her cool palm to his cheek. Her touch seared him with desire and longing, yet his emotions terrified him.

He was a loner, a man who had carved out a solitary life for himself, an existence unencumbered by love and emotion. His dispassion had served him well. Honor and loyalty were the manly traits he had cultivated; infatuation, love . . . he eschewed such schoolboy emotions. And considering his past, it was a good thing he could douse his emotions as easily as one snuffed a candle. Otherwise, he might never have survived as an exile. Indeed, he might never have had the nerve and fortitude to accept his brother's punishment as his own.

But Georgiana threatened to pierce his protective shield of aloofness. Which made his betrayal of her all the more painful. For whoever she was—and whatever her past might eventually reveal itself to be—he was unworthy of her affections. She knew nothing about him, and he prayed she would never know how black his heart truly was, how lonely he had been, or how deeply he had betrayed her.

But when she leaned over and gently kissed him on the cheek, his world tilted at a crazy angle, dislodging his logic, knocking him completely off balance. She drew back and looked at him, a slight curve to her luscious lips, a twinkle in her eyes. He loved her. God help him, but he loved the mysterious minx whose life he was dangling as bait to a ruthless killer.

An hour later, the two couples convened in Seybourne's drawing room to discuss the bizarre events of the evening.

Sir Morton, perched on the edge of a velvet love seat beside Madge, lifted his brandy snifter in the air in a mock salute to Georgiana. "Here's to our clairvoyant friend. Lord, what a show!"

Madge broke in. "All of London will be talking about tonight's performance at Astley's! Pity they will think that it was Lord Seybourne who stopped the performance, though."

"That is just as well as far as I am concerned," Georgiana said. She was settled comfortably in an oversized wingback chair, her feet pulled up beneath her, slippers strewn on the floor. "I prefer to avoid the limelight whenever possible."

At the mantelpiece Lord Seybourne stood sipping his brandy. "I am eager to hear what caused the horse's injury. I do hope the papers will report that part of the story, should they choose to report such a trivial occurrence at all."

"With Queen Caroline making her way across the Continent," Sir Morton said, "I'm not so sure an aborted animal performance at Astley's is likely to make the news."

"Let us hope you are right," Georgiana said, stifling a yawn.

Sir Morton and Madge exchanged a quick, knowing glance, then leapt to their feet.

"It is getting late," Sir Morton said, "Would you mind if your driver took us home, Lawrence?"

"We really should be going." Madge leaned down and gave Georgiana a peck on the cheek. "Enjoyed the evening, love!"

Sir Morton shook Lord Seybourne's hand, then turned and bowed low over Georgiana's. "I look forward to seeing you at Wolfharden next week, my lady. It is sure to be the occasion of the season!"

All smiles and giggles, Madge took her companion's arm. "Have you decided what you are going to wear yet, m'lady? I've changed my mind a thousand times! But I suppose you've got something grand to show off in. Oh, it will simply be the best ball ever! I do look forward to seeing you there."

The two young people left the room before Georgiana could respond to this amazing bit of intelligence. As the door shut behind them, she turned to Lord Seybourne. "A party? At Wolfharden? What on earth are those two talking about?"

His features tightened as he took another swig of brandy. Thus fortified, he moved to an armchair opposite Georgiana's and leaned forward, elbow on knees.

As always, her gaze was drawn to his long, lean, boot-encased legs. She had noticed that most men of the *ton* wore trousers, but Seybourne continued to wear the snug breeches of a decade earlier. She was glad he did; they showed the hard, sinewy outlines of his muscles and gave him a pantherlike, masculine look. Her pulse quickened a bit as she stared at his sleek thighs and rock-hard haunches. Rattled by her inability to ignore the man's sexual appeal, she took a quick sip of brandy and tuned her attention to her husband's voice.

"I must host—" he began, then started over. "I mean to say, I have the pleasure and the honor of hosting a dinner and dance for Caroline of Brunswick, the queen of England."

"Oh." Georgiana's knowledge of politics and world affairs

was gleaned from her casual eavesdropping on Sir Hester's conversations. She knew, however, that hosting a ball for the queen of England was bound to be rife with pitfalls for a new bride whose knowledge of etiquette and court protocol was limited. "Must I attend, my lord?"

His head jerked up and his eyes fastened on hers. "Yes, of course. You are my wife."

"Perhaps you could say I am ill. Not feeling well. Recuperating from that nasty fall I took on the day of our wedding."

"You have been seen in public since then," he reminded her. "No, Georgiana, it is imperative that you attend this ball."

She gulped convulsively, unable to clear the lump in her throat. "And where, might I ask, is Wolfharden?" The place sounded positively terrifying to her. Was it truly full of wolves?

" 'Tis the name of my family country manor in Kent near Wrotham. Less than a day's drive from here, if we get an early start. We shall leave next Tuesday, and that will give us a few days at Wolfharden before our guests arrive."

Georgiana shuddered as an ominous chill rippled across her shoulders.

Seybourne moved quickly, closing the space between them, half kneeling beside her chair. "Are you all right?" He clasped her hands in his, then rubbed her forearms to bring warmth back to her gooseflesh.

But the feel of his hands on her body merely doubled her discomfort. Terrified of the notion of being hostess to a party in honor of the queen of England at a place called Wolfharden, Georgiana had the insane urge to throw herself in Seybourne's arms. There was something comforting about his presence, his touch, his heat-filled gaze.

"I cannot hostess such a party!" she blurted. "I will be a total failure, Lawrie. I will be an embarrassment to you!"

His expression changed. His pale-blue eyes narrowed, and the skin across his cheekbones pulled taut. Georgiana thought an explosion of emotion was imminent, but then he tightened his lips and looked away. She thought she saw a glimmer of wetness in his stare, but he dropped his shaggy head in her lap before she could be sure.

And her hands went instinctively to his head, her fingers threading themselves through thick dark hair shot through with silver. The texture of it delighted her. She edged forward and drew him closer to her, so that her breasts cradled his head, and his cheek was pressed to her thighs. For a moment, the two held one another while the air in the room charged with tension. A need—raw and urgent—welled up in Georgiana.

She hardly knew she'd spoken the words till they tumbled from her lips. "Oh, Lawrie, I need you!"

What was she saying? Her heart beat mercilessly against her ribs. She wished she could recapture her words, but she couldn't. And she didn't know what to make of Seybourne's response to them.

He turned his face into her lap and wrapped his arms around her waist. She felt the wetness of his tears through the thin muslin of her dress, but the only sound she heard was her own labored breathing. Lawrie held her so tightly that she was powerless to escape. And she didn't want to. She wanted to hold him like that forever. Their physical joining seemed the only salve for her pain, and his, too, whatever had caused it.

At last, she cupped his jaws and lifted his head. Staring into his watery blue eyes, she watched with stark fascination as his expression changed again, going stone cold in the blink of an eye.

Clearly, he didn't want to share his emotions. His heart was as scarred as hers. They were both loners, two people who depended only on themselves. But now they faced a situation in which they needed one another. And that newfound hunger was terrifying. It drew them together . . . and it kept them apart.

Her voice was strained. "You are in pain, Lawrie. I will ask you what you asked me earlier this evening. *What can I do to help you?*"

He closed his eyes for a second, a cord of muscle rippling beneath his jaw. "There is nothing you can do, minx," he whispered. "Come, it is late. I must get you into bed."

His throaty voice—his mention of bed—stirred something deep inside her. An insatiable longing blossomed in the pit of her stomach. Acting purely on instinct—a new feminine instinct which seemed to have sprung up from nowhere—she lowered her head and kissed his mouth. "Yes, Lawrie. Take me to bed. Please," she whispered against his lips.

He gathered her in his arms, never taking his gaze off her. Lifting her as easily as if she were made of feathers, he carried her up the stairs and to her bedchamber, where he kicked shut the door behind him and laid her gently on the bed.

While she watched, he shrugged off his coat and ripped his shirt from the waist of his skintight breeches. The sight of his bare skin, the hard muscular planes of his shoulders, chest and belly, robbed her of breath. When at last he climbed onto the bed, her arms went around his neck, and her body pressed itself to his in an ancient ritual that seemed as natural to Georgiana as breathing.

She loved him that night with all her heart and soul and body. She knew, then, that she would never let him go, never let him leave her. For the first time in her life, Georgiana was willing to admit she needed someone. Lawrence deWulff, Viscount Seybourne was necessary for her survival. It was a terrifying realization, but one quite insignificant compared to the intense pleasure Seybourne gave her that night.

Afterward, she slept lightly for the first time in her life. In the middle of the night, her husband's nightmare awakened her.

"Guilty! Guilty! Guilty!" he cried out in his sleep. Then he muttered an unintelligible string of words Georgiana couldn't understand. Something about a person named Francis. Something about a boat trip to Australia. What in the world was he talking about, she wondered, stroking his shaggy head. Her touch calmed him, and, eventually, he fell silent again, although his breathing was harsh and raspy for many more minutes. Georgiana told herself she'd have to ask him the meaning of his nighttime talk, but for the time being, she was simply glad that his unpleasant dream had dissipated.

Slowly, her eyes adjusted to the subtle glow of moonlight bathing the room. Lawrie's head was nestled on her shoulder, his leg was thrown over hers, his warm body wedged beside her.

Rubbing a hand along her jawline, Georgiana tested the rawness of her skin. Her husband's bristly beard had nearly rubbed her raw in some extremely delicate places. Smiling, she held him tighter to her bosom, her chest rising and falling in deep contentment. She loved his smell; she loved his rough beard; she loved the way he touched and kissed her. She loved *needing him.* And she loved the fact that he needed her, too.

Drifting back to sleep, her acute senses dulled by the excesses of lovemaking, she failed to detect the tread of stealthy footsteps stealing down the carpeted corridor outside her bedchamber door.

Chapter Ten

Exhausted from the efforts of his lovemaking, Lord Sey-bourne snuggled up beside Georgiana, his head resting peacefully on her shoulder. He intended to doze a few more minutes. He knew from his previous experiences with mistresses and lovers, including Lady Spraddlin, that females valued their nocturnal privacy, even after a heady bout of bed play. Seybourne's own parents had never shared a bedroom; most aristocratic couples didn't.

So, he told himself, he would close his eyes only for a moment. Then, he would return to his own bed. Knowing Georgiana, she would want to sleep later than he the next morning, and she would be grateful that he didn't interrupt her rest with his constant jerking and flinching and talking in his sleep.

It was a curse he hadn't been able to shake in the five years following his conviction for smuggling and murder. He thought when he returned from Australia, his bad dreams might disappear. But they had not. His twin brother's face on the day the charges were made public was as vivid to him as ever.

And the nightmarish journey in the bowels of a prisoner

ship—rowing for days on end while shackled to a bench—was still as real and painful as if it had happened yesterday.

The scars he bore from his ordeal, and from the stigma of his conviction and exile, still chafed beneath his skin. Even in Georgiana's arms, he could not forget who he was, *who the world thought he was*. Five years had not erased the pain of being torn from his home, country, and family.

In his deep subconscious, Lord Seybourne was aware of Georgiana's heart thudding beneath his ear, her fingers gently stroking his hair. Inhaling, he breathed in the exotic scent of her—musky and sweet, with a hint of cinnamon. Like the spiced tea she loved so much. With his arm thrown across her waist, he nestled closer to her, his leg moving up and down her thighs, his skin burning with the sensation of her flesh beneath his.

Just before daybreak, his arousal woke him up. His hand slid up Georgiana's body, caressing her shoulder. Just as he rose to one elbow and gazed down at her sleeping expression, he heard the telling creak of a floorboard outside her door.

He froze, his senses triggered. Listening intently, he scanned the shadows. But he heard only the doleful voice of the night crier. Inside the house, a tense silence dominated.

Slowly, quietly, Seybourne extricated himself from the tangle of Georgiana's limbs and slipped from beneath the counterpane. Faint moonlight filtered through the window, washing the room in sinister shadows, dimly illuminating swatches of furniture, carpet, floral wallpaper. Seybourne could see in the semidarkness, but not clearly.

Without a sound, he slid from the bed and padded across the carpet to the pile of clothes he'd left on the floor. Silently cursing, he recalled leaving his pistol tucked beneath the mattress of his own bed. He had not carried the weapon to Astley's and had not retrieved it when he and Georgiana returned home.

In the corner of the room, a painted screen shielded an enameled tole bathtub from view. Hearing a scrabble at the door, Seybourne moved quickly behind the screen, peering through the cracks in its hinged panels. The doorknob turned. With agonizing suspense, it cracked open. For a moment, the heavy oaken door stood ajar ever so slightly, as if the intruder were debating whether to enter.

Seybourne held his breath. Every nerve in his body tingled; every muscle drew as tight as a bow. The silhouette of a man's figure, clad entirely in black, moved across the threshold like a wraith. Beneath a black hat, a black mask concealed the intruder's features. Pausing in the center of the room, he looked around. Then, with a pistol glinting in his gloved hand, he crept closer to Georgiana's bed.

Violent anger exploded inside Seybourne's belly. Stampeding from his hiding place, he let loose a gut-wrenching roar. The flimsy screen collapsed beneath him, crashing to the floor in a bent and broken heap. The intruder's head whipped round, and the point of his gun swung toward Seybourne.

A deafening crack split the air. Without pausing, Seybourne rushed headlong toward the intruder. Unconcerned for his own safety, he was determined to protect Georgiana from harm. He launched himself at the black-clad figure.

Georgiana awakened with a bloodcurdling shriek, just as the intruder got off a second shot.

The bullet's impact tore through Seybourne's shoulder like a scorching arrow. Stumbling backward, his arms windmilled crazily. Through sheer strength of will, he stayed upright, but his setback gave the intruder time to turn and flee the room. A black cape swirled behind the villain as he escaped.

"Lawrence! Oh, God! You are shot!" Georgiana flew to his side, the whites of her eyes flashing in the semidarkness.

He pushed her aside. "Only a flesh wound," he managed to say, lurching toward the door. But pain tugged at him like a muddy quagmire, and he barely made it to the threshold before he collapsed.

Instantly, the house came to life. Doors crashed open, and herds of footsteps pounded the carpeted hallways. A brace of servants appeared with lit tapers and sleepy eyes round with surprise.

Shocked murmurs among the servants reminded Seybourne that he was stark naked.

"Minx, be a dear and throw me a robe, will you?" he said, before everything went black.

No, you cannot die on me! Georgiana's worst fears rushed back to her in a split second. Every time she allowed herself to care about someone—every time she let down her defenses and allowed herself to depend on someone—*he died*. Sir Hester's death had shattered her world, but she had sprung back, resilient and feisty as ever. Lawrie's death would break her heart into a million pieces.

Servants pounded the door, demanding to be let in.

Terrified, Georgiana threw some covers over her husband's naked body. Amid the tangled bedclothes, she found her muslin wrap. Thrusting her arms into the sleeves, she quivered like aspic, and her teeth chattered uncontrollably.

She opened the door to a noisy jumble of servants. Two footmen, both dressed in flannel nightgowns and nightcaps, lifted the viscount off the floor and laid him carefully in the bed. One of the maids scampered off to fetch a basin of water, towels, and a flask of whiskey. Someone dispatched a courier to the surgeon's residence with strict instructions to bring him at once.

"Lucky bastard!" one of the servants cried. "The bullet missed m'lord's vital organs. He's losin' a right good amount of blood, but if the barber comes soon, he'll be awright!"

Relief mingled with fear and anger as Georgiana watched the chaotic scene in her bedchamber. She felt as if she were watching from a great distance. Her nose twitched at the odor of blood, and her muscles tensed in preparation for flight.

Arms encircled her shoulders, startling her. "He will be fine, my dear. Just stand here, out of the way for a moment, and tell me what happened." Aunt Inez's warm, ample body, clad in yards of white muslin, exuded strength and comfort.

It took a moment for Georgiana to find her voice. Then, sobs quaked her body, robbing her of speech.

Aunt Inez held her tightly against her cushiony bosom, while servants cleaned Seybourne's wound, wrapped strips of white cotton around his shoulder, and waved hartshorn beneath his nostrils.

"Oh, Aunt!" Georgiana's voice was muffled against Inez's tearstained shoulder. "Someone was in the room! It was not a dream this time. Lawrie attacked him and was shot. The man got away!" She buried her head against the older woman's shoulder and wept copiously.

"Poor Lawrie." Inez extracted a handkerchief from her cleavage and clasped it over Georgiana's nose. "Blow, child. La! But that boy attracts trouble like honey attracts bees!"

Georgiana took the kerchief and lifted her head. Between sniffles, she said, "I know I've been nothing but trouble to Lord Seybourne. From the day he saw me. He only married me to avoid scandal, I know that. As soon as the talk of our marriage has died down, I will quietly disappear, I promise."

Aunt Inez held her at arm's length and gave her a little shake. In a low voice not meant for the servants' ears, she said, "That was not the trouble I was referring to, child. But given that you have consummated your marriage, I should think twice about bolting from this house and abandoning your husband."

Georgiana drew her sleeve across her damp nose and hic-coughed as Inez's admonition sank into her brain. Her dishabille was proof that she had slept with Lord Seybourne. Now, there would be little chance of obtaining an annulment of her marriage. She felt as if someone had slipped a collar around her neck and tightened it another painful notch.

"Aunt Inez, what did you mean when you said Lawrence attracts trouble?"

"Well, I suppose I really shouldn't let the cat out of the bag—"

"I am afraid she is already out."

"Whatever do you mean by that? Are you referring to Lady Spraddlin?"

Georgiana shook her head. "Just a slip of the tongue. Tell me, Aunt Inez, what sort of trouble is my husband in?"

Inez drew her to a *chaise longue* strewn with the debris of the splintered screen. Brushing off the velvet cushion, she lowered her body and pulled Georgiana down beside her. Side by side, they sat, well out of the servants' earshot, but certainly within view of the goings-on surrounding the supine viscount.

"It is not my place to tell you—"

"He is my husband and I deserve to know," Georgiana argued.

"Quite so." After a brief hesitation, the older woman clasped Georgiana's hand and stared her straight in the eyes. "If I do not tell you, someone else will, perhaps even that meddling Mercy Mary. Whom I once liked very much, mind you, but now—"

"Aunt, I am not concerned with Lady Spraddlin!"

Inez averted her eyes, faltered a moment, then continued. "Very well, then. Seven years ago, your husband was convicted of smuggling French contraband—wine and brandy mostly—into this country. Napoleon was still raging around the Continent threatening to capture us all, then. 'Twas a very serious offense."

"A smuggler!" Georgiana stared at Lord Seybourne as if she'd never seen him before.

"That is only the half of it, dear. When the arrest was made, a scuffle took place. In the melee, a Bow Street Runner was shot and killed. So Lawrie was convicted of murder, too."

Shocked, Georgiana sat in stony silence. Could it be true? Could the man she married and made love to be a murderer and a smuggler? Had she at last overcome her fear of abandonment, only to fall in love with a ruthless killer?

Inez patted her hands. "Now, now, child, that is not the end of the story. Five years after Lawrie was transported to Australia, the king—he was prince regent, then, of course—intervened. He demanded that the King's Bench review the evidence, and when it was discovered an eyewitness existed who placed Lawrie at a St. James gaming-hell the moment of the murder, a pardon was granted. No one really knows why the king took an interest in Lawrie. Fat old thing really does have a soft heart, I s'pose. Anyway, Lawrie was recalled from Australia."

"Australia?" Georgiana pictured kangaroos and wilderness.

"He has been in London some two years now, slowly trying to rebuild his reputation. But, he still doesn't like to talk about his conviction, or anything that happened afterward. Including his twin brother's death. *Especially that.*''

"He had a brother? Tell me everything!"

"Francis died just months after Lawrie was convicted. Shot in the back, I'm afraid. It was a most unseemly affair." Aunt Inez pressed her fingers to her lips for a moment and shut her eyes tightly. Her features pinched together as if she were struggling to contain her emotions. Then, she opened her eyes and sighed.

"Go on," Georgiana urged her.

"It does no good to relive the pain of the past. Lawrie was not here when his brother died. Which was tragic. They were close, mind you. As all twins are."

"Did they resemble one another?"

"They were identical. That is Francis's portrait in your husband's study, child. Oh! Did you think it was Lawrie's?"

A thousand tons of ballast dropped in Georgiana's stomach. No wonder the viscount had glared at her so angrily when she commented on the portrait. But why had he not explained to her that he had a twin brother who died?

"I do not know what to say." Georgiana disengaged her hands from Inez's and dropped her head into her cupped palms. Frightened, exhausted, and confused, her mind simply refused to assimilate the information Inez had imparted to her. How could this man—so gentle hearted that he would risk public humiliation to save the hide of an animal—be a murderer?

Inez stroked the top of Georgiana's head. "Now you know, child. You must make the decision for yourself. Will you forgive him, or will you flee him?"

From across the room, Lord Seybourne moaned.

Georgiana's head snapped up and she leapt from the *chaise longue.* She crossed the room in a flash and wedged herself between the servants, bending over Seybourne as his eyes flickered open. A bandage, wrapped tightly around his underarm and shoulder, was soaked through with blood. Seybourne's face was nearly ashen, but his pale-blue eyes gleamed.

She kissed his lips, moistening his face with her tears. "Oh, Lawrie! Thank God you are going to be all right!"

Lifting one hand, he rubbed the pad of his thumb along her jaw. When he spoke, his voice was hoarse and cracking. "Had you been injured, Georgiana, I would never have forgiven myself."

And then his eyes fell shut again.

A surgeon appeared and, after a brief examination, pronounced Lawrie weak from fever caused by the bullet in his body. Whiskey was poured on his torn flesh and down his throat, but he was painfully sensible when the doctor cut the bullet from his shoulder.

Georgiana sat beside her husband throughout the ordeal, holding his hand and wiping the sweat from his brow as the doctor probed inside him with metal forceps. Her stomach flip-flopped when the doctor extracted a flattened bloody slug, and held it to the early-morning light. She'd never been queasy at the sight of blood before, but knowing how close Lawrence had come to dying, she couldn't help but feel sick.

Throughout the surgery, Lawrie never uttered a word. Sweat dripped from his body and, with the blood flowing from his wound, soaked the mattress through. When his wound was sewn up, he fell into a deep, fitful sleep.

The surgeon rolled down his sleeves and shoved off from the edge of the bed. Releasing her husband's hand, Georgiana accompanied the doctor to the door. They tiptoed, careful not to disturb Aunt Inez, who was sprawled on the *chaise longue,* snoring.

"He is out of the woods, now," the doctor said, pausing in the threshold. "If his fever does not break by tomorrow morning, I will bleed him with leeches to suck out the poison. At any rate, he is a strong man and he has survived worse, I suspect. Those prison ships kill more men than bullets, I can promise you that."

Pushing the door closed behind the doctor, Georgiana stood for a moment, her head resting on the cool oaken panels, her body weak with exhaustion. Never had she gone so long without sleep. Her limbs were wobbly with fatigue. But her mind gave her no rest. Georgiana's experiences on the waterfront had familiarized her with prison and slave ships. The idea of Lawrie, shackled to a bench in the galley of one of those floating hells, filled her with rage.

Crying silently, she wished she had never met Lawrence deWulff, Viscount Seybourne. If she hadn't, she'd never have known how happy she could be. If she never knew that, she wouldn't feel such despair now.

Why did everyone keep waking him to ask whether he was resting comfortably?

"Are you all right, boy?" Aunt Inez's voice accompanied an irritating plumping of pillows beneath his head.

Lord Seybourne opened his eyes and shifted his position, immediately regretting the movement. Wincing, he sucked air in through his teeth as shards of hot pain jabbed his left shoulder. His right hand flew protectively to the bandages that wrapped his bare chest. He attempted a smile, but judging from his aunt's wobbling chin, all that he accomplished was a wolfish snarl.

"Good morning, Aunt Inez," he said. "Where's Georgiana?"

His wife crossed the room in a faint rustle of muslin. Aunt Inez slipped out of the room as Georgiana leaned over the bed. Seybourne studied her creased brow and slightly swollen eyelids. Had she been crying? Over his misfortune? It was almost inconceivable that she'd have wasted a single tear over the likes of him.

With his right hand, he caressed her cheek, then pulled teasingly at one of the black curls that framed her face. He watched in amazement as the shiny tendril bounced back into place. Everything about Georgiana amazed him; especially the look of grave concern on her face.

Scooting toward the center of the bed brought sharp waves of pain to his injury, but he wanted Georgiana to sit beside him while he looked at her. Patting the bed, he said, "How in God's name did the servants prevent blood from ruining this mattress?"

Arranging her skirts around her, she sat on the edge of the

bed. "They did not. You have been unconscious for almost twenty-four hours now, my lord, during which the mattress has been discarded and a new one—"

"Twenty-four hours?" His head shot up, precipitating another jolt of razor-sharp pain in his shoulder. Sinking back into the pillow, he said, "I must get up and about, minx. There is much to do before next week's ball for the queen."

"You must rest, Lawrence. Your health is far more important than any silly ball. You will simply have to cancel the queen's entertainment."

"Impossible," the viscount said, more harshly than he intended. "The ball must take place."

"But, Lawrie, you can hardly lift your head from the pillow. You will certainly not be strong enough to host a dinner party for the queen's entourage a week from now."

But he had to. As he struggled to his elbows, sweat popped out along his upper lip, and a cold, nauseating wave of pain washed over him. He managed to sit up, blinking his eyes as black dots jumped before them. As he swung his legs over the bed, Georgiana stood and crossed her arms over her chest. The viscount's feet landed on the floor with a thud before he realized he was stark naked except for the bandage wrapped around his shoulder.

He turned and looked at Georgiana in time to see her gaze drop guiltily to the floor. Grabbing the counterpane, he held it to his body and stood, his knees wobbling precariously. Dizziness nearly swept him into unconsciousness again. The room tilted so violently that he dropped the bedclothes and stumbled sideways.

Georgiana caught his elbow, steadying him. "Listing a bit to the port side, aren't we, Lawrie?"

He was determined to show her he could withstand the trip to Wrotham and the party planned for the queen. Summoning all his inner strength, he walked across the room and back to prove he could. When he finally sat on the edge of the bed, his skin was coated with a sheet of cold sweat. "See there? I am perfectly capable of entertaining the queen."

"Ridiculous."

It was ridiculous, but Seybourne had no choice. If he canceled the party, he would lose his opportunity to nab Sir Hester's killer. And after the killer's recent bold attempt, he was more determined than ever to bring the miscreant villain to justice. The king would not be safe until he did. More importantly, neither would Georgiana.

"Did you get a good look at the intruder who shot me?" he asked her.

"No, I only saw him when he whirled and ran out the door. He was dressed all in black, I think."

"Yes, and he wore a mask to disguise his features. Do you remember whether Sir Hester's killer wore a mask?"

"I think—" She faltered, obviously shaken. "Yes, I think that perhaps he did. But I cannot be sure, you understand."

"What else do you remember, Georgiana?"

"Nothing."

But he didn't believe her anymore. Her gaze ricocheted around the room, and her body radiated tension. Yet, he couldn't bring himself to press her on the issue. He reckoned she was afraid to tell him what she saw because she didn't want to disclose the real reason she was found nude in Sir Hester's study. And if she'd been at Sir Hester's house for an afternoon of profitable bed play, then Lord Seybourne saw no reason to force such an unpleasant disclosure.

He had already made up his mind he loved Georgiana. He didn't care about her past. He hadn't been terribly shocked when he learned Lady Mercy Mary Spraddlin was a reformed cyprian. Why should he care if Georgiana was?

What was a checkered past compared to the aching love he felt for his new—temporary—bride?

Temporary? He'd be damned if he'd ever let her go!

As the viscount stood, the counterpane covering his loins slid to the floor. Georgiana's cheeks darkened as he lightly grasped her arms and drew her to him. He felt his arousal prodding her muslin wrap; so little was between them, so much held them apart.

He cupped Georgiana's chin and turned her face. "Look at me, minx." Drawing her against his naked chest with one arm, lowered his lips to hers.

He was tentative at first, and she was hesitant.

Then, they melted together, mouths clashing in a fury of passion.

Lord Seybourne whispered against the side of her mouth. "Come to bed, minx."

She gasped. "In the light of day? And in your condition? How could you—"

He cut off her objections with a deep, smoldering kiss. Pushing her onto the bed, he crawled atop her. And while the morning sun grew bright, he proved his physical stamina with astounding, if not multiple, results. By the time her husband had finished with her, Georgiana's argument that he was too weak to host a party for the queen had more than a few holes punched in it.

Chapter Eleven

The trip to Wrotham promised to be unusually uncomfortable for Lord Seybourne. At the insistence of his wife and aunt, he rode inside the carriage instead of on horseback to the family's country manor in Kent. He felt it rather silly to rest his head against plush velvet squabs when he should be riding alongside the carriage to ward off brigands and highwaymen. But, in the end, he was happy to spend the entire day cooped up with his new bride.

Aside from the dull soreness in his shoulder, Lord Seybourne actually enjoyed the trip. Watching Georgiana was a pleasure. Her amazement as she stared at the passing countryside both bewildered and amused him.

Early in the day, Lord Seybourne passed a copy of the morning paper to Aunt Inez. "Read the article on the second page," he advised her. " 'Tis all about how the horse and monkey act at Astley's was interrupted the other night. Seems that earlier in the day, a couple of groomsmen drew knives on one another, and the horse was injured in the fray. No one knew it, though. Had the act continued, the horse might have been permanently injured."

Aunt Inez glanced at the article, oblivious to the conspiratorial look exchanged between Lord and Lady Seybourne. After a short time, she returned the paper to the viscount and said, "Ooh, I should not have attempted to read that fine print. Dear me, my stomach . . ."

"Are you ill, Aunt?" The viscount leaned toward her. "Do you wish me to stop the carriage?"

Georgiana fished a small porcelain snuff box from her reticule. "Here, take a pinch of this. Just a pinch, no more. It will cure your nausea, Aunt, I assure you."

The old lady complied and, within moments, her complexion lost its ghastly green cast. "What sort of tobacco is that, Georgiana? Good heavens, it is an odd color!"

" 'Tis my own private mixture, Aunt." Georgiana smiled sweetly as Lady Twitchett's eyelids grew heavy. Turning to her husband beside her, she said, "I hope you do not mind, Lawrie, but I pilfered some of the snuff you keep in that box on your desk. I mixed it with a small amount of the herb that grows in the gardens behind your house."

"Our house, as long as you are my wife," he reminded her. "By the way, what sort of herb is that?"

She shrugged her shoulders. "I noticed a cat rolling in it just yesterday . . . as if it were a bed of clover! I think the herb is called catmint, but I am not certain."

The viscount chuckled as his aunt snored loudly. "Seems harmless enough. At any rate, I am now free to enjoy watching the passing countryside with you."

Smiling, Georgiana returned her gaze to the rolling fields outside the window.

At noonday, the carriage stopped at a country inn, where Lord and Lady Seybourne enjoyed a nourishing repast of pheasant pies, an array of cheeses, and a bottle of claret. Aunt Inez remained in the carriage and was still asleep when it resumed its trek eastward.

As the arduous journey continued, Seybourne clasped Georgiana's hand and pulled her toward him. Her closeness made the jolting ride over rutted roads tolerable, even enjoyable when her body rocked snugly against his. He could almost forget that he was going to dangle her as bait at the queen's party.

Her gaze strayed over his shoulder and out the window.

"You've never seen the countryside before?" he asked her.

She flashed him an apologetic smile. "Oh, I must be terribly boring to you, Lawrence. I cannot resist watching the scenery float by. 'Tis like being in a ship and sailing past the most exotic islands, full of surprises and treasures just waiting to be discovered."

"So, you have traveled by ship," he deduced aloud. "Can you tell me a little bit about your travels?"

"I do not remember much," she replied quickly.

"But you must remember something, minx. I can see it in your eyes, little flashes of memories that disturb you. You are not being completely honest with me, are you?"

For once, she found it difficult to lock gazes with him. His pale-blue eyes were so intense, so penetrating. When he stared at her that way, she felt transparent. She felt . . . cornered. Like a cat run down by a vicious wolf.

Swallowing hard, she turned her head from him. "I remember the masked killer, dressed in black. I am sure it was the same man who broke into my room a few nights ago and who returned to shoot you in the shoulder."

"What else do you remember, Georgiana? Tell me!"

"I just cannot remember anything else, my lord. Perhaps I never will."

He nodded, gently patting her hand. "I will not press you further on the matter, Georgiana. It is obvious that the man who killed Sir Hester is also the man who entered your room and shot me. You must take extra pains to avoid being alone anywhere once we are at Wolfharden. Aunt Inez or I must accompany you at all times. Do you understand me?"

A terrible thought occurred to her. "Oh, Lawrie! I have placed you in danger, haven't I? You married me to avoid scandal, and look what has happened! A murderer has broken into your home twice and nearly killed you. All because of me!"

His expression was inscrutable, but it was obvious to Georgiana that her outburst made him uncomfortable. His Adam's apple bobbed convulsively before he spoke. " 'Tis not your fault. But please promise me that you will be careful. Do not explore the grounds on your own, and whatever you do, do not wander anywhere without supervision."

She bridled at the thought that she was to be constantly watched. "I can take care of myself, Lawrie."

"I insist, Georgiana. You must not be alone." He squeezed her hands tightly.

"You are hurting me!" Yanking her hands from Lawrie's grasp, she tossed her head, refusing to look at him. "I will do the best I can, *my lord.*"

He sighed and leaned stiffly against the corner of the carriage compartment. "Very well, then. But I do not intend to let you out of my sight. Especially at night."

Because of Lawrie's injury, he was two days later in arriving at Wolfharden than he'd originally intended. True to their promises, Lords Whitney and Chumley had sent ahead huge staffs of servants to prepare for the queen's arrival. That was the good news. The bad news was that the other members of the Kit-Kat Club arrived within hours after the viscount and Georgiana.

Lord Seybourne was in the mansion's library, thumbing through a week-old copy of *The Morning Chronicle,* when he heard the first carriage rumble to a stop on the circular gravel drive fronting the house.

He stood beneath the portico of the redbrick Georgian mansion. As servants rushed to assist guests from the newly arrived equipage, Seybourne fixed a smile on his face. With open arms, he greeted Madge as she emerged, wilted and wrinkled from the rigors of travel.

Disgorged from the carriage was an only slightly less rumpled Sir Morton Drysdale; behind him alighted Sir Douglas Babworth and Lord Turner Pigott. The men dusted off their coats and stretched their limbs, while valises and portmanteaus were unstrapped from the top and boot of the carriage.

Madge offered her hand, and Seybourne politely bowed, allowing his lips to brush her kid glove. After exchanging pleasantries and trivialities concerning the trip, he ushered his guests inside.

Madge studied the foyer, with its gleaming parquet floor and alcoves that showcased an impressive collection of Greek statuary. An elaborately carved oaken balustrade and Oriental-carpeted steps ascended to a gallery above. The entire entrance area was bathed in muted sunlight filtered through a stained-glass dome high above their heads.

Tilting her head back, Madge spied Georgiana leaning over the upstairs railing. Her smile widened and her fingers waggled in childlike glee. "Hello, up there!"

"Come on up, and I will show you to your rooms." Georgiana accompanied Madge to her guest chamber, instructed a servant to fetch a basin of water, then backed out of the door. "When you feel like it, your abigail will direct you to me."

Below stairs, she settled on a velvet settee in the drawing room, awaiting her guest's appearance.

"Mind if we join you?" Lord Seybourne strode into the sunlit room with Sir Douglas, Sir Morton and Lord Pigott on his heels.

Georgiana smiled politely while the male guests squeezed her hand. While she'd been introduced to these men at her wedding, she remembered little about that day. The names and faces of her husband's friends had not yet coalesced in her mind. When Madge appeared, smiling and fresh faced in a low-cut pale-yellow gown that clung provocatively to her shapely figure, Georgiana was grateful for the distraction.

While the party made polite chatter, more carriages arrived, including one that carried Lady Mercy Mary Spraddlin and her companions, Henrietta and Julia. Before midafternoon, the drawing room was filled; the ladies grouped around a setting of settees and chairs in front of the mantel, the men huddled in cliques to discuss the day's events.

A country party held during the height of the London season was unusual. That this one was spectacularly well attended was not surprising, however, given the notoriety of the guest of honor, whose arrival was expected any minute.

Viscount Chumley pulled up a chair across from the small sofa where Madge and Georgiana sat sipping spiced tea.

"Oooh, I just adore this drink," Madge said, draining her cup.

Lord Chumley tasted a few sips, then replaced his cup and saucer on a nearby ormolu table. "A little exotic for my tastes," he said, smiling.

The man always smiled, Georgiana thought, judging him to be extremely good-looking. But, her gaze traveled inexorably to where her husband stood across the room, surrounded by Lady Spraddlin, Lord Pigott, and Mr. Craven.

Henrietta and Julia perched on delicate rosewood chairs with intricately carved backs. Georgiana offered them tea, pouring with a skillful grace that belied her inexperience.

With an ease that amazed her, she made polite, glib conversation with her guests. "I find that ordinary English tea is a bit bland for my tastes," she said, relaxing amid the comradery of the house party.

But the overall mood of the party was one of mounting excitement. Talk of the queen's imminent arrival buzzed around the room. Lady Spraddlin could be seen leaning close to Lord Seybourne, speaking to him intently and making little circles in the air with her hands. Georgiana kept one eye discreetly trained on her husband and the redhead occupying his attention, while she continued her conversation with Chumley and her female guests.

"I cannot wait to see her," Madge bubbled. "I've read everything about her I can possibly get my hands on. The papers describe her behavior as shocking!"

"Those are the Tory rags, m'dear," Lord Chumley said.

Undeterred, Madge continued in her recital of the queen's Continental escapades. When she had finished, Georgiana's lips were twitching with amusement.

"Why, she sounds delightful!" Georgiana finally exclaimed. She and Madge fell into gales of laughter, clasping one another's hands while tears slid down their cheeks.

"I am so pleased to see you enjoying yourself," Lord Seybourne said, appearing at the mantelpiece, his gaze twinkling.

Georgiana glanced up, smiling at her husband. She noted with interest that Lady Spraddlin, Mr. Craven, and Sir Morton Drysdale were now engaged in an intense discussion in the corner across the room. Her keen ears picked up a snippet of the exchange—something about the queen's being made to *"comprehend the enormity"* of something, but her attention was too easily distracted by Seybourne's presence to care what gossip her other guests were sharing.

He stood behind Lord Chumley's chair, one hip canted rakishly, his long, lean legs delicious in those snug old-fashioned breeches of his. Having experienced the most intimate of encounters with the man, Georgiana could not fend off the flush of heat that his penetrating stare generated in her.

To busy her hands, she poured herself another spot of tea. Sipping, she eyed her husband over the gilded rim of the Sevres china cup. Gooseflesh prickled up and down her arms as she met his predatorial, wryly amused gaze. She wondered if the tension that crackled between them was equally obvious to their guests.

Madge certainly wasn't blind to it. "Well, well. I see that the honeymoon isn't yet over. Come, Lord Chumley, what say we let these two lovebirds alone for a bit? Henrietta and Julia, would you care to stroll outside in the gardens a moment?"

"I suggest you not stray far," Lord Seybourne told the ladies. "A courier galloped up the driveway just a short while ago and informed the staff that the queen's caravan is less than a quarter mile away."

Lord Chumley rose, offered Henrietta one arm and Madge the other. Georgiana, embarrassed by her inability to control her emotions, could barely swallow. But she was relieved when the three ladies and Chumley wandered to the other side of the room toward the doors that led onto the immaculately manicured gardens. Upon their departure, her husband quickly took Madge's place on the settee beside Georgiana.

Her cup and saucer rattled noisily as she replaced it on the tea table. Lawrence touched her forearm, then allowed his palm to slide to her wrist. As his strong fingers clasped hers, a frightening frisson of physical awareness shivered through her.

Georgiana closed her fingers around her husband's. When she looked at him, noting the tightening of his features, the slight flaring of his nostrils, she knew he wanted her as badly as she wanted him.

"If it were not so rude, minx, I should gather you up in my arms right now and cart you off to bed." His whisper, throaty and portentous, raised the hairs on the back of her neck.

"If a carriage were not turning into our drive just now, my lord," she replied, her voice husky, "I should chase you up the stairs like a cat pursuing a hapless mouse."

A strident female voice interrupted. "A carriage is turning into the drive?"

Georgiana's head snapped up, and her gaze locked with Lady Spraddlin's. An uneasy premonition uncurled in the pit of her stomach.

Lord Seybourne tilted his head. "I cannot hear a thing, Georgiana."

Georgiana leaned into her husband and whispered in his ear, "I have the most acute sense of hearing, darling."

Within seconds, carriage wheels crunched on the gravel drive in front of the house. The drawing room buzzed with excitement.

"You were right, the queen has arrived." Seybourne kissed Georgiana and briefly nuzzled the soft, fine fuzz of her earlobes.

Sir Morton Drysdale tapped him on the back.

Sir Douglas Babworth hurried across the room in a comical, effeminate shuffle. "She is here, she is here!"

Mr. Craven and Mr. Higgenbotham, their expressions grave, proceeded toward the grand entrance hall.

Abruptly, the viscount straightened. As he stood, a marked change came over him; in the blink of an eye, he went from playful and seductive to cold and businesslike.

The quick alteration in her husband's demeanor alarmed Georgiana. She leapt to her feet, and followed him across the drawing room and into the entrance hall. The foyer was packed with guests and servants alike. Everyone was eager to get a glimpse of the queen and her entourage.

Lord Seybourne hesitated. Shooting his cuffs caused him to

wince at the pain that gripped his injured shoulder. But his features quickly resumed their stoical cast. He flashed his wife a conspiratorial grin, then flung open the great white lacquered doors of the house.

At that moment, arrived the first of six coaches, each emblazoned with the crest of some aristocrat whose fleet of rigs the queen had commandeered.

Georgiana stood beside her husband beneath the portico. As the last carriage rolled to a halt, a liveried footman placed a pair of steps beneath the door. Two young women, obviously the queen's ladies-in-waiting, emerged first. Next came a tall, mustachioed gentleman with thick, wavy black hair and foppish Italian clothes. Turning, he reached into the carriage. Georgiana held her breath as she awaited her first glimpse of the infamous globe-trotting queen.

Suspense rippled through the gathering beneath the portico. All eyes were on the open carriage door as first one dumpy stocking-clad leg, and then another, materialized.

The queen dipped her towering black coiffure, clearly a wig, to avoid smashing the great ostrich plume that bobbed from her elaborate curls. Taking the mustachioed gentleman's hand, she stepped inelegantly to the ground, skirts bunched in her fists and rucked around her knees, exposing flabby calves, the hem of a ragged petticoat and, to Georgiana's great astonishment, dirty ankles.

Lord Seybourne made a leg as the queen ascended the few steps and stood beneath the stucco overhang. Georgiana, limber as a cat, curtsied so low that her forehead touched the ground.

"You must be Lady Georgiana," the queen said. "How pretty you are. And how handsome your husband is!"

Rising, Georgiana met the queen's smile—radiant for its sheer simplicity, despite the tooth decay it so prominently featured.

Lord Seybourne guided his royal visitor into the foyer of Wolfharden Manor. Once inside the house, introductions continued apace. The queen announced her ladies-in-waiting, two young women named Lady Sophia and Lady Winifred. Her male companion was introduced simply as "the Baron," a moniker that aroused curiosity among the guests chosen to attend this very unusual country house party.

Despite having traveled such a far piece, the queen was eager to hold court in the drawing room. After a short retreat to her bedchambers—the best in the house, of course—she returned to the crowded drawing room. There, she ensconced herself in a comfortable chintz wing chair situated catty-corner to the French doors overlooking the Capability Brown gardens that spread to the northeast. Even Aunt Inez descended from her rooms, refreshed and bright eyed after a fortifying nap.

Georgiana, at the queen's behest, settled into a chair opposite her. Madge perched on the edge of a needlepoint settee, while the men circulated about the room, each one pausing to make his obeisance to the queen and engage her for a moment in polite chitchat.

Caroline basked in the attention of her captive audience. She peppered Georgiana about her marriage, asking impertinent questions that would have flustered the average dissembler. But Georgiana had prepared for the queen's interrogation, having heard of the woman's incessant desire for gossip and her compulsion to meddle in the private affairs of everyone who surrounded her.

After deftly explaining to the queen that she was the viscount's third cousin—laboriously tracing a lineage that was so completely fictitious it drew an openmouthed yawn from her royal listener—she summoned a servant with the lift of her brows.

"Yes, m'lady?" asked the servant, one of Chumley's, all decked out in full-dress black-and-white livery.

"We would like some tea," Georgiana said. "The spiced tea—cook has my recipe."

When the queen tasted it, she made a deep rumbling sound. "Umm, that is wonderful!" Her nose twitched and her eyes closed. The expression on her face was pure pleasure.

A few hours later, dinner was served in the richly paneled dining room. Twenty people gathered at the long mahogany table, and just as many servants stood against the walls awaiting orders. The atmosphere was festive, and the food—endless platters of beef, mutton, and roasted squab—was delicious.

Caroline, seated at the end of the table opposite Lord Seybourne, ate heartily. On her right side was Lady Georgiana Seybourne and on her left, Lady Mercy Mary Spraddlin. An unusual seating arrangement to say the least, but Her Majesty had totally ignored the tiny engraved name-cards when she entered the dining room, insisting instead that her two new "lady friends" dine beside her.

"How do you like married life?" the queen asked Georgiana.

It was a ridiculously personal question. Georgiana's cheeks warmed beneath the scrutiny of a tableful of sycophants who did not dare look askance on Caroline's impudence.

"I rather like it," she said, at last. "I didn't think I would at first, too many rules and restrictions. I was rather accustomed to coming and going as I pleased, living life according to my wants and desires, no one else's."

The queen slanted Georgiana a knowing look. "Ah, but all that changes when you marry an important man, does it not?"

"Yes, indeed! Why, he keeps track of every move I make!"

Caroline laughed and reached for her wineglass. When she discovered it was empty, she turned to a servant and demanded more. It was poured immediately.

While the queen threw back another glass of wine, Lady Spraddlin insinuated herself into the conversation with the provocative statement, "Men! They are such a bother, are they not?"

The queen set down her glass with a heavy thud. "Now, there's a cynical gel for you!" She extracted a pair of grimy quizzing glasses from her cleavage, lifted them to her nose and examined Mercy Mary through narrowed eyes. "What is your married status, pray tell."

Lady Spraddlin lifted her chin a notch. "I am a widow, ma'am. The late Earl of Spraddlin was my dear, departed husband."

"That old wretch!" The queen cackled, her double chins quivering in amusement. "He attended my wedding, that one.

He was a rabid reformer, as I recall, particularly interested in the rehabilitation of wayward women.''

Aunt Inez, seated halfway down the length of the dining table, overheard this last bit of gossip. ''The earl was a generous man,'' she inserted. With a dollop of pride, she added, ''Were it not for his selfless and unflagging devotion to the plight of London's working women, I would never have got the Society for the Rehabilitation of Wanton Women off the ground.''

The queen turned her scrutiny on Aunt Inez. ''Wanton Women? I wonder, is my husband a benefactor of your organization?''

This remark brought peals of laughter from Caroline's ladies-in-waiting, along with embarrassed simpers from Henrietta and Julia. The men joined in with good-natured guffaws, though the subject of Caroline's impending divorce trial was too sensitive a topic to discuss openly. It was the sort of thing Caroline could refer to with jocularity, but no one else dared to broach the matter openly with the queen.

Her Majesty leaned toward Georgiana. ''I wish to pursue our earlier conversation. Tell me, my sweet, how have you managed to control your impulse to roam about uninhibited, in the manner to which you were once accustomed, while at the same time conforming your behavior to that of a subservient little wife? I ask because I fear I have not yet learned the secret of living happily beneath the auspices of an important and domineering man.''

Georgiana stared at the queen, an unattractive dumpling with weak chins, deep-set eyes, and bad teeth. She pitied the woman whose behavior had brought down the scorn of half the nation and the entire Tory political party. Perhaps it was her old feline instincts, but she empathized with Caroline.

In an uncharacteristic show of affection, Georgiana reached out and touched the queen's bare arm. ''I have always believed that above all, one must survive. If no one else looks out for your best interests, ma'am, you must fend for yourself.''

The queen scoffed. ''But how am I to tell my enemies from my friends? Old Brougham says he's looking out for my interests, but I'll be damned if I know for certain what games that man is playing!''

"Trust your instincts," Georgiana replied. "A woman must live by her wits. Trust your fear. Use your head, but never ignore the dictates of your heart."

A tear sprang to the queen's eyes. A hush fell over the table as the older woman wiped her sniffling nose with the back of her hand. Overcome by emotion, she grasped Georgiana's hand and said in a husky whisper, "But it is so lonely, this solitary life! Not knowing whom to trust! Not knowing whom to turn to!"

How true, thought Georgiana, her gaze locking with Lord Seybourne's. She met his stare, and a wave of emotion washed over her. Suddenly, she realized the enormity of her own dilemma; it had taken the queen to put it into words, but now Georgiana knew the source of her inner conflict. She had always relied solely on her own wits to survive. Because no one took care of her, she learned to fend for herself. She was a survivor and she could land on her feet in any situation.

But even the strongest woman needed love, didn't she?

Tightening her clasp on the queen's fingers, Georgiana spoke with intense sincerity. "Every creature needs love, Your Majesty. Just as surely as tiny kittens need their mother's milk. A woman needs a man."

The queen's cleavage heaved with gut-wrenching sobs. Everyone at the table stared. The dinner party had turned from a festive affair to a dismally depressing display of feminine emotion.

Lady Spraddlin tossed her linen serviette on the table. "Now, look what you've done, Georgiana! You have gone and made Her Majesty cry!"

Caroline lifted her skirts and dabbed them at her rumpled cheeks. Sniffing, she replied, "No, no. Everyone needs a good cry once and again, I suppose. Georgiana is correct in all that she has said. I have been a fool to place my trust in untrustworthy men. And I have been a fool to abandon London and allow my husband and his Tory cronies to slander my name with all manner of scurrilous stories. One thing I have not been a fool in, though: I quite agree a woman's got to have a man! Now, for heaven's sake, let us forget our sadness for a while. I don't know about you good ladies, but I am in the mood to dance!''

With that, the queen pushed back her chair and hopped to her feet. Everyone at the dinner party hurried to rise, despite the dinner not being half over. If the queen wanted to adjourn to the drawing room, where furniture had been rearranged to accommodate the party and a small orchestra situated just outside the French doors, then that was what everyone would do.

And gladly. The queen's sudden transformation from despair to giddiness was a relief. Dancing on an empty stomach was far preferable to watching the queen blubber and sniffle at the dinner table all night.

Georgiana took the queen's arm, and they marched from the room ahead of the other guests. As she led Caroline across the room, she watched in wry amusement as Lady Spraddlin sidled up to Lord Seybourne, giving a little tug at the sleeve of his black cutaway coat.

Georgiana's ears pricked and she turned her head ever so slightly in an effort to hear Mercy Mary's words.

''Meet me in the library in a quarter of an hour, Lawrence. I must see you alone! 'Tis urgent!''

Teeth clenched in a rictus of a smile, Georgiana breezed through the middle corridor, which separated the dining room from the drawing room. Anger and resentment and jealousy boiled, welling up inside her like a cauldron of bubbling oil. The queen of England was not the only woman with man problems.

But unlike Caroline, Georgiana had no intention of fleeing to the Continent to evade her husband's jurisdiction. She would confront that redheaded tabby Mercy Mary head-on. The fur would fly, but Georgiana had never been the type of female to walk away from a fight. She saw no good reason to do so now—especially when her happiness was at stake.

Chapter Twelve

Barely aware of her actions, Georgiana guided the queen into the drawing room. A servant appeared on their heels bearing a silver tray laden with delicate crystal champagne flutes. Caroline grabbed one and tilted her head, giggling as the bubbles effervesced beneath her rather longish nose.

Luckily, the queen was surrounded by a swarm of people eager to entertain her. Laughing at Caroline's ribald jokes, they occupied her royal attention while Georgiana faded stealthily out of the picture.

Her heart fluttered as she crossed the drawing-room floor. *Why was she threatened by Lady Mercy Mary's attentions to Lord Seybourne? Why should it signify, given the fact that their own marriage was a sham?*

A hand on her arm halted her progress. Georgiana spun to face Aunt Inez's worried expression.

"Where are you going, as if I didn't know?" Lady Twitchett asked.

Georgiana's fingers closed over the older woman's dimpled hand.

The lady immediately cried, "Oh! Your fingernails, Georgiana, you are hurting me!"

Horrified, Georgiana released her grip on Aunt Inez. Had her survival instinct compelled her to act so violently that she'd risk injuring a sweet old lady? With a maelstrom of emotions swirling in her breast, she quietly asked Inez's forgiveness.

" 'Tis understandable," Lady Twitchett replied. "I suppose you are allowed a bit of jealousy notwithstanding the circumstances of your marrying Lawrie. Oh, dear, I fear my meddling has resulted in a dangerous bumble broth."

"Your meddling?" Georgiana drew the woman away from the center of the room. Glancing over her shoulder, she satisfied herself that her royal guest was well looked after. Then, training her intense gaze on Aunt Inez, she lowered her voice to a whisper. "What do you mean by that? Tell me."

Lady Twitchett fiddled with a square of linen, turning and twisting it in her fingers till it was nothing but a ragged strip of cloth. "I—I should not tell you this, Georgiana, b-but it has to do with the viscount's decision to marry you. You s-see, I more or less forced him into this union."

"You forced him? I'm afraid I don't understand." A sick, queasy feeling blossomed in Georgiana's stomach.

"Being caught holding a naked woman in his arms is nearly as damning as being caught *in flagrante delicto* in the bed of one's mistress! Oh, I know that Lawrie's reputation was already in tatters! For heaven's sake, he was convicted of smuggling and murdering! But during the past two years, he's redeemed his image and even taken on the role of political advisor to Lord Pigott. Pigott's campaign would be ruined if Lawrie's new indiscretions were brought to light. Which certainly they would have been, dear."

"Yes, I know all this," Georgiana said with a difficult swallow. "But how can you say you forced the viscount to marry me? After all, you did not orchestrate the scenario that led to my being found naked in Sir Hester's study."

"No, but I could have prevented the publication of the situation."

Georgiana pressed her fingers to her throbbing temples as the drawing room spun wildly beneath her feet. "Why then did you threaten to expose the **compromising situation? You** are an unlikely blackmailer, Aunt.''

"I had my own reasons for wanting the viscount to marry you, dear,'' Aunt Inez said. "And it had nothing to do with avoiding scandal or promoting the lofty objectives of the Society for the Rehabilitation of Wanton Women.''

"What, pray tell, was your motivation in threatening to publicly humiliate your nephew?'' Georgiana asked dully.

"I did not want him to marry Lady Mercy Mary Spraddlin.''

Georgiana's stomach lurched. "Was he planning to?''

Inez stiffened, her brows arching imperiously. "They were enjoying the fruits of a connubial relationship without benefit of clergy or civil ceremony of any kind. Does that answer your question?''

"And are they still . . . lovers?'' Georgiana's limbs burned with the desire to run from the room and track Lady Spraddlin down. In some part of her mind, she fantasized injuring the woman, then toying with her crippled body before finally putting her out of her misery for eternity.

But, she quickly squelched that impulse, reminding herself that she was a viscountess and the hostess of a country house dance in honor of the queen of England. The dichotomy of her natural instincts versus the restraints of her social station produced a drastic polarization of conflicting wants and desires. Patting an elegantly arranged tendril into place atop her head, she flashed on an imagined picture of Lady Spraddlin mangled and pleading for mercy . . .

Oh, stop! she told herself. 'Twas nonsense to entertain such thoughts. She was a lady and she was expected to behave like one.

But she did not have to let that redhead walk off with her husband. Even if Lord Seybourne eventually managed to untie their tangled bonds of matrimony, he had not done so yet. Tonight, the man was still her husband, and Georgiana intended to protect and enforce her marital rights.

She brushed past Aunt Inez, heading for the door.

"Georgiana, be careful,'' the older woman said in a hushed voice. "I truly fear that the woman is dangerous. That is why

I believe I made a mistake in setting up this horrible cat-and-mouse game!''

But Georgiana took no further note of Inez's admonitions. She strode purposefully through the middle corridors of the ground floor, turning left into the west wing of the house. At the end of a dimly lit hall was the closed door of the viscount's study. Heart galloping, she stood with her ear pressed to the mahogany panel, listening, thinking, waiting in vain for some inspiration to tell her what to do.

She had no cause to be jealous and she knew it.

Lady Spraddlin's intervention in her doomed marriage should be viewed as a godsend, a legal and moral justification for exiting her marriage without guilt, remorse, or regret.

Lord Seybourne had never lied to her; he had told her from the outset that their marriage was a sham. She should be grateful to the man for not tossing her into the streets, or handing her over to the Bow Street Runners. After all, she'd been found naked with her arms wrapped around a dead man's neck. She was lucky the viscount took her in.

But, to him, she was nothing more than a stray cat.

The thought filled her with rage and sadness.

Tears flowed freely down her cheeks as she silently cursed this human emotion called love. If she had never felt it, she would never have experienced such deep, gut-wrenching despair.

At last, her breathing normalized and she brushed the tears from her face. Quietly, she turned the knob and pushed open the study door.

Lady Spraddlin, standing in the center of the study with her body pressed against the viscount's, flinched, her startled gaze swinging to Georgiana's.

''Georgiana, this is not what you think!'' The viscount roughly shoved Lady Spraddlin away, then strode across the room toward Georgiana.

And in the other part of the house, a gunshot sounded. For a moment, the three occupants of the study stared at one another in stunned silence. Then, the din of frightened voices in another part of the house compelled them to action.

"Damme, that shot came from the drawing room!" Lord Seybourne rushed past Georgiana and down the long corridor. His boots pounded across the checkered foyer floor, fading as he entered the drawing room.

Lady Seybourne remained in the study with Lady Spraddlin. The air between them crackled with tension as their gazes locked.

Seybourne raced down the hallway, through the foyer and into the drawing room. His conversation with Lady Spraddlin had given him some inkling as to what was going on, but he was still shocked when confronted with the scene that greeted him.

Many of the guests, particularly the ladies, were huddled facedown on the floor. At the far end of the drawing room, just inside the French doors, Mr. Jack Craven kicked angrily at a wooden music stand. The members of the small orchestra had scattered, leaving empty seats and instruments behind. Pages of sheet music fluttered around Craven's feet as he stepped backward, crunching a delicate violin beneath his boots.

He held the queen against him, her back to his chest, and he had one arm crooked around her neck. In his hand was a nasty-looking pistol, its snout pressed to the queen's temple.

Caroline's expression was one of pure terror. "Release me!" she cried, jowls quivering, eyes as wide as saucers.

Craven gave the queen a rough jerk. "Shut your mouth, or I'll send you back to your husband in a coffin!"

"What the devil—" Seybourne reached inside his coat only to discover that his pistol was missing. His mind flashed on Lady Spraddlin and the way she had pressed herself against his chest, running her hands over his body even after he rebuffed her sexual overtures.

Damme, that conniving redhead had stolen his weapon! Unarmed, he rushed toward the front of the room. Threading his way around the huddled ladies, he noticed most of the members of the Kit-Kat Club crouched close to the carpet, as well.

He paused in the center of the room, staring down at Sir Morton Drysdale's puddled figure. "Get up, Morton! For God's sake, we can't let that idiot kill the queen."

Sir Morton uncovered his head and peeked from beneath his arms. Slowly, he rose to his full height beside Seybourne. His gaze darted nervously to the end of the room where Craven held the queen at gunpoint. "I am with you, Lawrie. Just tell me what to do."

"Follow me." Seybourne wound his way through the room, noting a few of the other members of the Kit-Kat Club rising to their feet. Among them were Mr. Sam Higgenbotham, Lords Turner Pigott, Hughes Chumley and Anderson Whitney. Where was the young, impressionable Sir Douglas Babworth, whom he had rescued from losing his last penny at Brooks's?

Seybourne halted about ten feet away from the orchestra area. Craven retreated to within a few inches of the open French doors. Against the backdrop of the darkened gardens spreading out behind him, his eyes glowed wickedly.

"Let her go," Seybourne said in a low, ominous voice.

"Ha! You must be crazy! Why do you think I arranged this dinner party, Lawrie! Did you think I merely wanted to meet the king's consort and pass a pleasant evening smiling at her dirty jokes? Damme, I don't even like to dance!"

The queen's eyes bulged at the insult, but she clamped her lips shut.

"You will be dancing in the wind before long, if you do not release the queen, Jack." Seybourne, hands at his sides, fingers spread, took one step forward. "Surely you are not planning to murder the Queen of England?"

"Murder her?" Craven smiled. "Not unless I am forced to. No, Lawrie, I intend to kidnap the queen and turn her over to the Italian revolutionaries."

"The Italians!" the queen cried. "The Italians don't want me. I just came from there, and I am quite certain they didn't take a fancy to me at all."

"Be that as it may," Craven continued, grinning. "Wouldn't it be grand if the Italian radicals held the king of England's wife as ransom? George IV would be hamstrung, would he not? He would be forced to send his troops to Italy, something he has thus far refused to do. Georgie's government would be thrown into total confusion. Boney might yet enjoy the last laugh.''

''What a dastardly plan.'' Seybourne turned to Sir Morton. ''What did you know of this?''

''Nothing!'' The man's voice betrayed his fear. Stammering badly, he continued, ''I thought we were simply going to bombard the queen with our political dogma. It all sounded terribly underhanded, I admit, to pounce upon the woman in her hour of vulnerability and convince her that her impending divorce was a partisan matter!''

Higgenbotham's reedlike voice replied, ''I had my own doubts about the ethics of what we were planning. But I never thought the queen was to be harmed in any way.''

''Nor I!'' The voice was Lord Turner Pigott's. ''Lawrie, I would never have embroiled you in such an evil plot, I swear it!''

''Fools and blunderbusses, all of you!'' Craven turned his head and spat. His eyes were wild, his speech more frantic with each passing moment. ''You all wanted to sit around and talk about the reforms that need to be made in government, but none of you wanted to do anything to force the Tories into action! Well, I am a man of action! King George and that pompous Liverpool will have to treat with me now! Or else, I will turn Queen Caroline over to the Italian revolutionaries!''

''You will never get away with it,'' Seybourne said, with suppressed violence.

''We'll see about that.'' Craven jerked Caroline toward the French doors and the shadowy stretch of lawn beyond them.

If Seybourne didn't act quickly, he'd be searching for the queen and her kidnapper in pitch blackness. Rushing Craven was an act of madness, but he had no choice. Looking about for a weapon, he saw only a chased-silver candlestick sitting on a small rosewood table. Grabbing it, he plunged forward.

Still clutching Caroline to his chest, Craven swung his pistol toward Seybourne's charging body. An arm's length from the gunman, Seybourne halted. Staring at the snout of Craven's pistol, he lowered the candlestick, allowing it to hang at his side.

The silence in the drawing room was punctuated only by the muffled cries of the ladies hunkered on the floor behind Seybourne. But his focus was so complete, so intense, that he heard nothing, felt nothing of the pain pulsing in his wounded shoulder. Cold moisture plastered his ruffled lawn shirt to his chest, but he was oblivious to his physical discomfort.

A subtle movement on the flagstone porch beyond the French doors caught his eye. Perhaps it was a breeze rustling the velvet curtains, or a bat swooping toward the light inside the drawing room. Whatever it was, Seybourne pointedly ignored it, his gaze fixed instead on the pistol aimed at him.

Craven waggled the gun in the air. "Back up, Seybourne, or I shall kill you deader than a red Spaniard."

"Sorry, old man," Seybourne said smoothly, "but I'm not ready to stick my spoon in the wall just yet."

Craven's grasp tightened on the butt of the pistol; his trigger finger twitched.

Caroline, Queen of England, gasped.

Suddenly, a gun slid through the opening of the French doors and pressed against Craven's temple. Attached to the gun, which Seybourne recognized as the one he ordinarily carried in his breast coat-pocket, was a slender, pale hand. Connected to that hand was a shapely female arm.

Lady Georgiana Seybourne stepped into view, crossing the threshold of the French doors with amazing feline stealth. Her movements were taut and languorous at the same time, tigresslike in their efficiency.

Holding the pistol at Craven's head, she spoke quietly. "Drop your weapon, Mr. Craven, and release the queen. *Now.* Or I will shoot you dead."

Craven's gun clattered to the floor. His arm loosened its hold around the queen's neck, and she promptly fainted, falling to the floor in a heap of flabby flesh, and not nearly enough muslin to cover it.

Slowly, Craven's hands lifted toward the ceiling. "Fool," he whispered, his gaze locked with Seybourne's.

The viscount exhaled a breath he hadn't known he was holding. He took a step forward, reaching for Georgiana's gun. Some of the people on the drawing-room floor behind him sighed with relief and began to scramble to their feet.

At that instant, Sir Douglas Babworth slipped through the open doors, grabbed Georgiana, and pressed a knife to her throat.

Craven quickly plucked Seybourne's gun from Georgiana's hand. Then, he pointed the pistol at the viscount and cackled with vitriolic glee.

"I won't hesitate to cut her throat," Sir Douglas said, his face flushed and damp with perspiration.

"She's been a thorn in my side from the beginning," Craven added.

Staring at the crazed villain, Seybourne seethed with rage and frustration. Unable to rush the men who held his wife captive, he stalled by initiating conversation. If he could keep Craven talking, perhaps an opportunity to free Georgiana and the queen would arise. "Why did you do it, Jack? Why did you kill Sir Hester?"

Craven smiled. "He had stumbled onto my plot. I had no choice."

"You tried to kill me, too," Georgiana said, her eyes round. "But why? I had no idea who killed Sir Hester. You wore a mask that day, and I didn't recognize you when I met you later."

Craven faced her. "How was I to know that? You might have recognized me from my voice, or the cut of my clothes, for all I knew. After all, you must have been in the room when I killed the old man; otherwise, how could you have been found nude in his study just moments after I left? Where were you hidden, gel? How is it that I never saw you?"

Georgiana's lips tightened. "I will not tell you."

The viscount took another step forward, but froze in his tracks when Craven waved his gun wildly in the air, and screamed, "Stay back, or I will shoot your precious wife!"

"Was Sir Douglas your only accomplice?" Seybourne asked.

Craven obviously enjoyed talking about himself. "Oh, no, Lawrie. You should have been more discriminating in choosing your mistresses. Lady Spraddlin was more than helpful. Why, I couldn't have pulled this off without her."

Lady Spraddlin's voice cut through the room. "Just so." In a rustle of pale-green taffeta, she brushed past Seybourne from behind, stepped over the queen's body, and stood next to Craven. "That jealous termagant attacked me, Jack. And robbed me of the pistol I took off Seybourne, too!"

"God, you look as if you've been in a battle." Craven referred to the two vicious red scratches marring Mercy Mary's cheek.

She touched her torn skin and frowned at the blood on her fingertips. "Let us just say I got involved in a catfight," she replied, looking pointedly at Georgiana.

Seybourne would have laughed, had there not been a knife pressing against the delicate skin of his wife's throat. "Good heavens, minx, were you truly jealous?" he asked in genuine surprise.

Her green gaze fastened on him. "You might have married me to avoid scandal, dear, but the fact remains you are still my husband. I admit to being a bit territorial. I am apt to fight for what is mine." Her voice was almost a purr when she spoke, a purr that sent tremors of arousal up and down the viscount's spine—a most peculiar reaction given the precariousness of their present situation.

He moved toward her, but Craven blocked his path with the snout of his gun. "Stay where you are, Lord Seybourne." Jerking his head in Mercy Mary's direction, he instructed her to rip the cords off the curtains and bind the queen's hands and feet. "We've got to get that Brunswick cow out of here if we intend to make Dover by morning!"

Seybourne remained motionless, his fingers clutching the silver candlestick at his thigh. Watching, waiting, constantly appraising his odds against a gun and a knife and a belligerent redhead, he dared a glance at Georgiana. When their eyes met, a preternatural awareness flickered between them. There was hurt and anger and betrayal in Georgiana's gaze, but there was strength, and determination there, too. Seybourne recognized the kindred spirit of a survivor, and it filled him with hope.

Lady Spraddlin gave an unladylike grunt as she yanked at the tasseled cord that held the curtains back. Connected to a plaster medallion, the heavy gold cord stubbornly refused to budge. "I need your knife, Douglas," she said.

Removing his knife from Georgiana's throat, Sir Douglas shoved her into the waiting arms of Craven.

Craven grasped her by the upper arm, his gun aimed at her midsection. Then, he turned a cold malicious stare on Lord Seybourne and said, "I have just conceived the most delicious idea, Lawrie. I believe we shall take Lady Seybourne with us on our journey. If you attempt to pursue us, I promise you that the first body to be tossed from our carriage will not be the queen's corpulent one. It will be your wife's pretty young body. Dead as dead can be!"

Seybourne stared at Georgiana. With his right arm held at his side, he reached toward her with his left.

She stretched out her arm, and their fingertips touched.

A current of warmth flowed between them just as Jack Craven jerked her backward. With the queen safely bound and gagged with a silk kerchief, the trio of criminals—Craven, Sir Douglas, and Lady Spraddlin—prepared to flee Wolfharden.

Craven and Sir Douglas strained to lift Caroline's bulky body from the drawing-room floor. "Seybourne, you will have to help," Craven said, passing his gun to Lady Spraddlin.

She trained the pistol on Seybourne as he stepped forward. "Drop that candlestick," she said with a mocking smile.

The heavy silver candlestick holder fell to the floor with a thud, along with Seybourne's hopes to prevent his wife's abduction. Recognizing the futility and danger of resisting, he bent over and grasped Caroline's ankles. It took every ounce of strength the three men had to carry Caroline out of the house and to a waiting carriage. Seybourne's shoulder was burning with pain by the time he released the woman's limbs.

Once the queen was loaded into the rig and propped against the leather squabs, Craven ordered him away from the carriage. Reluctantly, Seybourne retreated to the edge of the graveled drive as Georgiana was forced at gunpoint to embark the vehicle. Sir Douglas scrambled in next, and then Craven, who paused in the doorway to lean his head out and say, "Remember, Seybourne, if you follow us, you'll be a widower before morning."

Lady Spraddlin hopped in last, throwing Seybourne a victorious, arrogant look before she pulled the door shut behind her. A moment later, the carriage took off with an abrupt start crunching over the gravel driveway that led from Wolfharden to the main road running east toward Wrotham.

Chapter Thirteen

The house-party guests streamed from the drawing room and onto the front porch and steps, staring in wonderment at the departing coach.

Lord Seybourne stood on the graveled drive, fists clenched at his sides. "Someone hand me a pistol." His voice was menacingly quiet.

Sir Morton Drysdale appeared at his elbow, breathless and panicky. "What are we to do now, Lawrie?"

"Damned if I know," Seybourne replied, accepting a pearl-handled weapon from one of his guests. "But I will not abandon my wife to the clutches of that son-of-a—"

"Listen, boy!" Aunt Inez commanded, yanking at the sleeve of her nephew's coat. "There is a shorter way to Wrotham! If you get on your horse, you can intercept Craven's carriage about two miles down the road. That's where the back road and the main one intersect. If you hurry, you can beat them there and then—oh, well, I expect you will know how best to deal with those awful people!"

Seybourne spun around, his eyes lighting on a footman wearing Lord Chumley's colors. "To the stables, boy! Quickly. Fetch my mount and bring it round as fast as you are able!"

"I am going with you, Lawrie." Sir Morton rushed off to the stables to assist the servant in saddling the horses.

Meanwhile, Aunt Inez explained precisely which road Seybourne should take. Tears stood in her eyes as she clasped his hands. "Can you ever forgive me, Lawrie? I should never have allowed you to marry that girl. If I had minded my own business, her life would not be in danger now, and you would not be risking yours to save her!"

Bending down, Seybourne gently kissed his aunt's wrinkled cheek. "If I recall, it was I who suggested the surest way to avoid scandal was to marry Georgiana. You merely agreed with me, dear. Truthfully, I believe it was the most charitable thing you have ever done."

"But, what if you find out she was a . . . ."

"I don't care," he replied firmly. "I love her."

Sir Morton, mounted atop a spirited roan, galloped around the corner from the direction of the stables. Behind him was the young liveried servant atop a prancing black stallion. The boy slid from the horse's back and tossed Seybourne the ribbons. The viscount threw himself into the saddle, gritting his teeth against the searing pain that shot through his shoulder. Then, he gouged his heels into the horse's flanks and lifted his hand in farewell to the dozens of faces staring at him.

"Have some of that spiced tea ready when I return," he called out to Lady Twitchett. "I believe that Georgiana will fancy some after this adventure!"

The back road was treacherous, pitted with deep holes, strewn with tree limbs, and lit only by the glow of the full moon. The two men galloped at a dangerous pace, Sir Morton riding close behind Lord Seybourne. Between the tall hedgerows, the road wound its way northeast, bending sharply on the coast side of Wrotham.

Seybourne recalled his aunt's instructions: *When the road straightens, ride another three hundred yards and you will arrive at the intersection that connects it with the main thoroughfare to London.*

Thundering into the intersection, Seybourne and Sir Morton reined their horses to an abrupt stop. Peering up the main London road, Seybourne saw nothing but shadows; either Craven had already crossed the intersection, or he was yet to pass this point.

"What shall we do?" Sir Morton asked.

"We cannot stay in the middle of the road and simply flag down the carriage; that is for certain," Seybourne answered. "Craven has already made it clear what he will do if we attempt to apprehend his gang."

"We're not going to let them go—"

"Of course not! But we need to devise a method for stopping the coach. I want Craven to disembark before he realizes we have followed him."

Seybourne dismounted and scanned the dark countryside. A few feet back from the side of the road, silhouetted against the purple sky, rose an old oak tree, knotted and twisted. While Sir Morton tied their horses to a small maple sapling behind the huge tree, Seybourne inspected the old oak; it was ravaged by lightning, its limbs dead and rotten, ready to snap off with the least amount of pressure.

He gave the lowest limb a forceful kick. The limb fell off with a sharp crack, hitting the ground amid a spray of bark, twigs, and debris.

"Knock off as many limbs as you can," Seybourne told Sir Morton. "Then drag them into the center of the road and pile them one atop the other!"

The men were breathing heavily and soaked with sweat by the time a pile of rotten oak limbs rose from the center of the intersection. As Seybourne tossed a splintered log on the heap, he felt the rumble of hooves vibrating beneath his boots.

"They are coming, Morton! Hide yourself!"

The two men hunkered behind the thick trunk of the oak tree, peering through the tangled web of limbs that concealed them from view. Within minutes, Craven's carriage came roaring into sight.

The coachman saw the pile of logs in the nick of time. Yelling "Whoa!" at the top of his lungs, he reared back in his driver's seat and reined the horses to a skidding halt. Even in the semidarkness, Seybourne saw the cloud of dust that billowed from beneath their hooves.

Bellowing his outrage, Craven flung open the carriage door and peered out. "What in the hell are you stopping for?" The carriage lanterns shone on his gaunt face, lending it a sickly yellow glow.

Scrambling from his perch, the driver pointed toward the logs blocking the middle of the road. "Must have fallen out the back of some farmer's tumbrel, Mr. Craven. Looks like a pile of kindlin'. I 'spect some jackanapes is wonderin' where he lost his faggots about now."

"Well, don't stand there gaping, man! Clear the road. Quickly! That arrogant aristocrat will soon be on our heels anon, no matter that I threatened to kill his wife if he pursued us."

Without looking at Sir Morton, Lord Seybourne whispered, "Do not move until I say so." Then, body pressed against the tree, he drew the pearl-handled pistol from the waistband of his breeches.

The driver grunted as he hefted one of the rotten logs and threw it toward the side of the road. By the time he'd moved three of the cumbersome limbs, he was huffing loudly while Craven berated him from the open door of the carriage compartment.

"I'm movin' as quickly as I can, guv'nor," the coachman answered between ratchety breaths.

Another couple of logs were removed from the pile and tossed to the side of the road, just a few feet from the oak tree that hid Seybourne and Drysdale. Then, Craven, clearly unable to contain his frustration any longer, hopped from the carriage and stood on the rutted road, gloved fists propped on his waist. "Get out here, Douglas," he yelled. "And help this oaf clear the road. We haven't got all night, for Christ's sake."

Sir Douglas Babworth leapt from the carriage, his face aglow with sweat and gaslight.

Seybourne's muscles tensed and his fingers itched on the cool metal trigger-casing of the pistol. Nudging Sir Morton, he said hoarsely, "They are all three out in the open now. The women are in the carriage alone."

"Let's rush them!" The younger man's voice was full of charged impatience.

But, Seybourne was older, calmer, and cooler. He knew how to wait. Cuffing Sir Morton's biceps, he said, "Only when I give the signal! And then, you will leap up into the coachman's seat and start driving. Drive as fast and as far as you can, man! Do not stop until you reach London. It is up to you to get the women to safety. And no matter what happens, do not try to rescue me. Just get Georgiana out of danger and then tell her . . . tell her that I did love her very much."

In the dimness, Sir Morton's face was creased with confusion. "Lawrence deWulff, you can't be serious! We can take them all three out, old boy, I swear it. Only one's got a pistol and you'll shoot him dead before the other two make a rush at us. Then—"

The viscount spoke through gritted teeth. "Sir Douglas has a knife, fool! And God only knows what sort of weapon that driver has. A good coachman is well armed, prepared for brigands of the most despicable sort. We are two men and one pistol against three men and three weapons. No! I won't have Georgiana's life risked while we are waging a losing battle on some deserted country road."

"This is not a good plan," Sir Morton muttered.

"You will do as I say, or I will shoot you myself," the viscount replied tightly.

Sir Morton gulped convulsively, his gaze returning to the road where Babworth and the coachman continued their work. Though Seybourne and Morton had compiled the logs in less than a quarter of an hour, it took nearly twice that time for the other two men to move them. Behind the oak tree, Sir Morton fidgeted, eager to engage the enemy, while Seybourne stood motionless, muscles taut.

Through the open door of the carriage, the viscount caught a glimpse of white muslin, which interrupted the rhythm of his heart. He thought Georgiana must be cold in her flimsy evening gown, and he ached to hold her. Knowing that she was frightened and uncomfortable produced in him a blinding rage, an irrepressible protectiveness that overwhelmed any concern for his own safety. He would not allow Jack Craven, or anyone else, to harm a hair on her head. He would die before that happened.

The low guttural moan of a cat rent the still night air. Seybourne's ears pricked and his skin prickled as the moan turned to a series of chirrups and growls. The sounds seemed to emanate from within the carriage. *But that was impossible; there was no cat inside that carriage!* Shaking his head, the viscount concluded that the cold had clouded his senses.

"Do you hear that?" There was a quiver in Sir Morton's voice.

"Take it easy," Seybourne replied. " 'Tis just a cat."

The cat's moan, throaty and filled with animal desire, grew louder. From somewhere deep in the forest, another cat joined in. Then, a second and third feline voice added to the caterwauling, and soon, a symphony of strident moans and meows filled the woods and the moonlit night.

Craven, obviously disturbed by the deafening cries, paced beside the carriage with his hands clapped over his ears.

"Ready, now," the viscount whispered. "Those are the last two logs that the driver and Sir Douglas are lifting now. As soon as they drop them on the side of the road, we will make our move. Do not forget—drive straight to London and don't stop till you get there."

Sir Morton nodded.

Seybourne, his body coiled as tightly as a spring, watched. On the road, Craven gripped the handles on either side of the carriage door frame and heaved himself up. As he hovered in the threshold of the compartment, a female scream erupted.

The cats in the woods went deadly silent.

"Now!" Suddenly, Seybourne and Sir Morton were all movement. Dodging low-hanging limbs, they raced toward the road, boots crushing dry leaves and weeds. Over his shoulder, Seybourne yelled, "Get her out of here as quickly as you can, Morton!"

Craven's voice split the air like a rusty hatchet. "Good God, you conniving little wench! You have killed them."

Then, Craven fell backward—or was kicked—out of the carriage, landing on the dry, mud-caked earth with a thud. His angry curses were cut off by Lady Spraddlin, who tumbled from the compartment atop him, skirts and petticoats rucked about her stockinged legs, bare arms thrown akimbo by the impact of her fall.

Having dropped their logs, the coachman and Sir Douglas rushed to the side of the coach where Craven and Mercy Mary rolled in a heap. Seybourne and Sir Morton approached in a stampede of footsteps, however, drawing their attention. Weapons materialized, a small pistol in the driver's hand and a flashing knife in Sir Douglas's.

Sir Morton, to his credit, obeyed Seybourne's instructions and headed straight for the front of the carriage. But he was not quick enough. The driver fired off a shot in Sir Morton's direction just as the young man leapt toward the box. A blast of gunpowder burst orange in the night sky. Sir Morton, thrown against the side of the carriage, just managed to scramble into the driver's seat, where he slumped over and remained motionless.

Seybourne aimed his pistol and fired, knocking the coachman to the ground and killing him.

Sir Douglas disappeared inside the coach.

Craven heaved Lady Spraddlin, apparently insensate, off him and struggled to his feet. "You stupid oaf! I told you we'd kill your precious wife if you tried to interfere."

Seybourne lunged at the man. "You must have known I wouldn't let you get away with such a thing, Jack!"

A ruckus inside the carriage, however, caused both men to freeze, their gazes swiveling to the door as it snapped shut. From inside, a muffled scream sounded. The carriage rocked on its springs wildly.

Craven's hands moved a fraction.

"Go for your gun, and I will kill you." Seybourne's promise was delivered with an icy sureness.

Suddenly, the carriage door swung open, hitting Craven

squarely between the shoulder blades and knocking him to the ground. Just as he was about to get up—he was on all fours, shaking his head like a wounded animal—Queen Caroline came tumbling out of the coach. She landed on his back with considerably more force than Lady Spraddlin had landed on his stomach.

"Oomph!" Flattened, Craven's arms and legs splayed out in all directions. The queen rolled on top of him like an overturned turtle, her thick white limbs glowing obscenely in the dark.

Strangely, she rolled off Craven's back and landed next to Lady Spraddlin's supine body, a beached whale next to a slender orange-haired carp. Seybourne, puzzled by the two women's unconscious state, nevertheless turned his attention to the figures hovering in the threshold of the carriage compartment.

Sir Douglas shoved Georgiana to the ground; she landed gracefully on her satin slippers while he clumsily disembarked.

Craven lurched to his feet, producing a gun from inside his coat pocket. "Back up, Seybourne. Or I shall instruct Sir Douglas to slit her throat."

The pearl-handled pistol fell to the ground. "Let her go, Craven. You have custody of the queen, that is who you wanted."

"Aye, but it's getting her across the Channel and all the way to Italy that's got me worried now, boy. I am beginning to think Lady Seybourne may come in handy during our arduous journey. Perhaps if we can get some decent dowager's weeds on that fat lump of flesh who calls herself a queen, we can masquerade as a family on holiday. I, as the father. Douglas and Georgiana as our two adoring children. Caroline the cow, of course, as my dowdy wife."

"You will never make it to safety," Seybourne said, his eyes locking with Georgiana's. In the moonlight, her neck gleamed white and swanlike; the pulse point in her tender throat throbbed.

He marveled that she could be so self-contained at a moment like this, when her very life was at stake, when a single wrong movement or word could result in that hideous knife slicing her silken white skin. He met her stare, and a strange otherworldly awareness passed between them—it had happened before. He couldn't escape the feeling that they were kindred souls, loners who needed no one else . . . *but each other.*

Christ on a raft, he loved her! Heart pounding, Seybourne glanced up at the driver's box. Sir Morton remained slumped over and unconscious. The viscount's plan had failed. He had no choice but to retreat and allow Craven to gallop off with Georgiana in his clutches. She might survive on her own. She wasn't helpless, after all. But, if he didn't retreat now, Sir Douglas would surely slit her throat.

"Of course, we cannot leave you behind to cause more trouble for us," Craven said, cruelly sneering.

"Kill him!" Sir Douglas said. "Don't waste another moment on him, kill him!"

Craven's thumb drew back the hammer of the pistol, and his fingers tightened on the handle. Seybourne stared at the short snout of the weapon aimed at him, quite certain he was about to die. Closing his eyes, he imagined Georgiana's face and knew that he had truly loved her.

Suddenly, an eerie keening filled the woods behind him. Seybourne's eyes flew open and he stared disbelievingly at Craven's fearful expression. The night air came alive again with the voices of hundreds of cats crying and moaning and growling. They seemed to be invading the countryside, moving toward the road, encircling the men and the carriage.

The crickets' racket and the owls' hoots were drowned by the cacophony. Gentle meows mingled with trilling crowlike caws. The sounds became deafening, blotting even the roar of blood through Seybourne's veins. The invisible cats moved closer, their cries growing louder by the moment.

Craven's jaw worked furiously. Above the din, he yelled, "Douglas, what in the devil is going on?"

"Hell if I know!" the younger man yelled, clutching Georgiana tighter against him.

Seybourne met Georgiana's gaze. Rather than the fright most sane women would have shown, a smoldering sensuality burned in her eyes. She gave the viscount a half smile, a knowing look that caused his loins to prickle.

He thought he had lost his mind. He was on the verge of

being killed, yet his wife's slight smile had him physically aroused! The notion that he was fit for Bedlam flitted through his brain. But in a flash, it was gone, replaced by an alarming revelation.

Seybourne lifted his brows in a question, and Georgiana nodded almost imperceptibly. Yes, it was *she* causing the commotion which filled the air! Georgiana had drawn the cats to her with a power that Seybourne would never comprehend.

What was she?

Staring at her while the rasping cries of angry cats intensified, Seybourne experienced a burst of insight.

Georgiana had been naked, her arms entwined around Sir Hester's neck, her fingers clutching a balled-up bit of paper.

A balled-up bit of paper.

Much the same way a kitten batted a bit of paper around with its paws.

A trickle of understanding flowed through Seybourne's body. He held Georgiana's gaze while the woods folded in around them, heavy with the sound of cats screaming, thick with the danger of a thousand vengeful felines. *He thought of Georgiana falling over the balcony; Georgiana dipping her nose in a cup of milk; Georgiana spicing her tea with an herb amazingly similar to catmint.*

But the thought was just too insane to seriously consider. Still, when he looked at her, mouth tipped up in an enigmatic smile, heavily fringed eyes twinkling with mischief, he knew it was true.

The way she slept all day.

The way she craved her solitude and bolted from the room whenever she felt her privacy had been impinged upon.

Her keen sense of smell; the way she could tell who had been in a room simply by sniffing the air.

Most of all, the way she curled up in his arms and purred each time he kissed her. . . .

She lifted her chin a notch, oblivious to the sharp edge of the knife pressed against her throat. Her green gaze locked with Seybourne's pale-blue one, affirming his suspicions.

She knew that he'd discovered her identity, that he'd figured out who she was, and what she'd been before he met her.

"I don't care, Georgiana," he blurted out, his words inaudible above the roaring sound of the cats moving closer.

But she heard him. Her eyes glowed brighter, hotter, clearer. Her lips parted.

Even amid the deafening tumult of the cats' cries surrounding them, Lord Seybourne could feel the warm vibration of her feline purr. It moved through him like a soft moan. It ruffled the hair on his nape and stroked the most intimate parts of his body. It aroused his imagination, as well as his loins. And it cemented him to Georgiana in that moment; he knew that no matter what else befell them, he would never let her escape him. She was his, now and forever.

Craven made a wild gesture with his gun, waving Sir Douglas toward the coachman's box. "Forget Seybourne, let's get out of here! Douglas, grab the reins and get these horses moving!"

Sir Douglas tossed Georgiana into the carriage, and Craven climbed in behind her.

"Haven't you forgotten something?" Seybourne asked coolly.

With one foot in the carriage threshold, Craven halted. He whirled around, his gaze fastened on the inert figures of Queen Caroline and Lady Spraddlin. Waggling his gun at Seybourne, he said, "Get them into the coach and be quick about it!"

It was a good way to stall for time, Seybourne thought. The cats were all around them now. Though their moans and shrieks had lulled somewhat, their nearness was as palpable as the chill breeze that lifted Seybourne's shaggy hair.

The viscount leaned over Caroline and grasped her beneath the arms. Straining to drag her toward the carriage, he reckoned she must have weighed close to thirteen stone. After a few steps, he released her and she slumped to the ground. Turning, he sent Craven an apologetic look, shrugging to indicate the queen was simply too fat to be moved any farther.

But Craven didn't fall for the ruse. The man stepped to the ground and prodded Seybourne's back with his pistol, urging him to move the queen. When the viscount finally got the

THE MINX OF MAYFAIR 199

woman's unconscious body to the edge of the carriage, Craven took her feet. Between the two of them, they slid her into the compartment like a slab of pickled beef. Peering inside, Seybourne could see Georgiana sitting primly on the squabs, her face serene.

He scooped Lady Spraddlin off the road and easily handed her inside the carriage.

Forced at gunpoint to retreat, Seybourne stumbled backward, out of the coach. He stood on the rutted road, staring up at Craven, who loomed in the doorway of the carriage compartment. Sir Douglas, seated in the coachman's box beside Sir Morton's crumpled body, called over his shoulder, "Ready, Jack?"

Craven pointed his pistol at Seybourne and smiled. "Say goodbye to your wife, Lord High-and-Mighty. And thank you for your gracious hospitality. The party was wonderful!"

And then the first cat emerged from the darkness. And in the time it took for Seybourne's heart to stop and start again with a thundering boom against his ribs, the balance of power shifted and the villains became the victims.

Chapter Fourteen

The cat flew at Craven's extended arm, blotting the pistol aimed at Seybourne's chest.

A terrible screech and a menacing growl split the night. Screaming, Craven reared back as the cat's claws found his flesh, dug into the sinews and muscles of his arm, sliced through the gaunt skin that hung slack at his jaws.

"Help me!" Craven's arm shot up reflexively, fingers grabbing the pistol trigger. The gun fired with a deafening crack, shattering an oak limb overhead and sending it crashing to the ground in an explosion of bark and splinters.

There wasn't much time. The cat's distraction provided Seybourne with a window of opportunity, but he couldn't waste a second. Craven would not be felled by a single cat, not for long.

The cat mauled and clawed and screamed like a banshee. Craven fell to the ground, kicking and cursing and wrestling the animal. The scene would have been comical were Georgiana not imprisoned in the carriage, a murderous Sir Douglas at the reins.

"Help me!" Craven cried.

Sir Douglas leapt from the coachman's box, unwisely thrusting his hand into the fray. For his troubles, he received a shredded coat sleeve and an arm bloodied and torn. Yelling his pain and indignation, he retreated quickly, leaving his partner in crime to fight the cat alone.

Carefully skirting Craven and the wild cat, Seybourne leapt to the doorway of the carriage. Peering inside, his eyes adjusted to the darkness of the compartment's interior. Georgiana's hands flew to her throat, and an expression of pure relief spread across her face.

But Sir Douglas was not to be so easily got rid of. While Craven wrestled with the cat, Douglas flung himself at the viscount and pulled him out of the carriage. The two men fell to the ground and rolled atop one another, their limbs entwined. Sir Douglas emerged on top and astride Seybourne. He reared back his fist, then slammed it into the viscount's face.

Seybourne's head rang like a cracked bell. Raw animal instinct surged through him, strengthening him, inuring him to the pain in his shoulder. He threw a blow at Sir Douglas's head, and the man slumped over and sprawled on the ground.

For a moment, the fight stalled. As the cat shot across the road toward the woods, Seybourne gasped for breath. Craven, his face a tattered, bloody mess, lay beside him motionless.

The collective voices of the cats in the forest disappeared, their plaintive cries fading into the black forest.

Seybourne scrambled to his knees and looked up just in time to see Sir Douglas coming after him again.

To Georgiana, crouched in the threshold of the open carriage door, the fight lasted an eternity. Her heart raced as the men made it to their feet and began slugging one another. Their fists slammed into one another's faces and jaws. The sounds of fists hammering flesh, cartilage snapping and bones crackling, caused her stomach to spin.

At last, Seybourne stood, his chest heaving. Sir Morton remained unconscious, moaning unintelligibly. The coachman lay lifeless in the spot where Seybourne's bullet had felled him. And Jack Craven's cold eyes stared heavenward in a gruesome death mask.

Silence enveloped the night. The faint chirrup of the cats'

cries was replaced by crickets sawing, owls hooting, and, in the distance, a cow lowing balefully.

The carriage lamps dimly lit the carnage strewn on the rutted road. Seybourne looked up at Georgiana, standing in the open doorway of the carriage.

Georgiana's knees wobbled beneath her gown and her voice quavered uncontrollably. "Are you . . . all right?" she asked him.

He drew in a deep breath and cringed. Blood trickled from a deep gash above one eye. But, a crooked smile crimped the side of his mouth and, even in the shadows, his eyes sparkled brilliantly. "I suppose I will mend rather quickly. I am a pretty tough old brute, you know."

"That you are." Georgiana stepped from the carriage into Seybourne's open arms.

He held her closer and longer than he needed to, but not nearly long enough to satisfy her thirst for him. His hands encircled her waist; they were strong and comforting.

"Georgiana, there is something I have neglected to tell you." His breath warmed her lips, fanned gooseflesh across her bare shoulders and neck. "I am glad I married you."

Despite the chill of the night air, a wave of liquid heat flooded Georgiana's body. She placed a fingertip on his lips. "So, you do not resent your aunt's interference?"

His expression altered. "Well, that is not precisely why I married you. In due time, I hope that I can explain everything. But for now, minx, you must know that I love you. I have no intention of inventing some spurious impediment to our continuing as a married couple. I want you to be my wife, Georgiana, now and forever."

But there was much about her that the viscount didn't know. A niggling kernel of doubt twisted in Georgiana's belly. "I love you, Lawrie." Her voice was hoarse, seemingly ripped from her throat. "But, there is also something I have failed to tell you."

"I think I know what it is. I do not care." He lowered his head and kissed her savagely.

A weak moan sounded from the driver's box. "Lawrie, for God's sake, get me home, old boy!"

Seybourne drew in a ragged breath as he set Georgiana at arm's length. Then, he bolted to the coachman's perch and yelled, "Georgiana, get inside. Quickly! I am going to return this rig to Wolfharden."

Georgiana scrambled inside, seated herself between the still unconscious bodies of the queen and Lady Spraddlin, and rode in desolate silence the short distance to Wolfharden. As the carriage jolted over the uneven road, she worried about Sir Morton's physical condition. He had a bullet wound, and he had been exposed to the cold air for far too long.

Sir Morton's welfare was not, however, her only concern. Deep unhappiness clutched at her throat. The words Lord Seybourne had spoken to her were full of love and hope and promise. But would those words be as true once Seybourne discovered the truth about her identity? Would the viscount be able to accept the truth about her past?

Another new human emotion—hopelessness—engulfed her. Georgiana's heart ached so violently, she thought it might literally break open inside her chest. Her entire body ached for the man who had rescued her from the evil clutches of Jack Craven.

Stifling a sob, she thought disconsolately of Sir Hester, who had once rescued her, taken her in as a stray and fed her, given her shelter and affection. Lord Seybourne had taken her in, also, but he had given her something she never knew existed. He had awakened in her emotions and feelings she'd never experienced. Damn him! Though she loved him with every fiber of her being, she couldn't help but resent him for demonstrating to her the painful depth of human love and emotion.

When the carriage rumbled to a stop in front of Wolfharden, Georgiana's nerves were taut and jumpy. The carriage door opened and the viscount reached in for her, his somber expression lit by gaslight fixtures beneath the portico. She grasped his hand, clutching her skirts as her slippers touched the graveled drive.

"We must talk, Georgiana," he said, drawing her close to him.

She opened her mouth, but couldn't speak over the painful lump in her throat. Lord Seybourne's mouth was set in a grim straight line. His touch was hot, but his gaze was icy, sending a shiver up Georgiana's spine. *Had he reconsidered his rash words of love? Had those assurances of love and fidelity been made in a moment of passion, when he was overwhelmed by relief at having survived Jack Craven's villainous attempt to kidnap the Queen of England?*

Lady Twitchett, emerging from the front door, rushed with arms outstretched toward her precious nephew. A dozen servants followed in the woman's wake and quickly began the arduous task of extracting Caroline from the carriage and carrying her into the house.

A pair of sturdy footmen gently lowered Sir Morton from the driver's box. A dark stain marred the shoulder of his evening coat, and he tucked one arm close to his side, but a rakish smile twisted at his lips. "Could use a bit of doctorin', I believe."

Seybourne and Georgiana followed the young man into the house, assuring him in tandem that he would receive the finest medical attention available.

Aunt Inez scurried along behind the servants. Inside the foyer, she directed Lady Spraddlin be returned to her guest chambers. Then, she sent a young courier off to Wrotham to fetch the doctor. "Take the queen to her chambers—Lawrie's, that is! And see that she is made as comfortable as possible."

Sir Morton gave a brave chuckle. "They must have gone mad here, wondering whether we'd make it back alive, Lawrie. And wondering whether we'd bring the queen with us when we did return."

"Well, we're back," Seybourne replied. "And the doctor will be here soon enough. To bed with you now, Morton, and I will see you shortly."

"Aye, my lordship." Knees sagging, Sir Morton made it up the steps, his weight largely supported by the two footmen.

Georgiana and Seybourne stood for a moment in the center of the tumult. The house was lit like a bonfire with branches of candles, chandeliers, and wall sconces ablaze. Servants scampered all about them, carrying out Lady Twitchett's orders, or conveying messages from one visitor to another concerning the viscount's arrival and the queen's condition.

An uncomfortable moment of silence passed between Lord and Lady Seybourne. At last, the viscount looked at Georgiana. "Come, surely we can find some privacy in the library."

She followed him into the deserted room, lit dimly by several strategically placed candelabra. When the viscount closed the door, Georgiana's pulse skittered. Settling on a dark cracked leather sofa, she looked around her. This room was so much like her husband, she thought, so dark and brooding, full of secrets that he was reluctant to share.

He stood in the center of the room, hands behind his back, feet planted far apart. The blatant hunger in his stare frightened her. "There is something I must tell you, Georgiana."

She nodded, swallowing hard.

His voice was clipped and raspy, as if he were attempting to suppress whatever emotion tugged at him. "It concerns my motivation for marrying you."

"Lawrie, don't! I know why you married me. Your aunt explained it all to me. She thought you had formed an unhealthy connection with Lady Spraddlin, and when she saw the opportunity to marry you off to someone else, she made a snap judgment. A complete unknown was better than that hussy, in her opinion. I hadn't thought she was correct until tonight, but now I am afraid your aunt was quite prescient in predicting the widow's bad intentions—she is an evil tabby, that one, and the less said of her the better!"

Sighing, Seybourne ran a hand through his shaggy hair. "Yes, I suppose I was quite taken in by Lady Spraddlin, in the beginning at least. I was grateful to her for befriending me—how foolish! But then, I've been known to be slavishly loyal to the most disloyal people."

"I do not know what you're talking about, Lawrie."

"Hasn't anyone recounted the sordid details of my past to you, Georgiana? Don't you know that I've been convicted of smuggling and murder?"

"I do not care about your past."

Anger spilled into his voice. "Well, you should! For I am

branded a criminal in all of England! Never mind that I was innocent, that it was my twin brother, Francis, who was guilty! Francis begged me to stand in for him and like a fool, I was persuaded by his eloquent speeches."

Georgiana gasped. "You allowed yourself to be convicted of a crime you did not commit? Out of loyalty to your brother?"

"My late brother. Shortly after I was transported to Australia, Francis was shot in the back by an angry husband who made a quite untimely reappearance at his own home around nuncheontime. Seems Francis was taking his own repast with the gentleman's wife. The whole thing was exquisitely bloody. Aunt Inez was mortified with shame. By the time I returned to London, she had begun to think of me as the *good twin*— imagine that!"

"Does your aunt know that you are innocent?"

The viscount rubbed his face with his hands. At length, he replied tightly, "You are the only one who knows that, Georgiana. What good does it do to condemn a dead man of his crimes? Once Francis was dead, I had no interest in shifting my guilt to him. I suppose I felt guilty enough of *something*— even if it was not exactly what I was convicted of—to justify the punishment meted out to me. After all, I never was a very good sort of person. I broke a lot of hearts, Georgiana. I was callous in my treatment of women, and downright cruel in my dealings with men."

Georgiana met his cold, challenging stare. "Lawrie, your past does not matter to me. I don't care what you've done."

The viscount turned his back on her, and for a long moment, the study echoed with silence.

At last, Georgiana spoke very softly. "I should hope that my past does not prejudice you against me, either. We are not children, you know, either one of us, with clean slates to be scribbled freely upon. We are adults, fully grown, with experiences that have shaped us and molded us. We cannot erase our pasts, Lawrie. Nor would I want to. I love you for what you are. Would you hold it against me if I told you that in my former life I was—"

"No!" Pivoting, the viscount crossed the room in long pantherlike strides. Kneeling at Georgiana's feet, he clasped her hands and touched his forehead to her fingers. "No, Georgiana, it isn't important what you were. I am not a jealous man! I do not want to know—"

" 'Tis not what you think—" Georgiana clamped her lips shut, wondering how to continue, how to explain her past to this tormented, noble man. Stroking his coarse gray-flecked hair, she said, "I wish I could be good like you, Lawrie. You are kind and courageous and loyal, while I am aloof and selfish and incredibly vain. You are everything I am not. And I love you for it."

He lifted his head slowly, staring at her through watery eyes. "How can you love me, Georgiana? How can you love me when I used you, dangled you as bait to lure a killer into the open? I see the look of shock on your face, minx. You didn't know that, did you? *You cannot forgive that, can you?*"

The room fell deadly quiet.

Georgiana blinked back tears, struggling with her confused emotions. Finally, she managed to speak in a low, throaty, trembling voice. "You—*used*—me?"

All her life it was she who used others. Now she knew the pain of being used. Fearing that her muscles would snap from tension and anger, she held on tightly to the viscount's hands, forcibly tamping down the urge to fly into a rage and scratch his eyeballs out.

His words came out in a tumble, as if he wished to rid himself of them. "The king granted me a reprieve from my exile, allowing me to return to England on the condition that I spy for him. I insinuated myself into a group of Whig politicians known as the Kit-Kat Club. Sir Hester was a member of the group, as was Lord Pigott whose candidacy for the Commons I endorsed and campaigned for."

"Go on."

"At first, I thought the Club was merely a harmless clique of eccentrics, progressive thinkers, and frustrated poets. Sir Morton Drysdale befriended me, but the others remained wary of my presence. For months, I attended meetings, socialized with these men, entertained them in my home. And I repeatedly informed the king that his suspicions of a Radical plot were groundless.''

"But Sir Hester's death changed all that,'' Georgiana whispered, her mind leaping back to that horrible day when she witnessed her patron murdered.

"Yes, and the note I found crumpled in your hand indicated a far deeper intrigue than I'd ever imagined.''

"Did you recognize the author's hand?'' Georgiana asked.

"Not at the time, but it is clear Craven must have written it. To whom remains a mystery. I only knew that I had to discover who killed Sir Hester before the evil plot to topple the king's government was carried out. Since you had been at the murder scene, I used you to draw out the killer. Never in my life have I done a more loathsome thing, Georgiana. But I had a duty to the king and to my country.''

A wave of coldness swept over Georgiana. Withdrawing her hands from Seybourne's, she rubbed her arms. "So, Mr. Craven and Sir Douglas had planned all along to kidnap the queen as soon as she set foot on English soil.''

"Precisely. No one else knew of the scheme, however. When Sir Hester intercepted the incriminating note, he tried to warn me. Before he could, Jack Craven killed him. It was Craven who broke into my town house and tried to kill you. He must have slipped away from Brooks's while Sir Douglas distracted me with his reckless gambling streak. And, of course, it was Craven who shot me.''

"Thank God he is dead,'' Georgiana said, shuddering.

Seybourne stared at her intently. "Georgiana, there still remain some unanswered questions. You were present when Craven killed Sir Hester.''

"I remember very little of that day,'' she replied, rubbing her temple to emphasize her head injury.

Standing, he backed away, studying her as if he were seeing her for the first time. "I suppose that the blow you sustained on your head robbed you of your memory. But you were there, Georgiana. You must have been.''

She shook her head, angry to learn that Seybourne had used her, that he had drawn a killer to her, a killer that never would have known of her presence in that study. "Listen to me, Lawrie! Jack Craven did not see me in the study the day he murdered Sir Hester."

A sultry female voice interrupted the tense silence that covered the library. "She is telling the truth, Lawrie. Jack did not see her in the room when he shot Sir Hester."

Georgiana's head snapped up. Lady Spraddlin, hair a puffy mess, dress dirty and bedraggled, stood in the doorway. Though she clutched the frame for support, her expression was gloating.

"How the devil did you get here?" Seybourne took a step toward her.

"I walked downstairs. Damme, but it is difficult to get any attention when the queen is laid up and bellowing like a cow!" She stepped inside, slamming the door behind her. As she did, she pulled the pearl-handled pistol from the folds of her ragged gown. Raising her arm, she leveled it at Seybourne, halting his advance. "That snuff you gave me and the queen was pretty strong medicine, Georgiana. But I wasn't quite as knocked out as Caroline, thank God."

Georgiana stood beside Seybourne, shoulder to shoulder. She was mad as blue blazes at her husband, but she had no intention of allowing Lady Spraddlin to end his life with a bullet.

The redhead, punch-drunk and weak kneed, pointed the gun first at Seybourne, then at Georgiana. "She's a feisty wench, that one! I've yet to figure out how she landed on her feet when I pushed her off the balcony."

"If you harm a hair on my wife's head," Seybourne said quietly, "I shall tear you from limb to limb with my bare hands."

Lady Spraddlin's pistol wavered in the air. "Defending the little strumpet now, are we? Despite her questionable origins?"

"Damme you, Mercy Mary! I have no interest in any woman's past, not yours and certainly not my wife's. I love her regardless of what happened before I met her."

"How noble," Lady Spraddlin replied sarcastically. "And

has she told you how she performed her famous disappearing act, yet? La! I admit Jack and I could never quite figure that one out! Come, gel, tell a kindred spirt how you done it! Were you behind the sofa, or hidden in the folds of the curtains?''

"Shut up, woman!" Seybourne's voice was a ferocious growl.

"Or were you beneath the desk—on your knees perhaps! That was my theory. Jack said he never saw you when he went to visit Sir Hester, but you must have been there the entire time! Why, I spied Jack running down Theobold Street, I did, just as Lady Twitchett and me, we crossed the intersection. He had just left Sir Hester's house minutes earlier. There weren't time for you to leave, gel. You must've been there!''

Georgiana glanced at Seybourne, furious that he had betrayed her. She had trusted him, and he used her for his own purposes. Perhaps he wasn't the good, noble man she thought he was.

His voice charged the air with a rumbling undercurrent of violence. "Hush, Mercy Mary, or I shall be obliged to close your mouth for you.''

The redhead responded with a shrug of her bare shoulder, and a snort of derisive laughter.

Emotion raged within Georgiana's chest. *How could she reconcile her love for the viscount with his newly revealed betrayal of her?*

On the other hand, how could she maintain her anger toward him in the face of his steadfast defense of her character, her reputation, her womanhood?

She closed her eyes, remembering the night he'd loved her as only a husband could love a wife. She felt the anguished hunger of his kiss, the urgent need his touch had conveyed. The words he had whispered—so intimate her cheeks pinkened to think of them—echoed in her mind, filling her with a hot, primeval desire.

But he had betrayed her, used her, endangered her life.

And then he had loved her, protected her, rescued her, and defended her against the vilest slanders ever leveled against a woman.

He didn't care who she was, or what she had been. He loved her now, and he promised her he'd love her forever.

Removing her hands from her face, she turned and met his level gaze. A strange tingling sensation overwhelmed her; it was the same dizzy feeling that had preceded her transformation from an unfeeling animal to a thinking, living, breathing, red-blooded, compassionate woman. Her legs were damp and trembling beneath her skirts. Blood coursed through her veins, deafening her to Lady Spraddlin's scurrilous denouncement of her.

But the viscount's lips mouthed the words she longed to hear. Three short, simple words that rang as loud and clear in her heart as a gong. And with those words, the odd otherworldly sensation that invaded her body vanished. Her limbs felt strong again, while her heart thumped steadily against her rib cage.

Inhaling deeply, she lifted her chin, tore her gaze from the viscount's and stared at Lady Spraddlin. She suddenly knew that she had learned another emotion, and experienced the sweetness of a feeling many humans never understood.

Forgiveness.

"Put the gun down," Georgiana said.

Lady Spraddlin pointed the barrel directly at Georgiana's heart. "I think I shall kill you. I'll be hanged for my part in this conspiracy, won't I? So, hadn't I just as well kill you?"

Without warning, Georgiana flung herself at Lady Spraddlin, reaching for the gun and knocking the woman backward.

An explosion tore through the room, and Georgiana felt the whistle of the bullet pass her ear.

Then, Seybourne yelled "No!" and threw himself in front of Georgiana.

Lady Spraddlin got off another shot before falling to the ground beneath Seybourne's weight. Then the gun fell with a dull thud to the carpet, and three people lay sprawled on the floor, their bodies tangled in a mass of limbs and muslin. Lady Spraddlin struggled at the bottom of the pile, kicking and clawing and muttering obscenities. But without her weapon, she was defenseless against Seybourne's greater strength.

Georgiana rocked back on her heels and slowly straightened.

Lady Spraddlin wriggled from beneath Lord Seybourne's body and lunged for the gun. But as her fingers closed around the handle, Seybourne's hand cuffed her slender wrist, and Georgiana's slippered foot descended on the small of her back. Defeated, the redhead sighed heavily. "Damn you both to hell," she muttered before closing her eyes and succumbing to a faint.

Only then did Seybourne roll to his back on the floor. And only then did Georgiana notice the black stain, thick as syrup, spreading from beneath him like a grotesque silhouette.

Swept inside a maelstrom of churning colors and bitter memories, Lawrence succumbed to the tug of senselessness. A tunnel of bright lights and images from his childhood sucked at him. His mind spun and twisted round old slights and resentments. His brother's pleading eyes—so much like his own, ice-cold and clear blue—impaled him, haunted him, tormented him.

"I cannot bear prison, brother! You are stronger than I. And as I am the older brother—if only by a few seconds—'tis I that must remain behind to handle the family estate. Please, Lawrie, please! I shall be in your debt forever!"

For what seemed an eternity, Lord Seybourne struggled against the encroaching demons of his past. Confronting Francis in his dreams, he denounced him, castigated him, told him he hated him. Then a fire-snorting dragon, with claws that dripped blood, chased the firstborn deWulff twin through a sunless forest. Lawrence unhesitatingly brandished a medieval sword, pommel glinting with crusted jewels, and pursued the monster that threatened his brother.

He ran till sweat poured down his brow, and his heart pounded. With his magic sword, he sliced the dragon's tail clean off its body, then buried his weapon between the monster's eyes, clear up to the dazzling gem-encrusted hilt.

A grinning Francis, barely having broken a sweat, embraced his brother and planted a kiss on his cheek.

"*Forgive me,*" he said, holding Lawrence at arm's length.

"I forgive you," was the younger brother's reply.

Lawrence awoke to the sound of his own voice, his own

hoarse words repeated over and over. His eyes flickered open, and the veil of darkness surrounding him slowly lifted. Candlelight lent a golden glow to the scene that faded into view. His body ached everywhere, but his shoulders, now with bullet holes in each of them, hurt the worst.

Georgiana hovered over his bed. "Lawrence? Can you hear me? Do you know where you are?"

His lips were cracked and dry, his voice a rough croak when he answered her. "I am in my bedchamber at Wolfharden."

"That is right. Queen Caroline would not hear of remaining in your quarters after she learned the terrible injuries you'd suffered. She and her heavily guarded entourage have journeyed on to London, dear. It seems you are quite the hero among both the Tories and the Whig politicians; the former for saving the king from the ignominy of having to ransom his errant wife from the Bonapartist sympathizers in Italy, the latter for rescuing their spokesperson."

Seybourne closed his eyes a moment, ruminating on Georgiana's news. He swallowed, relieved when she held a glass of cool water to his lips. When he'd moistened his tongue and laid his head back, he stared at her. Perched on the side of his bed, her black hair done up in a loose chignon, tendrils of it spilling down around her forehead and cheeks, he thought she was the most angelic-looking creature he'd ever seen.

He found her hand and closed his fingers around hers. "There is still so much I do not understand."

"Is it necessary to understand all the mysteries of life?" she replied.

Her upturned nose, her sly, coy smile, her half-lidded green eyes, reminded him of a . . .

Seybourne shook his head, dispelling any thoughts he might have had of forcing Georgiana to divulge the true facts of her past. *Her past didn't matter.* What she'd been before she met him was unimportant. Only her future with him signified now.

"My lady, you owe me no explanations concerning your past. But, perhaps you can answer a few of my other questions. For example, how did Lady Spraddlin come to be involved in this conspiracy to kidnap the queen? What could she possibly have gained by throwing in her lot with Jack Craven and Sir Douglas Babworth?''

"She was blackmailed, Lawrie," Georgiana said. "Oh, she did quite a bit of talking once the sheriff appeared to escort her in shackles to London. It seems that in her former life as a courtesan, Craven was a favored customer. After she was rehabilitated and married respectably to the Earl of Spraddlin, she tried to disinherit her past, but she couldn't. Not with men like Craven around to haunt her.''

"She should have simply let the sharpster reveal all to the *ton*," Seybourne said. "There is a very good chance his nerve would have faltered. There is also the chance the *ton* wouldn't have believed him—or wouldn't have cared.''

Georgiana's lashes flickered. "Not all men are as forgiving or as understanding as you.''

Forgiving? Lawrie cringed inwardly. Yes, he'd let go of his resentment at having been used by his twin brother, Francis. But it had taken him so long! For years, the chip that he carried on his shoulders had pinned him to the earth. He had turned the key that locked his own shackles, no one else had done it. Not even Francis could be blamed for the years Lawrence deWulff, Viscount Seybourne, had lost to bitterness and anger.

He thought of Lady Spraddlin, so frightened of her past that she allowed herself to be used in a criminal conspiracy to kidnap the queen. "Poor woman," he mused, his mind flashing on her unconscious body tossed to the road beside the carriage. "But, Georgiana, what happened to the queen and Mercy Mary that rendered them insensate during the carriage ride?''

Georgiana gave a light shrug. "It seems they shared a bit of snuff that had the effect of knocking them for a loop.''

"Snuff? Why, I knew they both had a fondness for it, but where on earth did they acquire tobacco leaves that rendered them unconscious?''

"I really couldn't tell you, Lawrie, but wasn't it lucky that I didn't join them in a snort while we were toddling down that nasty road in that nasty carriage, jammed together like matchsticks between Craven and Sir Douglas?''

"Did the men partake?''

"Oh, no! Just the women. I couldn't get the men to—"

Seybourne lifted his head, but the bend of his neck strained his muscles and sent a searing pain through his body. Slumping back on the pillow, he said, "You drugged them, didn't you? To protect the queen and to render Lady Spraddlin helpless, was that it?"

"My herbs are much stronger when you sniff them than when you brew them, my lord."

He chuckled despite the band of pain that encased his ribs. "You are clever, minx, aren't you?"

She answered by stroking his bare arm, running the palm of her hand over his hot feverish skin. Her touch was cooling, healing. When he smiled, the weight of five years' bitterness rolled from his chest.

"What else did Lady Spraddlin confess?" he asked in a hoarse whisper. His lids grew heavy as Georgiana's presence soothed him.

"It was she who dropped the note in Sir Hester's study. She lost it the day she went there to solicit a donation for the Society for the Rehabilitation of Wanton Women."

"How careless of her."

"It seems Sir Hester found the paper on the floor, balled it up, and allowed his pet kitty-cat to play with it. Eventually, when the cat tired of the game, he retrieved it. For some strange reason, he uncrumpled it and read it. He summoned you because he knew you bore no dangerous grudges against the king and couldn't possibly have written the note."

Seybourne's lids fell, then rose again as a thought assailed him. "How on earth would you know that the cat batted the crumpled note about and—"

"Just conjecture," Georgiana said. "At any rate, Craven killed Sir Hester when it was clear the old man would expose his plot. Craven was fairly certain you had not learned the contents of the note. And he didn't dare murder you outright; that would have drawn entirely too much attention to the Kit-Kat Club. But, he instructed Lady Spraddlin to train a watchful eye on you, anyway."

"Lucky that Craven did not find the note when he killed Sir Hester in the old man's study."

"He knew he could not dawdle, or spend too much time looking for the note. After all, there were servants in the house. So, it was agreed that Mercy Mary would contrive a reason to visit, shortly after Craven's murderous call. If Craven had not found the note, Mercy Mary was supposed to search for it. Aunt Inez didn't notice, of course, but Craven left the door ajar to indicate he'd not recovered the note; 'twas a signal of sorts."

"They must have been in a panic when you were discovered in Sir Hester's office. They knew there was a witness to the crime."

"Umm, odd thing about that," Georgiana said. "Mercy Mary says that Craven swore no one was present in the study when he murdered Sir Hester."

Barely able to focus his gaze, Seybourne mumbled, "Where were you, then, minx? Will you ever explain that mystery to me?"

Tilting her head, she appraised him with that sparkling green gaze. Meeting her stare, the viscount felt a wave of warmth wash over him. Did it matter what part she played in Sir Hester's death, as long as she was safe now? Did her past signify, as long as she was his?

"Do you trust me, Lawrie?" she asked.

What it all boiled down to was, did he love her enough to take that leap of faith? Could love replace his need to know what happened in that room on the day Sir Hester was killed?

"I suppose I will never know what really happened in that room," he said groggily. "What in the devil will I tell the king?"

"Tell him our first son shall be named George." Lady Seybourne bent over and pressed her lips to her husband's.

They sealed their oneness with a kiss, long and deeply felt. The viscount felt his breath drawn from him and, for a moment, a strange woozy sensation quaked through him. Georgiana's sigh was the breath of angel wings, sweet and secret and rare. His arms ached to hold her. He never wanted to be alone again.

When she drew away, just before the edges of his world faded to black, he managed to say, "I love you, minx, and I shall never let you go."

She murmured a throaty, "I love you, Lawrence."

He could have sworn she said it with a purr.

AUTHOR'S NOTES

Queen Caroline, wife of King George IV, did return from Italy to England in June, 1820, in order to defend herself against her husband's bill for divorce. She was an eccentric, colorful woman, reviled by her philandering spouse and loved by the king's political enemies. Viewed somewhat as a martyr by the common people, she did, in fact, become a symbolic figure around which many Whig politicians raised their reformist standard. There is no evidence, however, that a Whig conspiracy to kidnap her existed.

Nor is there any historical evidence linking the Italian revolutionaries of 1820 to Napoleon Bonaparte, who had been imprisoned on St. Helena under the watchful eye of an English governor since 1815. It is true, however, that shortly after his final capture and exile, Napoleon inexplicably became a romantic figure to reactionaries all over Europe who were disgruntled with the results of the Congress of Vienna. His memoirs, which he dictated in the years before his death in 1821, were obviously slanted to glorify himself and justify his motivations. Amazingly, his *apologia* appealed to liberals and nationalists in the very countries he previously trampled.

I have also taken liberties in describing the herb catmint. Though the herb, *napata cataria,* does grow in rich, sandy soil, its presence in a nineteenth-century Mayfair garden is doubtful. In areas where the herb proliferates, it is often used in tea, but I highly recommend Georgiana's Spiced Tea recipe instead.

The tea is actually Indian Spice Tea, or *Masala Chai.* The recipe was made available by the gracious people at Taj Mahal Indian Cuisine Restaurant in Metairie, Louisiana. It was originally created by Mr. Har G. Keswani and has been a favorite among the customers at Taj Mahal for years.

WATCH FOR THESE REGENCY ROMANCES